FLORISSANT

FLORISSANT

P.H.C. MARCHESI

Bink Books YA
Bedazzled Ink Publishing Company • Fairfield, California

978-1-949290-58-5 paperback

Cover Design
by
BetiBup33 Design Studio

Bink Books YA
a division of
Bedazzled Ink Publishing Company
Fairfield, California
http://www.bedazzledink.com

To mom and dad
(on the other side of the door now, but always here)

Contents

Chapter 1

Misfits

THEY SAY TRUTH is stranger than fiction. I say dreams are stranger than both.

Sylva and I didn't always have strange dreams. There was a time when we dozed off peacefully under the stars and the rustling leaves. Maybe that sounds super corny to you, but that's how it was. We were happy. We were home.

I was about ten when they took us away, and Sylva was about five. It's all a blur when I try to think about it, a collection of sounds and images. A gunshot. A faceless man. Sylva and I running through the forest and then onto a road. A car hitting the brakes. People staring at us and asking us questions. All I could say in reply was that someone had killed our mother.

I said it over and over again. And I dreamed it over and over again. Sylva did too, poor thing. It was definitely worse for her.

Reader, what can I say about the next five years? We don't blame any of our foster parents. We weren't easy kids. It's a miracle we were placed together in the first place. It was probably because Ms. Williams, the Social Services person in charge of our case, figured Sylva wouldn't make it on her own. You have to understand: from the moment we'd been found, Sylva was clutching a sapling planted in a piece of burlap. She went everywhere with it. She even slept with it right next to her. Our first foster parents wanted to plant the sapling, but Sylva refused to let them touch it. They tried a few times, but her dark brown eyes stared so fiercely at them that eventually they gave up. She was just too "out there" for them. One time, they found her outside, with her feet under the earth (all the way to the ankles). She sat there, smiling, her hair decorated with leaves and flowers (I thought she looked cute, actually). When they asked her what she was doing, she said she was being herself. They finally took her to a therapist.

"Do you have any friends, Sylva?" the therapist asked.

"Wynd," said Sylva. She didn't speak much, my sister, and I'm sure that didn't help.

"You mean the wind?" asked the therapist, looking puzzled.

"Wynd is my sister," said Sylva.

"Your sister's the wind?"

"My sister's name is Wynd."

It wasn't a promising start. Sylva finally gave the therapist a list of her friends: air, sunlight, trees, rainfall, earth. Oh, and wind.

"Isn't there something we can give her?" I heard our foster mother say. "She thinks she's a tree. She thinks her hair's a canopy, and won't let anyone cut it."

"It does look a little like a canopy," said the therapist, smiling at the thought of Sylva's bushy and disheveled hair. "Give her time. She'll grow out of it."

Not fast enough, apparently. Time is a difficult thing for people to give. That's why we ended up with our second foster parents. Ms. Williams told us they loved the outdoors, and Sylva got very hopeful. Maybe they would let her sleep outside during the summer and let her go to school under a tree.

I tried not to be too excited. I could do well anywhere, as long as it wasn't a concrete parking lot with nothing living in it. Pretty much any place would be awesome as long as Sylva did okay.

Our hopes were dashed on our first day with our second foster parents. It was true that they liked the outdoors—especially fishing. I almost choked on the diced potatoes when they said that, and Sylva literally let her piece drop from her mouth onto her plate.

"You'll see how much fun it is," said our foster dad, encouragingly.

"It's not fun to kill friends," said Sylva. When she *did* say something, it was always short and honest. She never tried endearing herself to anyone.

"Fish aren't friends, sweetie," said our second foster mom, looking to me for support.

"Sorry," I said, shrugging. "Killing things for fun is lame."

Before I tell the rest of our story, I just want to say this: it's not that we weren't eager to belong to a family. It's just that we couldn't be who we weren't. And we knew who we were, even at five and ten years old. That scared people.

"I just don't think they're the right fit for us," our second foster dad told Ms. Williams, one day.

"You knew Sylva had special needs," replied Ms. Williams, as Sylva and I eavesdropped from behind the staircase. "You knew she required a lot of patience. You said you were willing to work with her."

"She's beyond what we can work with," we heard. "The teacher at school says she's not making any progress. She scribbles a bunch of scratches and claims she's writing, but the teacher says she can't even tell letters apart—at her *age*."

That was true. But Sylva wasn't stupid. She couldn't tell letters apart because she was miserable. She'd sit inside, looking longingly at the window. I told the teacher she should try teaching Sylva outside, under a tree, but the nearest tree was a block from the school, in a busy street, and that would have been unsafe. Regulations wouldn't permit it. So Sylva stayed inside, safe, and learned nothing.

Maybe if we had been placed with some ex-hippies, they might have understood Sylva and sent us to some type of experimental nature school. I often thought that might have done the trick. Then again, maybe not. In any case, we were in Georgia, so ex-hippies were hard to come by.

"It's not just Sylva, though," continued our second foster mom. "Wynd is worse."

Sylva looked up at me and grinned. I tousled her hair, because she was so cute when she was smug.

"Worse?" repeated Ms. Williams, baffled. "She's doing well in school, isn't she?"

"She's getting excellent grades, but she's not doing *well*," insisted our second foster mom. "She and Sylva hide in the school library every second of recess."

"I love the library," said Sylva, proudly.

Sylva's love of the library went like this: she'd sit next to me and smell the books. Sometimes she would hug them. My love of the library went like this: it was a peaceful place where no one could tease Sylva, push her around, throw her sapling on the floor, or snatch her backpack from her. Being able to read while having peace was just an added benefit.

"We don't know how to relate to them," confessed our second foster dad.

They really didn't. Since fishing wasn't an option, they tried giving us new clothes, a Nintendo, and expensive cell phones. To their disappointment, those things didn't seem as exciting to us as they had anticipated.

And every day, what we really longed for them to understand was that Sylva just wanted to be left alone so she could be a tree, and I just wanted Sylva to be happy.

Since that was too simple, I guess they never got it.

"When she's not being a loner," continued our foster mom, widening her eyes at Ms. Williams, "Wynd gets into fights."

"I would too, if my little sister were being bullied," retorted Ms. Williams, sounding slightly annoyed.

"But she fights like . . . a wild thing," said our foster father, lowering his voice. "She bites and scratches and won't back down."

"To be honest," added our foster mother, almost in a whisper. "Wynd kind of scares us. The other day, she climbed up a tree in the middle of a windstorm, and wouldn't come down no matter how much we begged her to."

I cringed. I liked Ms. Williams, and I hated that she had to find out about this. I had to listen, mortified, as they recounted how I had seemed to be in a trance until Sylva had shouted my name.

"Wynd!" she had shrieked, in a desperate voice I had never heard before. "Don't leave me!"

And I had suddenly come to my senses. I had climbed down, and Sylva had hugged me, sobbing.

"I won't leave you," I had whispered. "I promise."

I had always loved any kind of wind, from the softest breeze to the most violent storm, but that day something had changed. Suddenly, I had felt a powerful longing to *become* the wind, weightless and free. I had forgotten everything else—even who I was.

"Did Wynd give you any explanation for her behavior?" asked Ms. Williams, clearly disturbed by this turn in the conversation.

What explanation could I have given? I wasn't even sure *I* understood. I was afraid of how much I wanted it, that feeling of nothing and everything at once. I made up some story about how some kid in school had dared me to do it—something about him promising to leave Sylva alone if I did.

"That makes sense," said Ms. Williams, breathing a sigh of relief.

"If you believe it," said our second foster dad.

"Wynd is not the type to hurt herself," said Ms. Williams. "She doesn't fit the profile."

She was right on that one. I had never thought of hurting myself. Neither had Sylva. We had to be around for each other—which is why I kept ignoring my strange longing for the wind, even though it was always there, lurking in the background.

You've probably guessed by now that foster parents #2 didn't work out. They were the ones who tried the hardest, and after them it was just a downhill slope, so let me go over them with just a few highlights.

Foster parents #3: their big thing was sports and exercise. Because of them, I found out I could run fast, but I didn't see the point of joining the track team. They couldn't understand my lack of competitiveness, and they were appalled at Sylva's complete lack of ambition. One time they asked her what she wanted to be when she grew up. You can guess what she said.

Foster parents #4: couple with two kids of their own who wouldn't get off the phone—ever—and were always worried they'd be seen with the "orphan freaks" (or so they called us on Snapchat). I can't actually remember their names now.

Foster parents #5: weird people who lived in the middle of nowhere and tried to homeschool us. Pretty soon, they came to the conclusion that Sylva was possessed. I called Ms. Williams and told her I had overheard them talking about an exorcist (I'm not kidding, by the way). Ms. Williams came and had a brief chat with them. Then she told us to get in the car with her.

Foster parents #6: thought what Sylva and I needed was good old-fashioned discipline. They said Sylva was too attached to her sapling, and actually locked it in the basement, where it began to wilt for lack of light. Sylva could only "visit" the sapling for a few minutes every night, and if she had learned her lessons and finished her homework. Sylva begged them to at least put it near a window, but they told her they were doing her a favor and she would thank them later. Gradually, Sylva became lean and pale. One day, she was too sick to get up. Our foster parents thought she was "acting up" and threatened to throw the sapling away if she didn't get out of bed.

"You'll kill it!" moaned Sylva, tears running down her face. I had never seen her like that, and it scared me.

"That's the sound of the trash truck coming," said the foster dad, firmly. "Are you going to get up?"

Sylva couldn't, so the sapling was thrown in the bin and hauled up into the truck. Our foster parents seemed proud of it, too, like they had done something worthy of praise.

I think I kind of lost it at that point. I'm not even sure how I did it, but I caught up with the truck, grabbed onto the end, and jumped inside the trash. I think that's what happened. A few seconds later, I jumped out with the sapling. We were both a little worse for wear but otherwise all right. The truck drivers didn't even see me.

I ran back to the house, fully ready to confront foster parents #6 (I had done that a few times already, and our arguments had been getting steadily worse). But the front door was locked.

I couldn't believe it. It was cold, and it was beginning to rain—so I pounded on the door. They ignored me and raised the volume of the TV. They were trying to teach me a lesson, obviously. I was beginning to shake with cold, and they hoped I would apologize, beg, and all that good stuff.

I had to think fast. I was sure they were watching me from someplace inside the house. Too bad the cell phone Ms. Williams had given me was someplace inside the house also.

So here's what I did: I turned around and ran through the trees. Then I hid and watched. There was a gas station two miles away, and a police station maybe a mile farther, and I was hoping they'd think that's where I was headed. If they got out of the house, I could get Sylva out of there.

Bingo! A few minutes later, the garage door opened, and they drove out in a hurry. Both of them. They knew it would take two people to force me back into the car. I had counted on that, and as soon as the car was out of sight, I sprinted back to the house.

The front door was locked, so I grabbed a rock and broke the glass pane. Then I stuck my hand through the glass and opened the door. I got a few cuts on my hand, but I didn't care. I wanted to get to Sylva as quickly as possible. She needed her sapling. She would die without it—I had finally understood that. This was why I hadn't begged to be let inside the house again. I knew foster parents #6 might even let me in, but they'd destroy the sapling to teach us a lesson. I couldn't let that happen.

"Sylva!" I cried, stomping up the stairs. "Sylva, I got the sapling back!"

I stormed into the room, triumphantly, but Sylva didn't even prop herself up.

"I brought it back," I said, sitting next to her. "Look."

"Your hand is bleeding," she whispered.

"It's fine—don't worry about it," I said, hiding it from view. "You don't look so good, Sylva."

"Wynd," she said, so softly I could barely hear her, "I think I'm dying."

"I'm calling 9-1-1," I said, jumping up in a panic. "They'll send an ambulance."

"It won't help," she said, and I sat back down next to her, because I knew that she was saying the truth. I could feel it, her life draining away.

"But I brought the sapling back," I said, pitifully. "Look, it's mostly in one piece . . . wait—what's this?"

The string tying the burlap around the root base had come undone, and something was sticking out—something made of plastic. I pulled it out, carefully, and discovered it was a folded Ziplock bag.

"Sylva, there's something in here," I whispered, pulling out a faded piece of paper and two acorns. I unfolded the paper, trying not to tear it. Inside was a hand-written note, all blurry but still readable:

Eat the acorns to come home.

"Sylva," I said, feeling goosebumps on my arms, "I think someone left a message for us."

It seemed too good to be true, but I was too desperate to question. Sylva was fading fast, and I could hear a car turning into the long driveway. Foster parents #6 had guessed my strategy. They'd be walking through the door any moment now.

"How would you like to go home, Sylva?" I asked.

"Where's home?" she replied, ever so faintly.

"I don't know," I said, cracking each of the acorns and retrieving the nuts. "Shall we find out?"

"Okay."

I helped her to put her backpack on, and carefully stashed her sapling inside it. Then we each ate a nut.

They tasted like freedom.

Chapter 2

FLORISSANT

THE FIRST THING I saw were the wolves.

Wolves in Georgia? I knew there weren't any. I was a good student, *and* I read. Any and all wolves in the state had been killed in the distant and not-so-distant past. But the many trees around us *looked* like Georgia, and the temperature and humidity were more or less the same. I had read there were still some red wolves in North Carolina somewhere—but these weren't red wolves, either. They were grey wolves or timber wolves: large and tall, with massive paws and yellow or grey-green eyes. They were inquisitive eyes, curious eyes, and maybe even cautious eyes—but definitely not eyes that meant harm.

I watched, fascinated, as they trotted calmly toward us. One of the grey wolves had the handle of a lantern—with a candle and everything—firmly in its mouth. The fire from the candle seemed to fizz and sparkle, and I understood this was no ordinary candle, any more than these were ordinary wolves.

A thud forced me out of my amazement: Sylva had fallen on the ground, and I knelt down and tried unsuccessfully to wake her up.

She was cold. For a horrible second, I worried she might be dead.

"Don't die, Sylva," I cried, pathetically.

A long snout came between me and Sylva. I looked straight at a pair of yellow eyes and a black, furry face.

"Please," I asked the wolf, "can you help us?"

The black wolf licked me, so I took it as a yes. He took two steps, stopped, and looked at me, as if to certify to himself that I was following him. Meanwhile, the grey wolf with the lantern came and stood next to me. Clearly, his task was to guide my steps in the darkening (and now rainy) forest.

"I'm coming," I said, carrying Sylva. She didn't seem heavy at first. For a ten-year-old, she was underweight and shorter than average, and I thought carrying her would be easy. As I followed the black wolf, however, it got harder. The terrain was all uneven, and the floor was slippery with wet leaves. I nearly fell several times, and my pace slowed as I got more and more tired. The black wolf trotted more slowly ahead, as did the two other wolves behind him, the lantern-carrying wolf next to me, and the one that kept the rear.

You might be wondering if I was insane to be following a pack of lantern-carrying wolves, but I had the strange feeling that something mysterious—something that was clearly on our side—was at work here. And I was *desperate* to save Sylva. You'd be amazed what strange feelings you trust in when you're desperate.

It was raining hard now, though, and I was drenched, and hot, and exhausted. My legs were wobbly, and I was out of breath. The forest seemed endless, and I wondered how much longer I could do this.

"Sorry, guys," I said, leaning against a tree. "I have to catch my breath."

The black wolf turned around and regarded me with his yellow eyes. He was the only black wolf of the pack, and his eyes were like two orbs of fire.

"Yeah, I know," I said. "You want me to keep going, don't you?"

He blinked, and then *barked* at me. Nothing subtle about that.

"Let me just take a break for a second," I half-panted. The grey wolf with the lantern whined impatiently, and the other wolves whined and barked. The one behind me actually *nudged* me forward.

"Okay," I said. "Let's go."

I honestly can't say how much longer I stumbled along. I was half-conscious and numb from exhaustion when the black wolf finally stopped. Then he howled. It was a melodious, haunting howl, and the other wolves quickly joined him. It wasn't completely dark yet, and I could still see an octagonal building—three, maybe four stories high—in front of us with windows of various shapes and sizes. Two enormous trees seemed to blend seamlessly into the structure, flanking a heavy, arched entryway and a massive, wooden door. The archway over the door displayed, in elaborate golden letters, the following words:

Florissant Academy

Torn between total amazement and total exhaustion, I knelt (okay, more like collapsed), and waited to see what would happen. And what happened was that the door opened, and two women came running out. The black wolf went to meet them, and stood in front of the shorter one, as if telling her something.

"Thank you, Grimsby," she said, glancing at me. "Go and take shelter."

The black wolf—Grimsby, apparently—trotted unceremoniously away, and I felt slightly hurt that he hadn't even glanced back at me. The rest of the wolves followed him—including the wolf with the lantern—and within seconds they had blended into the forest, like ghosts into the fog.

"Can you help us?" I asked, not sure which of the two women I was addressing now. Taller and shorter—that's all I could tell about them out there, with the rain pounding against my face.

"Come inside," said the shorter woman, and both ushered me through the door and into a type of covered mud room, beyond which I thought I glimpsed a large, round courtyard. But my powers of observation weren't very sharp just then: I was dizzy, beginning to shake uncontrollably, bone-weary. I had been ignoring my hand the whole time, but it was swollen and throbbing now.

The taller woman took Sylva from me, and I leaned against the wall.

"My sister needs her sapling," I said, trying hard to make the words come out right. "She can't be separated from it."

"It couldn't be . . . ?" said the taller woman, with a bit of an accent that indicated English wasn't her first language. "Could it?"

The shorter woman unzipped Sylva's backpack and looked inside.

"I can't believe it," she muttered, turning in amazement to me. "How did you get here?"

"Acorns," I said, too tired to do anything but comply. "I found them hidden with her sapling. Can you help her? She's really sick."

"Home-sick," said the taller woman.

"Huh?"

"She needs Florissant earth," insisted the taller woman, sounding urgent. "I'll take her to Giniana."

"Wait—what?" I asked. But—get this—the tall woman waved her hand and *disappeared* with Sylva.

"Where did she go?" I cried. "Where did she take her?"

"You need medical attention, too," said the shorter woman, worriedly. "Your hand—"

"I don't care," I said, feverishly. "Why didn't that woman take both of us?"

"Because your sister is a tree fairy, and you're a different kind altogether. Mariposa is not going to stick *your* feet in Florissant earth."

I stared at this woman, a woman who smelled noticeably of flower petals and had vibrant, green eyes, like the leaves of the forest on a sunny day.

"What did you just say?" I asked. I was burning with a fever now, and my entire body shook.

"You and your sister are fairies," said the woman, smiling. "Welcome home."

Just as she finished speaking, I passed out.

Chapter 3

Tania Greenwood

WHEN I OPENED my eyes, the first thing I realized was that I had never felt so good in my life. I wasn't even tired. My hand looked perfectly normal—not a scratch on it—and my clothes were dry.

"Just in time," the taller woman said.

I scanned the room: clearly, it was an infirmary of some sort, but instead of the usual boring medical posters, there were tapestries of medicinal flowers and herbs on the walls, and where there weren't, vines and flowers seemed to grow *out* of the walls. The whole room had the stuffy, fragrant atmosphere of a florist shop, or a greenhouse.

"In time for what?" I asked. "Where's my sister?"

I now noticed that this taller woman had brown-grey hair and bushy, brown eyebrows. She seemed to really like brown, because she wore a kind of brown dress tunic over her jeans. As she stood by the one open window in the room, she struck me as restless.

"My name is Mariposa. Your sister is in the courtyard, with Giniana," she said. "Don't worry—Giniana is taking good care of her."

It was dark now, but the rain had stopped, and the clouds were letting the stars and a bright full moon through. I looked out and thought I distinguished Sylva's shape, asleep by a large tree—Giniana, I guessed—in the middle of the courtyard.

"You left Sylva out there?" I cried, outraged. Don't get me wrong: I knew Sylva needed some sort of unconventional medical help, but leaving her outside under the care of a tree seemed a bit too . . . unconventional.

"She's recovering," said the woman, defensively. "She would have died if I hadn't planted her in some Florissant earth. You can go downstairs and see for yourself—the door is over there." She pointed to an oval door that had moss and tiny flowers growing out of it, and that might have taken me a while to find.

"I'm leaving now," she continued. "Don't close the window. Buenas noches."

Then Mariposa turned into a moth and fluttered out the window. I'm not kidding.

Still somewhat in shock, I walked out of the infirmary, trying to figure out how to get downstairs. Another corridor, this one full of doors, each with two or three names on them. I guessed I was in some sort of dorm, so I looked for some sort of exit sign. There wasn't one, but I finally got to a spiral staircase and ran down. Another corridor, another set of doors with names, another spiral staircase—nope, this one only went to the next floor up. What kind of quirky architecture was this? Okay, finally found the one going down, and eventually got to some kind of living room or lounge with windows, a massive fireplace, and a door to the courtyard that wasn't locked.

Reader, the courtyard smelled a-ma-zing after the rain. Each breath seemed to carry all the fresh and wet earth in the world. This was the smell of my childhood, alive and around me—for a second or two, I was five years old again.

As I skipped puddles to get to Sylva, I saw the reflection of the moon and the quickly disappearing clouds. And then I noticed there was something else in that reflection: moving specks of lights.

I had seen fireflies before, but never so many. It seemed as if, from the moment I had stepped outside, they had appeared out of nowhere to fill the courtyard. It was the most beautiful thing I had ever seen. Eager as I was to check on Sylva, I stopped for a moment, lost in wonder.

"They're welcoming you," said a voice by the door.

I recognized the smell of flower petals even before I turned around. There she was, the shorter woman, leaning with her arms crossed and observing me with interest. She had brown hair in a pixie cut (no pun intended), and wore jeans and a long, sleeveless tunic that seemed to have been made of green felt or some other similar material. The buttons of the tunic seemed to be made of twigs or bits of wood.

"Go ahead and check on her," she said, encouragingly. "What's her name?"

"Sylva."

"Of course," she said, nodding. "Amazing."

I had no idea what she meant, but I had other stuff to think about, because Sylva was awake. For the first time in a *long* time, she didn't look pale. She jumped up, feet still covered in earth, and ran toward me with her sapling, which had been replanted into a larger vase. It looked considerably less wilted than it had been before, which was incredible considering its recent ride in the backpack.

"We made it, Wynd!" she cried, excitedly. "We're home."

She grabbed my hand and pulled me toward the tree. It had to be some kind of oak, because there were hundreds of acorns on the earth all around it.

"This is Giniana," said Sylva. "She's been telling me all kinds of stuff."

I wondered how Sylva knew the tree's name, and then I wondered what kinds of things a tree might say. But, if anyone could keep a conversation with a tree, it was Sylva.

"Hey, you're all wet," I said. "Let's go inside so you can change into some dry clothes."

"No! I want to stay here."

"You'll get sick. You're all—"

I was going to say "wet," but the shorter woman waved her hand, and Sylva was suddenly dry. Even her hair had mushroomed into its usual canopy.

"Thank you!" cried Sylva.

"You're welcome," said the woman, giving Sylva a playful wink. "Now you can stay out here without your sister worrying."

"All night?" asked Sylva, widening her eyes. "Out here with the fireflies and Giniana?"

"Well, it *is* June, and it *is* Georgia, so it *is* warm enough to spend nights outside—especially for a tree fairy like you."

Sylva jumped with joy, and then went to check out the fireflies. She giggled in a way I had never seen her do before.

"Is it safe enough for her to be outside all night?" I asked.

"Yes. The courtyard is inside Florissant Academy," explained the woman.

"This is a boarding school?"

"For fairy youngsters. As you've seen, there is a lot of fairy magic around here."

I stared at her. "Honestly, I'm having a hard time with this whole thing."

"Why? Didn't you want to come home to a place like this?"

She regarded me for a moment, and only then did I notice that she had remarkable green eyes. They made me feel hopeful and at ease, like the beauty of the woods with all its various shades of green.

"I did, but I wasn't sure a place like this existed," I confessed. "Why is it called Florissant Academy?"

"Florissant is the name of the forest."

I thoug\ ht I detected the slightest hint of an English accent—or what I thought might have been one at some point.

"Let's talk in my office," she said, turning around and marching away. "There's too much to say out here, and Giniana can be a bit of an eavesdropper."

"Sylva can't just wander off, can she?" I asked, rushing after her. For someone who wasn't very tall, she sure could walk fast.

"I suppose she could, technically, if she went back inside and meandered around until she found the front door."

"But you're not worried."

"Not particularly, no."

"Why not?"

"Even if she went out into the forest, she'd be protected."

"By Grimsby?"

"Grimsby is the pack leader, but she would also be protected by Gwaelrod, Whitby, Antrim, and Etain. And Madog would be guiding her with that lantern if she got lost."

"Still," I insisted, "it's a forest. Forests can be dangerous."

"But they can also be places of opportunity, adventure, and sanctuary."

I hadn't thought of forests that way, and I secretly hoped Florissant would be all three for Sylva and me.

"In any case," she continued, "magic cannot exist without danger."

I wondered if Ms. Williams would agree. The smartest thing to do would probably be to leave both *magic* and *danger* out of our next conversation.

"There's Trego," she continued, gesturing to a pair of shiny eyes following us from one of the sofas. "He's one of our feline residents."

"Is he enchanted?"

"Not enchanted, but enchanting—once you get to know him. All of our cats are, in their own way."

"No one here's allergic?" I asked.

"Fairies? Allergic to animals? They'd need to be under a curse."

"Any dogs?"

"None yet."

I wondered if the wolves scared away any potential stray dogs. It had to be a scary prospect, *not* having those wolves on your side.

"So, you from Georgia?" I asked.

"Not originally, no," said the woman. "I came here a long time ago."

"From England?" I asked.

"You could say that," she said. "Any other guesses?"

"You don't believe in elevators?"

"No need for them."

"What happens if someone breaks a leg?"

The woman stopped on the landing.

"*This*," she said, waving her hand. We were suddenly in a cozy office full of books, tapestries, and a fireplace—oh, and a cat. This one was a calico.

"Hello, Calumet," she said, as the cat looked up and chirped. "I brought a new resident."

Calumet regarded me with condescending boredom, staying exactly where she was.

"Have a seat," the woman told me, sitting in an armchair by the fire. "As you probably guessed, this is my school. I'm Tania Greenwood."

"I'm Wynd," I said.

"Of course you are."

I wasn't sure what she meant, and I hesitated to sit across from her. I was afraid that, if I looked into her eyes, I'd fall on my knees and thank her for taking us in—even for one night—and making us a part of that world full of magic, guardian wolves, and fairies. I was afraid I'd cry.

"You have a lot of books," I said, scanning her shelves. "There's a lot of Shakespeare."

"I used to be a professor. You've read some Shakespeare?" she asked, and seemed pleased when I nodded. "*Romeo and Juliet*, I suppose."

"*Midsummer Night's Dream*," I said.

"My favorite," she said, with a flash of mischief in her eye.

I finally decided to sit down, but I avoided looking straight at her.

"How old are you?" she asked.

"Sylva's ten, and I'm fifteen."

"Ten and fifteen," she repeated. "I still can't believe it. I've been looking for you—both of you, for several years now."

"For *us*?"

"I was a friend of your mother's, back in the day."

I knew she was speaking the truth. Those eyes.

"My mother was murdered," I said, surprising myself. I was usually so guarded about this topic.

"I know, Wynd. I know."

And now I had tears running down my cheeks. I hated it. I quickly wiped them away, and then realized her eyes were brimming with tears also, although she had enough self-restraint for them to stay put.

"Are we really, um, fairies?" I asked, eager to change the subject.

"You know you are."

"Sylva is a tree fairy?"

"We call a young one like her a tree child."

"What kind am I?"

"You know what kind."

I knew, but I averted the green gaze once more, because I didn't want to confess that being a wind fairy frightened me. Wind was unpredictable, free, boundless. I had Sylva to think about.

"Are we allowed to stay here from now on?" I asked.

"I would be very happy if you did. I created Florissant Academy to give those kids of the fairy world who are orphaned, abandoned, or rejected a place to call home."

"Sylva and I don't have any money," I said, somewhat ashamedly. I knew things were expensive: tuition, boarding, books, and so on. I had heard foster parents #4 and their kids talking about college. I had never considered it, because leaving Sylva behind would have been madness. I didn't even think about the money issue.

"You've spent too much time in the human world," said Tania. "Magic is more important than money—and love, of course, is more important than both."

I understood love. What I wanted to learn more about was magic.

"Why didn't you use your magic to find us?" I asked.

"My magic doesn't work outside the forest."

"Then why didn't you use the internet?" I asked, immediately thinking I might have sounded too harsh.

"I *did*," she said, with a chuckle that indicated she wasn't in the least bit offended. "Either I'm really bad with computers, or I'm guessing you were given other names."

I had completely forgotten about that. In the foster care system, Sylva and I were officially Kaitlin and Jennifer Flynn. We hated the names.

A soft knock on the door prevented me from telling Tania about our alternate identities. A tall, black woman popped her head in. She had a warm smile and round, yellow glasses.

"Mustardseed," said Tania, pleasantly surprised. "Come in. Wynd, Mustardseed is our kitchen master and chef extraordinaire."

First Moth, then Mustardseed? This *had* to be a joke.

"Are you all named after the fairies in *A Midsummer Night's Dream*?" I asked.

"They're the ones named after us, sweetie," said Mustardseed, placing a bowl in front of Tania. "Berries and more berries with maple sauce: your favorite."

"You're a lifesaver," said Tania Greenwood. "I was in need of a treat after this late-night activity."

"It's more like early morning," Mustardseed said, giving me a bowl as well. "I hope this is to your liking, Wynd. Welcome to Florissant."

I was also seriously in need of a booster, and the berries with more berries and maple sauce were the best thing I had ever tasted. I suspected there was some magic in them, but I was too blissed out to bother asking.

"I took some to the tree child, but she seemed asleep by Giniana, and I didn't want to disturb her," said Mustardseed.

"I'll take her upstairs in a second," said Tania. "I thought about letting her sleep downstairs, but I don't want her to get startled by the kids in the courtyard tomorrow morning."

"I thought Mariposa might like some," said Mustardseed, "but she must be out now with the full moon."

"Luckily, it was raining when Wynd and Sylva arrived, so she was around," said Tania, cheerfully wiping her mouth with one of the beautifully embroidered napkins that Mustardseed had given us. The bowl, too, was porcelain, and the spoon and tray were silver. I had never eaten on something so fancy, and I found the whole thing almost more wonderful than an infirmary medic who was a fairy and routinely turned into a moth.

"Do *you* turn into anything?" I asked Mustardseed.

"No, but I make a mean mustard sauce," she retorted, smiling.

"Is there a Peaseblossom and a Cobweb as well?" I asked, proud that I could remember the names of the other two fairies from *A Midsummer Night's Dream*.

"As a matter of fact, yes," said Tania. "You will meet them—but it's getting very late, and the rest of us have to get up in just a few hours. Any other burning questions?"

"Two, actually," I said. I had finished eating, and was beginning to feel really drowsy, but there were two things I still wanted to know.

"Okay. Go ahead," said Tania.

"The first one is: if magic doesn't work outside the forest, how come the acorns brought us here?"

"There's one type of acorn that *does* work anywhere, and I'm guessing it's the one that brought you here. The tree it came from is on the very edge of the forest, which is where you were transported to."

"Okay."

"What's the second question?" she asked.

"I just realized it's not a question," I said, feeling a little embarrassed. "I meant to say that there's no character in *A Midsummer Night's Dream* called Tania Greenwood."

"You are right about *that*," said Tania. "But let's continue this conversation in a few hours. Good night, Mustardseed."

"Good night."

Tania waved her hand, and the two of us were transported to a simple but cozy room with two twin beds and a sink, and two rectangular windows (the windows were open to let in the pleasant summer breeze). With another wave of Tania's hand, Sylva materialized on the bed near the window, sleeping—and, if you can believe it, smiling as she slept.

"Now that she's in Florissant, she may not feel the need to sleep outside as much," said Tania. "She must have been longing for the forest all these years."

"Uh-huh," I said, sleepily.

"Good night, then," said Tania. "Sleep well."

She waved herself out, and I climbed into bed and lay down. I liked Tania Greenwood, even if she wasn't named after a fairy from *Midsummer Night's Dream*. If she had been, she would definitely have been the queen of the fairies and the forest, Titania.

As I breathed a deep sigh of contentment, I remember thinking that it was odd that *Tania* was pretty similar to *Titania*, and that *Greenwood* basically meant forest. Then I fell asleep.

Chapter 4

The Academy

FOR THE FIRST time in years, I didn't dream about the gunshot in the forest. Instead, I dreamed I was sitting in the forest, with Sylva, and we were both surrounded by wildflowers. We were drenched in sunlight, and happy. A woman wearing a white dress patterned beautifully with silver, gold, and copper threads emerged from the trees. She had brown skin and long hair with gentle waves, as well as captivating dark eyes. A golden aura radiated from her.

I knew who she was, of course. She was Mom.

"Wynd, Sylva—welcome home," she said, and as she hugged us, her aura spilled over to us, and it was warm and wonderful, like basking in the first warm rays of the morning.

I woke up, feeling strangely at peace. I knew, somehow, that I'd never dream about the gunshot again.

"Wynd," said Sylva, who had also just woken up. "I dreamed about Mom."

I was about to say we'd probably had the same dream—but instead I blinked and jumped out of bed.

"Sylva," I whispered, not sure if I was alarmed or amazed. "Look at the room."

Sylva's eyes widened. The room looked completely different. The walls were made of some type of wicker fencing, and there were all kinds of flowers, plants, and even mushrooms exploding from every little crevice. Vines with tiny flowers hung from the ceiling, and—yes, I'm not joking—soft moss covered the floor. The sink had turned into a bubbling water fountain, large enough to step inside and take a bath in. Even the windows had changed into round windows, with glass so clean and transparent that you could swear there was nothing there (later I found out they're made of fairy crystal).

"Giniana said everything would look different in the morning," said Sylva. "She said it would take a few hours to see all the magic clearly."

"Well, she was right," I said, thinking this was the coolest thing ever. "What else did Giniana say?"

"That the oldest tree in Florissant is in the deepest part of the forest and doesn't like anyone."

I couldn't help but laugh. A tree that liked to gossip and another that was antisocial. This place was getting better and better.

"Good morning, young ladies," called a voice we immediately identified as Tania's. "Are you ready for your first day in Florissant?"

I should quickly mention here that the door was no longer a door, but a giant leaf, heavy as a rug when we tried to push it aside. We finally managed to step outside, and—

"It's just like our room," cried Sylva, jumping barefoot onto the mossy corridor floor.

"I see the magic has kicked in," said Tania, pleasantly. "I brought you both some new clothes."

She handed me a folded bundle, and Sylva another. "I suggest a shower, and then breakfast."

"Where's everyone else?" I asked, seeing the hallway empty.

"Either somewhere in the Academy or out in the forest."

"They can do that? They can just be out?"

"Well, it *is* the summer," said Tania, shrugging. "Summers are for reading or wandering outside all day."

I liked the sound of that. I *really* liked the sound of that.

"Why don't you come to the kitchen when you're ready?" she asked. "I'll meet you there."

She vanished before I could ask where the kitchen was, and how she'd know we were ready.

"Wynd, look, she guessed my favorite color," said Sylva, excited at her outfit, which basically consisted of a cute light green shirt and dark green pants—except that the colors were, somehow, *glowing*.

"I think these colors are alive," I said. I had yellow pants, and an embroidered pink, blue, green, and orange shirt. If the combination of colors sounds horrible to you, I'm the first person who might have agreed—before seeing the outcome in front of me. I couldn't believe it. No one could get away with this much color. Could they?

I guess fairies could.

To conclude here: the outfit was gorgeous, and for the first time in my life, I was excited about wearing something. I rushed Sylva back into the room and tried everything on while she splashed around in the water fountain. I felt strangely beautiful, and marvelously bold. I felt I could take on the world.

"Come on, Sylva," I said, finally. "We'll never get to breakfast like this."

Sylva obliged, and I had to admit I would have also stayed longer in the fountain if I hadn't been so hungry. Even though the water was cold, it was refreshing, and made me feel alive, as if the water itself had been charged with some kind of special energy.

When Sylva and I stepped outside, both barefoot and with wet hair, a cat was waiting for us. It wasn't Trego or Calumet, but a small tuxedo cat with yellow eyes. He weaved himself between our legs a few times, purring, and then started walking down the corridor, turning around and meowing a few times.

Remember, reader, that the corridor also had life all over it: moss and mushrooms on the floor, flowers and plants on the walls, and vines and ferns hanging from the ceiling.

"He wants us to follow him," cried Sylva, skipping cheerfully on the moss and trying not to step on any mushrooms. "I bet he's taking us to the kitchen!"

"I hope so," I replied, as my stomach growled persistently. "I wonder what time it is."

"It's ten," said Sylva. Oh—that was another thing about Sylva: she always knew, with uncanny precision, what time it was.

Mr. Cat took us down a spiral staircase (now covered with moss) and we arrived on the ground floor. We went into the large living area, which still had an impressive fire place, but was otherwise a meadow complete with logs and giant mushrooms to sit on.

Tania Greenwood was sitting on the floor, leaning against a particularly large grey mushroom, reading a book.

"I knew Celynnog would have to go through here to take you to his treasure trove," she said, looking up at us.

"Treasure trove?" I repeated, confused.

"Probably some mice he's killed," said Tania. "He tries to show everyone. Mariposa goes crazy trying to revive them."

"We thought you'd sent him to take us to breakfast," I said.

"That would have been exceedingly convenient," said Tania, "but cats are immune to any kind of coercion—magical or otherwise."

"I'm sorry, Celynnog" said Sylva, crouching down and petting him. "I don't want to see dead mice."

The tuxedo cat was mightily baffled by this.

"Come on, Celynnog," said Tania, "how about a snack in the kitchen?"

Apparently, the word "snack" was one Celynnog knew well, because he perked up and followed us, chirping happily as he trotted along. We stepped out into the courtyard, and as we crossed it, another cat—this time a fat gray tabby with green eyes—started following us as well.

"That's Griggles," said Tania. "Some of the kids found him when he was a kitten, screaming from the highest branch of an apple tree."

"Speaking of kids," I said, as we crossed the courtyard, "is everyone really out in the forest?"

"Yes—with Peaseblossom, collecting flowers and herbs," said Tania.

Of course. Peaseblossom *had* to be connected to flowers.

"Where is Cobweb?" I asked.

"Not sure, but she's around here somewhere," said Tania. "She's our facilities director, so to speak. She takes care of the grounds. If we look hard enough, we can probably spot her fixing something. Let's see . . . there she is."

She pointed to a shape crouched on the thatched roof.

"Cobweb!" cried Tania, squinting against the sun. "Come down to meet Wynd and Sylva!"

To our surprise, Cobweb climbed down the outer walls on all fours, the way a spider might if it only had four legs. I have to say it was kind of creepy—all the more so because Cobweb's hair was thin and silvery, and so light it seemed to float around her face. Her eyes were pitch black, and her grin made Sylva and I take a step back: her teeth seemed sharper than a regular person's, though when I looked again, they appeared absolutely normal.

"Well—Wynd and Sylva—well," she said, and we couldn't figure out if she was surprised, shocked, or pleased.

"We're on our way to the kitchen," said Tania. "Would you like to join us?"

"Too much to fix, Majesty," was the reply. "Too much to fix."

"Very well."

I was glad she didn't come with us. Sylva was too, I think.

"Cobweb can be kind of intimidating," said Tania, as if she had read our thoughts. "She may like to eat the occasional bug, but she's a loyal and devoted friend."

"She eats bugs?" whispered Sylva, shocked.

"I think that's part of what she does on her rounds," Tania whispered back.

"What if she eats Mariposa?" I asked.

"A very good question," said Tania. "I *have* caught Cobweb eyeing Mariposa rather suspiciously, but Cobweb assures me the kind of moth Mariposa turns into is not her favorite."

"Not very reassuring," I said—and then I tripped so badly I nearly fell flat on my face.

"Are you okay?" asked Tania.

"Something tripped me," I said, scanning the ground but seeing nothing. "There was definitely something there."

I could have sworn I had just tripped over a root, but the only tree in the courtyard was Giniana, and there were no exposed roots in sight.

"Your foot looks red," said Sylva.

"It's fine," I said. "Just bruised."

"If it's just a bruise, Mariposa can check it out afterward," said Tania.

She seemed out of sorts as she said it, and I thought I detected a suspicious glance back at Giniana. I, too, glanced back at the tree, but she was wearing her poker face. I wondered what reason she might have not to like me, and then I forgot all about it as I followed Tania and Sylva through a small wooden door with a sign saying *Good digestion wait on appetite, and health on both!*

"It's Shakespeare," said Tania.

"What does it say?" asked Sylva, innocently. "I can't read."

"They didn't teach you in school?" asked Tania, and I was glad there was no disapproval in her voice.

"They did," said Sylva, lowering her eyes. "I just couldn't learn it."

"Would you like me to teach you?" she asked. "We can start right after we eat something."

"Okay," said Sylva, with a shy smile.

"Come on, then," said Tania. "Your sister looks like she's about to pass out."

Giggling and full of hope, Sylva opened the door and skipped in—and then stopped dead on her tracks. Here's why: the kitchen of Florissant Academy was a long, rectangular room, and its walls were almost entirely covered in vertical gardens with an incredible assortment of vegetables, fruits, climbing beans, and other stuff I couldn't even identify. There was this one spot where there was a super long stovetop and oven, and an industrial-looking refrigerator. Even in that spot, though, the fruits and vegetables threatened to take over.

"Good morning, I just pruned the blackberry, raspberry, and strawberry bushes," said Mustardseed. "Who'd like some berries? I also have a loaf of bread coming up—and juice and coffee."

"Coffee for me, please," said Tania, sitting down by an enormous round table just like King Arthur's, and with three placemats waiting for us.

"Coffee coming up," said Mustardseed. "Guess what else I made?"

"Your incredibly delicious mustard sauce," said Tania. "We couldn't very well have the bread without it"

"Bread? With mustard?" I asked.

"Trust me," said Mustardseed, "it's *good*."

When the bread came out of the oven, it turned out Mustardseed had been right: I had never tasted mustard (or bread, for that matter) that was so *good*.

"I'll have another slice," said Tania. "Magic uses up a lot of calories, you know."

Sylva and I also had another thick slice before we turned to the berries. And, apparently, Tania never said no to berries.

"Sit down with us, Mustardseed," said Tania. "Have something."

"Don't mind if I do," said Mustardseed, going for a slice of bread with a chunk of mustard on it.

"Do you cook for everyone here?" I asked.

"I don't actually cook a lot of the time, though I generally plan the menus," she said, after swallowing a morsel and approving the taste with a *hmmm!* sound. "In any case, I do a lot of supervising. It takes a lot of students to wash, chop, season, cook, serve, and clean."

"Students do that?" I asked. It was the first I had ever heard of something like this.

"Of course," said Mustardseed. "We have shifts, though. It's a lot of fun."

"And don't forget the compost crew," said Cobweb. "That's my favorite."

I nearly jumped. How was Cobweb sitting next to me all of a sudden? I hadn't heard her come in and pull up a chair at all.

"I—I thought you would just be using magic to do all that," I said, trying to regain my focus. "Can't you just wave your hands and have everything ready?"

"Handwaving is not something fairies can do until they're adults," explained Tania.

"Is this why Mom left us acorns?" asked Sylva.

"Precisely why," said Tania. "Your mom's acorns were special, because they could bring you all the way back to the forest. There are only a handful of trees on Florissant that have such acorns."

"Magic doesn't seem all that awesome if you can't use it everywhere," I said.

"Then tell me," said Tania, sitting back and crossing her arms. "Do you think electricity's awesome?"

"Pretty awesome—yeah."

"Can you use electricity everywhere?"

"Yeah."

"Even if there are no posts or outlets?"

"No—I mean—of course you need posts and outlets."

"With magic it's the same thing, Wynd," she explained. "Think of it as a current. You can only tap into the current if the posts and outlets are there."

"But you don't have magic posts and outlets," I said.

"Sure we do," said Tania. "They are called trees."

"Magic comes from trees?"

"From the forest," she said. "And you can't have a forest without many, many trees."

"Does that mean there's magic anywhere there's a forest?" I asked. I wanted to get it right.

"If the forest is ancient enough and hasn't been tampered with—yes."

I thought about it for a moment. "But there are hardly any forests like that anymore," I said, finally.

"And *that* is why magic is so hard to find these days," lamented Tania. "Thankfully, Florissant—at least what's left of it—is such a forest."

"Can we go into the forest?" asked Sylva, jumping out of the chair with excitement. "Can we go right now?"

"We sure can," said Tania, smiling. "It's a beautiful day to be out on Florissant. We may even run into Peaseblossom and the other students."

We put our dishes in the dishwasher. Yes, reader, there were dishwashers in Florissant Academy, and laundry machines, and computers and telephone landlines—all somehow mingled with the living walls and the magic hallways and staircases and courtyard. One time, when Ms. Williams asked Tania where the electricity came from, the answer she got was solar panels, backed up by a generator. But I never saw the solar panels, or the generator, and I always had the feeling that even the appliances in Florissant Academy were strangely alive and temperamental. It wasn't unheard of for a dishwasher door to "nip" at a student's hand, or playfully squirt water on someone. The clothes dryer routinely "swallowed" socks, and computers sometimes decided on their own screensavers (usually nature-themed). I honestly think they were fed by the current of magic that runs through the school, but I could never prove it. I could never even find out how the Academy had been built. It was definitely not the work of architects or engineers. Eventually, I came to the conclusion that Tania Greenwood must have used her magic to manifest it into being. Everything in there had her wildness, her mischief, her life-force. It must have taken some *serious* handwaving. It must have taken the magic of a fairy queen.

But I'm digressing here. What I *should* actually be saying is that, as we were leaving the kitchen, we spotted Mariposa rushing toward us, waving a crumpled newspaper in her hand.

"Majesty!" she cried, worriedly. "Majesty!"

In spite of her apparent hurry, however, Mariposa seemed unable to walk in a straight line. Her steps were irregular, restless, almost dance-like. She was moth to the last, even in human form.

Cobweb smacked her lips. Words can't convey how creepy it was.

"One day," she muttered, her dark eyes fixed on Mariposa.

"Hush, Cobweb," said Tania, disapprovingly.

"I remember I almost got her one time," said Cobweb, with noticeable regret in her voice. "I was close."

"Good thing you all lost your memory when I did," said Tania. "Maybe pursuing a degree in civil engineering was better than pursuing a moth."

"Debatable," said Cobweb.

Tania laughed. "Well, I'm glad Mariposa went to medical school, or we wouldn't have someone to staff the infirmary."

"Peaseblossom could never do it, that's for sure," retorted Cobweb. "Went and got herself a degree in flowers."

"Botany is a lot more than that, Cobweb," said Tania, gravely. "We could have never created the kitchen living walls without her. You all chose worthy pursuits in the human world."

"All *I* did was open a restaurant," said Mustardseed, embarrassed.

"Oh, come on," said Tania, nudging her with encouragement. "You became a famous chef, and earned a fortune."

"Yes, okay—that *was* pretty cool," said Mustardseed, with a proud chuckle. "This one article said I was a queen in the kitchen."

"And so you are," said Tania, playfully. "So you are."

I really wanted to know more about this new piece of information—memory loss in Tania's inner circle—but now Mariposa was there, restlessly shoving the newspaper into Tania's hands.

"*Ancient Tree in Town Square Brought Down by Last Night's Storm,*" Tania read, looking as if she had just received the worst news possible.

"The storm was much worse ten miles from here," said Mariposa. "The gales blew right through the downtown square."

"I remember when there was no town square, no town, no road," said Cobweb, looking over Tania's shoulder. "Just forest."

"I suppose we were lucky Ysador was spared to begin with, when they first built the town," said Tania, sighing. "It was such a majestic tree, of course, that they built the town square around it."

I suddenly caught myself wondering how old the three of them were. If they remembered a time before there were even roads there—when there was nothing all around but forest—they couldn't be in their forties, which is what I had originally guessed. Maybe they were a lot older than I had imagined.

"Poor tree," lamented Sylva, tears running down her face as she saw the picture of the toppled giant. She always cried over dead trees and plants. I put my arm around her shoulder for moral support and scanned the article the three ladies were huddled reading. The phrase "powerful winds" caught my attention, but I didn't get much besides that because Tania folded the article and returned it to Mariposa.

"Of all the trees," muttered Mustardseed.

It was clear to me that they were sad for this ancient tree, but there was something else going on that I couldn't quite put my finger on. Tania seemed uneasy—and Mustardseed, Mariposa, and Cobweb looked positively worried.

"It won't all start again, will it?" said Cobweb, abruptly.

"No," said Tania, with determination in her voice. "Things are different now. I've learned my lesson."

"But has he?" asked Mustardseed.

"*He*?" I repeated, dying to know more. "He *who*?"

"I'll ask Nick to give me a ride to town, to see for myself," said Tania, completely ignoring my question. "Wynd, Sylva—I'll be back later tonight, okay?"

"What about going into the forest?" said Sylva, unable to hide the disappointment in her voice.

"I'll take you first thing tomorrow," promised Tania. "Peaseblossom and all the students will be coming back for dinner, so you'll get to meet everyone in a few hours. Until then, you can hang out with Giniana, or explore the school. Florissant Academy is pretty big. Try the library."

Now she was talking. As far as I was concerned, if the forest wasn't a possibility, the library at least was a good consolation prize.

"I'll be back for dinner and dancing," said Tania.

"*Dancing?*" I cried.

"Of course," she replied. "It's Midsummer Night. There *has* to be dancing."

She waved her hand and disappeared.

Chapter 5

THE OLD ONE

"WHAT'S SO SPECIAL about Midsummer Night?" I asked.

"It's the summer solstice," said Cobweb. "Longest day of the year."

"So?"

"The summer magic of Florissant Forest is at its peak today," explained Mustardseed. "Flowers and herbs contain extra magic."

"Seriously?"

"I'm hoping Peaseblossom can collect them before noon," said Mariposa. "I should check on her."

She rushed off without further ado, with the same restless and winding steps that never went in a straight line.

"Why doesn't she just turn into a moth and fly off?" I asked.

"She only turns into a moth on full moon nights," said Cobweb. She smacked her lips, but checked herself.

"And she hates handwaving," said Mustardseed. "Says it messes with her moth radar."

"She and Peaseblossom are going to get into it again," said Cobweb, shaking her head. "They fight every year over this."

"Over what?" I asked. (By the way, don't think that Sylva wasn't there. She was. She just didn't say much. But she always paid attention.)

"Peaseblossom loves ornamental flowers and tends to forget the stuff Mariposa wants for the infirmary."

"If Tania would just let me be" said Cobweb, dreamily, "the bickering would stop."

"And who would take care of the infirmary, and the sick kids—and *you* in the winter?"

"My cocoon is low maintenance, thank you very much," snapped Cobweb.

"Do you have tons of little babies in the spring?" asked Sylva. (See? I told you she was there.)

"No," lamented Cobweb. "I'm a fairy, not a spider. I have a special connection to the spider world, and I've absorbed some spider behaviors because of spider magic, but in the end I'm still a fairy."

"What about you, Sylva?" asked Mustardseed. "Do *you* go dormant during the winter?"

"No."

"That would have made things even harder for you," said Cobweb. "Human beings would not understand you losing your hair in October and wanting to sleep until April."

"That would have *really* freaked them out," said Sylva. I could tell, from the way she said it, that all her bad memories were becoming distant, the way a pleasant summer takes the edge off a cold and rainy winter. She meandered over to the courtyard to see Giniana. Mustardseed went back to collect the dishes, and I asked Cobweb to show me where the library was.

"Very unusual," she said, as I followed her past the courtyard and through a door that led to a steep spiral staircase.

"What is?" I asked.

"For your type of fairy to enjoy spending time in the library."

"My type of fairy? What do you mean?"

"You know what I mean."

I did. I could pretend all I wanted, but I knew that even my name gave me away. Problem was, I didn't want to be who I was. I was afraid of it.

"I've always loved the library," I said, rather dismissively. "I've always found answers there."

Cobweb glanced back at me but said nothing, and I decided it was time to change the subject.

"Did you know my mother?" I asked.

"Yes."

"What kind of fairy was she?"

"Alchemy fairy. She could transform metals."

"Oh," I said. Somehow, that didn't seem very exciting to me.

"Very rare, alchemy fairies," said Cobweb. "We were all a bit jealous of her when she and Tania became best friends in India."

"What was Tania doing in India?" I asked.

"Tania has been all over the world," said Cobweb. "She met each of us in a different place. That's when there used to be forests, and magic, everywhere in the world. Fairies could come and go as they pleased."

"That sounds amazing," I said, lamenting something I knew I'd never be able to see.

"Your mother was technically never part of Tania's entourage, though, so she wasn't affected by the curse. But in any case, she paid dearly for it."

"I don't actually know anything about what happened to her," I said. "I only have a few memories."

I was hoping, of course, that Cobweb would tell a long story that would answer every question I had ever had about my mother. What she did, instead, was stop in front of a red wooden door at the top of the spiral staircase. In the middle of this small door hung an unassuming gold sign with, predictably, the word *Library* etched in the middle.

"Open the door, then," said Cobweb. "Maybe there will be some answers inside."

The door had no lock, and when I opened it my heart sank. I had expected a mega-library, enormous, with shelves and shelves brimming with books, elegant reading chairs—and maybe some pictures or inspirational quotes on the walls. What I walked into was a narrow space, like a turret, with what looked like tiny wooden drawers covering the walls from top to bottom.

"This can't be the library," I said. "Where are the books?"

But Cobweb had already left, and I didn't want to chase after her, so I just stood there for a few seconds, trying to make sense of what I saw. I now realized that the tiny, wooden drawers weren't actually drawers, but miniature doors, each with a tiny key in the keyhole. I picked a random key, turned it, and—

No. Freaking. Way.

I was standing in front of an avenue of trees, but the trees' branches were full of books instead of leaves. On the nearest tree hung a sign that said, "Thought is free."

Pretty cool idea, I had to admit. Trees of knowledge. I wondered if Tania had come up with that. Then I climbed up the tree—each tree had a rope ladder attached to it, by the way—and opened one of the books, wondering if it would do something extravagant, like surround me with its letters, or magically inject me with its contents.

It didn't. I was glad. Books were still books, apparently. You simply had to put in the effort.

Encyclopedia of the Fairy World was the first book on that first branch. That branch also boasted *A History of the Fairy World, A Fairy Atlas, Magical Forests of the World, Masterpieces of Fairy Literature, Music, and Art,* and *The Diversity of the Fairy World.*

At first, I wasn't exactly thrilled that I had landed in the reference section, but I ended up learning a lot as I leafed through the volumes. Here's what I discovered:

1. Magic is old. Really old.
2. Fairy magic can only exist in undisturbed, ancient forests and islands.
3. All people—humans—used to be fairies at one point. Some eventually forgot how to do magic. No one knows why.
4. Kids here and there are still born with fairy powers. These kids generally do not do well in the human world. If they do not make it to an ancient forest by a certain age, they either lose their magic or die. Tree fairies generally die instead of losing their magic.
5. Alchemy fairies can turn almost anything into gold. Pretty awesome, if you ask me.
6. There are only two types of fairies who can perform magic outside the forest: mischief fairies and wind fairies.
7. Most wind fairies are unable to resist the "call of the wind" by the time they turn fifteen.
8. Most wind fairies disappear at around the same age, because when they allow themselves to become wind, they tend to lose themselves in it.
9. Wind is the enemy of trees.

Reader, can you imagine how I felt as I came across all this information? I was flushed with excitement to read about this other reality, and yet already felt dissatisfied with my lot. Why couldn't I have been an alchemy fairy, or a mischief fairy?

"You look miserable!" shouted Tania, her voice coming from below. I was so startled that I actually fell off the branch. Thankfully, I landed on an enormous pile of leaves that seemed to have appeared out of nowhere.

"I knew the leaf pile spell would come in handy," said Tania, pleasantly. "You're not the first one to fall from one of these trees."

"I didn't hear you coming," I said, scrambling to get up.

"I didn't *come*," she said, grandly, "I *appeared*. It's what I used to do when I was queen, and I'm afraid I haven't gotten rid of the habit entirely. Sorry if I startled you."

"How did you become the fairy queen?" I asked.

"The moment I turned of age, a crown appeared on my head."

"Subtle," I said. "What if you wanted to stop being the fairy queen?"

She thought for a moment. "I doubt I could."

"How come?"

"Because that's who I am," she said, exuberantly. "Why would I want to be someone else?"

"Because it could mean you'll abandon your sister, and drift away forever."

"I see," she said, taking her exuberance down a notch. "I gather you've been reading about wind fairies."

"Just a thing or two—enough to know that my chances aren't great."

"And yet here you are."

"I read that most wind fairies don't make it past fifteen."

"Then you've surpassed expectations already. You're ahead of the game."

"I don't want to be a wind fairy," I protested. "I promised Sylva I wouldn't leave her."

"Speaking of Sylva," said Tania, putting my existential crisis on hold, "where is she? I came to get you both for dinner."

Dinner? It couldn't have been more than three o'clock in the afternoon.

"It's too early for dinner . . . isn't it?" I asked.

"It's seven o'clock," she replied.

"Seven o'clock? Is the library in a time loop or something like that?"

"Something like that," said Tania. "Dinner has already started—and my guess is that the dancing will start soon."

"And you can't find Sylva?"

"I've searched for her everywhere," said Tania. "Where could she be?"

"I bet that tree in the courtyard knows."

"My thoughts, exactly," she replied. "Come on."

She walked past a wooden *Exit* sign, the kind you might find on a trail. I hadn't seen it before, but I couldn't tell if it was because I hadn't paid attention or it simply hadn't been there earlier. Magic was funny that way.

I followed Tania Greenwood, and in fewer than three steps, we were back in the turret with all the wooden drawers. The little drawer I had opened closed on its own, and we walked out and down the spiral staircase.

"Can you do magic on me so that I'm not a wind fairy?" I asked, going back to my existential crisis.

"I can, but I won't. Keeping fairies away from their essence is too cruel."

"I reject my inner essence," I said.

"You don't know what you're saying."

"Wind is the enemy of trees," I said. "The wind raises storms and destroys trees. I read in one of the books that trees in Florissant hate wind fairies above all."

"Not entirely true," said Tania. "They hate human beings above all."

"I know—because they cut down trees."

"Exactly."

"But after human beings, trees hate wind fairies the most," I said. "According to one book, wind fairies cause all this horrible damage when they turn into wind the first time—not to mention they lose themselves in the wind and disappear."

"They *can* cause terrible damage, and they *can* lose themselves in the wind and disappear," said Tania, somewhat impatiently. "But let's continue this conversation *after* we find your sister, okay?"

"Can't you just give me something to prevent me from turning into wind?" I insisted, as we went out into the courtyard.

"Like what?" she asked, without slowing her pace.

"I don't know. Something that won't let me fly away. A magical leash or something."

"Nope," she said. "All good things are wild and free, even if they cease to be."

"Who said that? Shakespeare?"

"No—a writer called Henry David Thoreau said the first part, and I made up the second. It means it's better to be wild and free, even if it costs you your life."

I was too out of breath to really consider a reply. As we hurried through the courtyard, the delicious smell of dinner wafted past me, and I half-wished I could go inside to grab a bite to eat. The chatter of voices, too, was inviting, with its mingling of laughter and excited conversation.

"Giniana," said Tania, taking a stand in front of the oak tree and crossing her arms. "Where's Sylva?"

If the tree said anything, I did not hear it. What I did hear was Tania cursing under her breath.

"Let's go," said Tania. "She's pretending to be asleep."

"Can't you *make* her tell you?" I protested, running after her once more.

"You can't force trees. You can destroy them, but you can't force them to do anything they don't want to do."

"Like cats?"

"Much worse than cats."

We reached the front door, and Tania unceremoniously opened it. Twenty-four hours earlier, I had walked through that door—drenched to the bone—carrying Sylva.

"We'll find her," said Tania, summoning with her hand a pair of tall boots, and then putting them on. "I bet she decided to plant her sapling. Did she mention anything to you about that, or about the forest?"

"Only that there's a really old tree that doesn't like anyone."

"That's where she must have gone, then. Here," she added, waving her hand and handing me another pair of boots. "There's plenty that can sting you out there."

"Doesn't magic protect us?"

"Boots do a better job. Besides, stinging insects and snakes have as much a right to the forest as we do. I'm already pushing it by not letting them come into Florissant Academy."

I put the boots on, and they adjusted to fit my feet. They were the most comfortable shoes I had ever worn, reader.

"These are awesome," I said. "But why can't you just *handwave* us there?"

"There where?" she asked, closing the door. "I'd need a destination."

"Maybe we could split up. Do you have a map of the forest I could use?"

"A map of Florissant? Of course not."

"Why not?"

"Because, Wynd, a map suggests that only a few things are important. It includes those things and leaves everything else out. But in the forest, *everything* is important."

I stared at her. How could everything be equally important? I wondered if she was joking, but she looked dead serious.

"You have to get out of the human mindset if you want to be a fairy," she continued. "Everything in Florissant has magic. Everything is, potentially, its own destination. To navigate the forest, you must feel it with your heart."

"I don't know how to do that."

"Of course not," she said. "You just got here. But it'll happen. Take a good look. Do you feel anything?"

I stared at the forest. A strange—but pleasant—sensation of excitement came over me.

"I do," I said. "The forest feels familiar, somehow."

"See?" she said. "Some part of you remembers you were born here. Now come on—keep up."

With Tania Greenwood, keeping up was no easy feat. In spite of being relatively short, she had *the* fastest pace I'd ever had to keep up with. Besides, I kept tripping.

"Sorry," I said, after it had happened a few times. "I guess I'm not used to walking in the forest."

"The trees are tripping you."

"Are you serious?"

"You're lucky some of the willow trees haven't tried anything worse," she said. "It must be because I'm here. Willow trees like to tiptoe behind people. And the birches aren't called the trees of death for nothing. Once they hold a grudge, they'll—"

"You told me Sylva would be safe in the forest," I said, panicking. "Now you're telling me there are killer trees!"

"No tree would raise a root or branch against *her*," said Tania. "But we can't make progress like this."

She glared at the trees all around us, and then stomped her foot. It might have been ridiculous if someone else had done it—but, in her case, the earth shook slightly.

"Stop doing that!" she bellowed, in a voice that was surprisingly strong. "This is the tree child's sister, the one who has kept her safe all these years. No more tripping from now on!"

The echo of her voice—yes, there was an echo—faded. For a moment, complete silence reigned. It was pretty impressive, no sound in the forest for a second or two.

Then everything went back to normal. The forest was full of the droning of insects and toads and frogs and whatever else makes sound at night. You get the idea.

"We're getting closer to the deepest part of the forest," said Tania, quietly. "This is why the trees are so bold."

I didn't know trees could be bold.

"The less contact with the outside world, the wilder and more magical the trees are," whispered Tania, as we continued. "We're still far from the Old One, though."

"I can't believe Sylva ventured out here alone," I said.

"You're not a tree fairy," said Tania. "She wants to be rooted, more than anything else. That's the essence of a tree."

"And what's the essence of wind?"

"Movement."

I could feel the truth in her words. Even as we kept walking, I was restless and eager to get to the next step. I felt the same way when I read: I was always on a feverish search for the next word. My eyes were always on the move, even when the rest of me wasn't.

"If the sapling dies, does Sylva die?" I asked.

"Yes—but you already knew that."

"So, if Sylva dies, does the sapling die?"

"No."

"That's unfair!"

"Only because you are thinking of them as two separate beings," said Tania. "They are not entirely separate, even though they're not the same, either. The sapling holds Sylva's memories and wisdom. It's Sylva, in tree form. The oldest trees in the forest are the ones who know the most, even if their tree fairies are gone."

"Gone where?" I asked.

"When the great deforestations of the world began," explained Tania, "the tree fairies started to get depressed and ill. They withdrew into the trees to escape the pain. They never came back. Eventually, there were no tree fairies left. Until your sister came along, there hadn't been a new tree fairy in Florissant for a long time."

"What kind of fairy are *you*?" I asked.

"I don't have a type," said Tania. "I've a ton of magic, without a specialty. You could say I'm a generalist."

"Seriously?"

"Seriously."

"Is that why you're queen?" I asked.

"I'm actually not queen anymore," she confessed.

"You're not?"

"Do you see a crown?" she asked.

"No."

"Precisely."

"Well, who . . . de-crowned you?" I asked.

"The trees."

"Seriously?"

"You say that word a lot."

And she slowed down and stopped.

"For a long time, I was a good queen," she muttered.

"For how long?"

"Until I wasn't. Time goes by differently in the forest."

I was about to use that word (the one I say a lot, apparently), but I checked myself in time.

"Then I became an irresponsible queen," she lamented, "and your mother and the forest paid for it."

My mother. Just hearing about her made my heart beat faster.

"I remember the gunshot," I said, my voice quivering in spite of my best efforts. "It's weird, but I don't remember much else—not even from beforehand."

"The forest kept most of your memories to spare you from excessive pain," said Tania. "Now that you have returned, you'll slowly remember everything."

"I wish I could forget the gunshot," I admitted. "That sound haunted our childhood."

Tania placed a sympathetic arm on my shoulder.

"Your mother protected Florissant when I was absent," she said. "It's my fault she was murdered. If I had been here, I would have protected her—or at least died in her place. It's really my fault that you and Sylva grew up without a mother."

For all of two or three seconds, I hated Tania Greenwood with an intensity that surprised me. Then I saw the expression in those green eyes—full of guilt and regret—and something within me softened.

"I won't blame you if you hate me," she added, humbly. "Honestly."

It was painful seeing her like that. Humility didn't suit the fairy queen.

"I *don't* hate you," I said. "I hate whoever killed her."

"So do I," she said. "I fully intend to find out who it was. If only the trees would tell me," she added, lowering her voice. "Ever since they dethroned me, they've shut me out."

I felt an involuntary shiver go down my spine. We were surrounded by trees, and for the first time I sensed their power. It was ancient, raw, deep. It made me afraid.

"This Old One . . ." I continued, barely above a whisper, "are we getting closer?"

"Very close."

She pointed to the ground, but all I could see were leaves, pine needles, and the roots of a tree sticking out. She made a slight gesture with her hand, and the leaves and pine needles scattered, revealing several moss-covered roots that grew thicker and thicker as we followed their meandering paths.

"Just how big is this tree?" I muttered, nervously. I swear I could feel something pulsing through the powerful roots. If this particular tree decided to kill me, I wondered if even Tania Greenwood could do something about it.

"Do you see them?" asked Tania. "The marks on the roots?"

I looked down. Tania was right: the roots were covered in glowing marks that seemed a lot like the kinds of lines Sylva always made whenever someone tried to teach her to write.

"What are those?" I asked.

"It's TreeSpeak," said Tania.

"What does it say?"

"I don't know," said Tania. "I forgot TreeSpeak."

"Like when you forgot you were a fairy?"

"Yes."

"But at some point, you remembered you were a fairy," I said. "Can't you remember this?"

"Not if the trees don't want me to."

"I can't believe we have to look for Sylva in the middle of a bunch of trees that hate us," I said.

"I don't know if they hate us," mused Tania. "They might hate *you*. I think they just dislike me at this point."

"They can hate me all they want," I said, boldly. "I'm going to find Sylva, and no tree's going to stop me."

I followed the roots to the massive trunk of the Old One. Reader, this magnolia tree was so gigantic it took up a whole chunk of forest. I began to think that maybe I shouldn't have been so bold. I began to think that maybe Tania and I should head back.

"Well, at least we know your sister *was* here," said Tania.

"How?" I asked. "Do you suddenly understand TreeSpeak again?"

"Her sapling's over there."

I would have never noticed it, had Tania not pointed it out. It had been planted a few feet away. Directly above the sapling was a gap in the Old One's branches—enough to let light through and allow a new tree to grow. Yet the sapling looked so small, and so fragile in the immensity of the forest, that I decided I'd scoop it up and take it back home, where it'd be safe.

"Wynd, let it be," warned Tania, seeing me kneel down and stick my hands around the roots.

"I really think Sylva should keep the sapling a little longer," I said.

"Wynd, it's *really* not a good idea to uproot anything here in Florissant, least of all a tree fairy's—"

And that's when everything happened: the loud tearing sound, and the cold, powerful root around my neck.

Turns out the tree marks had been a warning.

"I can't breathe!" I gasped, as the root tightened its grip. It hurt so badly I was sure my neck would snap any second.

"Old One, no! That's my sister!"

It was Sylva's voice for sure—but clearly the tree was *not* listening.

"She saved my life!" insisted Sylva. "Don't hurt her!"

"Stop this, Old One!" said Tania, with a voice as powerful as thunder. "You know very well that trees can't exist without wind. Who would bring rain? Who would take seeds where they need to go? Do not blame this wind fairy for your friend's death. You are old enough to know that the wind is good *and* bad, the same way nature is life *and* death."

The root loosened its grip on my neck somewhat, as if thinking it through.

"If you want someone to hurt, hurt *me*, for I well deserve it," said Tania, her green orbs on fire.

The root relinquished its grip on my neck and sank back into the earth as quickly as it had jumped out of it. I fell on the ground, gasping miserably for air.

"Are you okay, Wynd?" asked Tania, quietly. I nodded. My neck was bruised, and I was shaking, but I could breathe.

"Old One," said Sylva, affectionately putting her hand on the ancient trunk, "don't hurt anyone. It won't make you feel better."

Several TreeSpeak lines glowed on the trunk.

"I know you're sad about Ysador," said Sylva, nodding sympathetically. "But I'd be really sad if I lost Wynd."

New TreeSpeak lines appeared. Sylva smiled.

"When you get to know her, you'll like her," said Sylva, eagerly. "I promise."

Tania and I watched the whole exchange, amazed.

"Well, what do you know?" said Tania, turning to me. "Your sister *can* read, after all."

Chapter 6

Grimsby's Revenge

I LEARNED TWO important things when we were walking back to Florissant with Sylva. The first came from noticing that Sylva wasn't wearing any shoes. It didn't seem to bother her, for she was walking happily next to me, oblivious to the pine needles, sticks, and stones she was stepping over.

"Is it okay for Sylva to go barefoot in the forest?" I asked Tania. "You said we could get stung out here."

"We can," said Tania. "But tree fairies hardly ever get stung or bitten by anything—good thing, too, since they generally hate wearing shoes."

So true. Sylva always took off her shoes whenever possible, and she absolutely refused to wear socks—even on the frigid winter mornings we occasionally get here in Georgia. I guess it was a good thing we weren't in New York, or Vermont.

"But what if they do?" I insisted. I was sure there were copperheads and scorpions in Florissant, for all its magic.

"I didn't tell you this before, but fairies are immune to venom," said Tania.

"So why are we wearing boots?" I asked.

"Because I hate getting stung—and I don't much like snake bites, either," said Tania. "You're welcome to go barefoot like your sister, if you'd like."

At night? In the thick of the forest? Uh—no thanks.

Anyway, the second thing I learned was that Sylva could identify several trees: alder, ash, beech, birch, cedar, dogwood, and so on. She also insisted on the fact that every tree had a name. This one here was

Matilda Birch, that one there Deva Dogwood, and that one way over there was Olaf Oak.

"And Sylva Magnolia," said Tania, affectionately. "You're the same type of tree as the Old One."

"Magnolias have always been my favorite tree," I said, "until I met the Old One."

"You'll like her when you get to know her better," said Sylva.

Somehow, I doubted that.

"You'll be huge like her one day," I said. "And you'll have those amazing flowers."

"When I grow up," said Sylva, earnestly. "I'm still tiny."

She was so cute, my little sis—I could barely stand it.

"Did Old One teach you about all the trees?" I asked.

"Uh-huh."

"She's taken you under her wing—her branch," said Tania, with a chuckle. "How about you teach me TreeSpeak, and I teach you how to read the human alphabet? Does that sound like a good plan?"

Sylva thought it was a fantastic plan. Almost as good as dinner. She was hungry from all that walking.

"So am I," said Tania. "What do you say we cheat a little?"

"Does it involve handwaving?" I asked. "If so, I'm for it."

"Me too," said Sylva.

A handwave later, the three of us were standing in front of the massive wooden door of Florissant Academy.

"I can hear music," said Tania, smiling. "We're still in time."

Just as she was about to open the door, however, we heard growling and barking nearby.

"Is that the wolves?" asked Sylva. I could tell she was scared.

"You two go inside," said Tania. "I'll check it out."

I wanted to tell Tania that she probably shouldn't go alone, but she had already run off, so I took Sylva inside and told her to close the door once I left.

"Where are you going?" she asked, nervously.

"After Tania," I said. "She shouldn't go alone."

"She told us to come inside," cried Sylva. "What if something happens to you?"

"Nothing will happen," I reassured her. "I'll be back in a bit. Let the others know, just in case."

Sylva rushed down the corridor, and I went outside again. I ran in the direction Tania had gone, guiding myself by the ruckus the wolves were making. It was a horrible sound—clearly, a fight had broken out.

When I found Tania, she was kneeling by an injured wolf. He was whining, and I saw blood. I couldn't figure out which of the wolves he was, and then I realized that the Guardians of Florissant were all watching from a distance. I counted. They were all there (no welcoming lantern from Madog this time), seemingly ready to bolt into attack again. Grimsby, in particular, had his yellow eyes fixed on the injured wolf.

I shuddered. The yellow fire that burned in Grimsby's eyes was frightening. Terrifying, actually.

"What happened?" I asked. "Why did they attack another wolf?"

"He's not a wolf," said Tania. As if to confirm what she was saying, the wolf morphed into a man in his late thirties, maybe—and a man who was in a lot of pain.

"Here," said Tania, giving him to drink from a vial. "I'm glad I carry this on me."

"What is that?" I asked.

"Healing water."

The man started breathing more easily, and finally sighed with relief.

"I have to admit that did *not* go well," he said, wincing as Tania helped him up.

"You're supposed to stay in the Academy during the full moon," Tania said, as we walked back to the door. "Why did you come out? Grimsby won't forgive you that easily."

"No kidding," he said. "Who's this?"

"This is Wynd," said Tania. "She and her sister are new in Florissant."

"Nice to meet you, Wynd," he said. "I'm Nick."

"You're bleeding, too," said Tania. "I only had enough water on me to stop the pain. Here"—she opened the heavy door for him—"let's get you to the infirmary. Wynd, make sure you close the door behind you."

She waved her hand and disappeared with Nick, and I was just pushing the heavy door closed when Grimsby tried to jump in (he must have been trailing us, stalking Nick). I'm not sure exactly how it happened, but when I used my body to block him, he staggered back, his thick fur blowing wildly as if a giant hairdryer had been pointed at him.

I quickly closed the door. I felt nauseous, as if I were about to throw up. My entire body shook—ever so lightly, but it shook.

"Wynd!" cried Sylva. "You okay?"

"Grimsby was trying to get in, but Tania told me to close the door," I said, realizing that I was slurring my words, as if my brain and voice were on two different speeds.

"I think you used wind magic to keep him out," said Mustardseed, whom Sylva had apparently brought with her. "Why is he not allowed in?"

"The wolves attacked Nick," I said. "Tania took him to the infirmary."

"Let's get you there as well," said Mustardseed. "You look a little sick."

"I'm okay."

I tried to stand up, but my eyes went dark, and I quickly slid down again.

"The infirmary it is," said Mustardseed, helping me up and handwaving the three of us there.

Nick was sitting on a stool, with his left foot in a basin and Mariposa pouring water over his calf. Reader, even though I felt super sick, I knew I wasn't dreaming when I saw the wound healing before my eyes.

"I think Wynd needs some help also," said Mustardseed.

"What happened?" asked Tania, rushing toward me with concern.

"Grimsby tried to get in," I said, relieved to notice I wasn't slurring as much. "I pushed him out."

"With wind magic," added Mustardseed.

"Mariposa, she needs stabilizing salts," said Tania.

"You want to diagnose her, do you?" said Mariposa, grumpily.

"Just look at her," said Tania, with a gesture of impatience.

Mariposa peered quickly into my eyes.

"I hate it when you're right," she said, rushing to a drawer and coming back with an ornate box, from which she took a little pink pebble.

"What is this?" I asked.

"Put this little salt pebble under your tongue, and let it dissolve," she said, giving it to me.

"Is Wynd okay?" asked Sylva, nervously.

"She will be, in a second," said Tania.

"Making predictions now, are we?" snapped Mariposa.

"I know it's after hours, Mariposa," said Tania, "but must you be in such a foul mood?"

"Sorry," said Mariposa. "It's just that these medical emergencies always happen when the moon is calling."

"Take off, then," said Tania, sympathetically. "Everything is under control now. Honestly—you may go."

"Thank you, Majesty," said Mariposa, gratefully. "I will see you in the morning."

Once again, Mariposa turned into a moth and fluttered away. I briefly wondered what would happen to her if she ran across a hungry bat. Would she turn back into her regular body? Would she become dinner? If I'd been feeling better, I might have pursued the subject, but I was still nauseous—and then there was the howling.

"They're out there," said Tania. "I must go and speak to Grimsby, or they'll do this all night."

"I will go with you," said Mustardseed.

They handwaved themselves away, and Sylva decided talking to Nick was the more interesting option now.

"Are you a fairy?" she asked him.

"I'm not so lucky, no. I'm cursed."

"Who cursed you?" she asked.

"The forest did," replied Nick. "I shot one of the Guardians of Florissant—Grimsby's mate, apparently—and that is why he hates me."

"You shot a wolf?" she asked, shocked.

"I used to be a jerk," he said. "Now I have to pay the price."

"*I* wouldn't forgive you," she said.

"Me, neither," he said. "Looks like I'll keep turning into a wolf every time the moon is full, and Grimsby will keep trying to kill me."

"That doesn't sound so bad for what you've done," I said, deciding I was getting well enough to venture an opinion.

"That's because you don't know what it's like," he said. "If I go anywhere near the town, people try to shoot me. And if I get close to Florissant, Grimsby tries to kill me. That's why I have to stay in the Academy when the moon is full."

Sylva went to the window to see if she could spot the wolves, but she was too short to see out of it. Nick got up from his stool, pushed it to the window, and lifted her onto it.

"There you go," he said.

He seemed nice, reader, and I wondered how someone like that could have shot a wolf and killed it, just like that. I couldn't wrap my mind around it.

"So, what do you do besides hunting?" I asked.

"I don't hunt anymore," he said. "I like to think of myself as an actor, actually."

"There's work for actors around here?" I asked.

"Not much," said Nick. "I earn a living mostly as a handyman. I act on the side. Community theater—stuff like that."

"I guess it's a pretty small town," I said, not sure what else to offer. "Do you ever think about leaving?"

"I sure do," he said.

"So why don't you?" I asked.

He turned to the window. The howling had stopped.

"Tania got them to stop," he said. "She's amazing, isn't she?"

Aha! So *that* was the reason he stayed.

"Your last name isn't Bottom, by any chance, is it?" I asked.

"No. It's Hintern. I know what you're thinking: the age difference is too great."

Had never occurred to me. I thought about it for a second. He looked about ten years younger than Tania—but then again, Shakespeare was already writing about her in *A Midsummer Night's Dream*, so she had to be at *least* some four hundred years older than him. Maybe that was a deal-breaker.

Or maybe it was the fact that he turned into a wolf every month.

"How long before you turn into a wolf again?" I asked.

"Not long," he said. "As soon as I'm all healed, it'll happen."

"How did she heal you so quickly?" I asked.

"Healing water. It works so fast you wouldn't believe."

But I did believe—especially as I saw him turn into a wolf right then and there, in front of Sylva and me.

"He's such a pretty wolf," cried Sylva, running her hand through his fur. "He's got green eyes."

Wolf Nick nudged Sylva, licked her hand, and then whined as the infirmary door opened. Tania came in and received a tail wag and a bark.

"I had a feeling he'd be back in canine form," she said. "Are you feeling better, Wynd?"

"Much better. Are the other wolves gone?" I asked.

"Yes. I persuaded Grimsby to leave. It's hard work, persuading a wolf."

"I think Nick wants to go out," said Sylva, as the wolf paced restlessly and whined.

"He can stay in the courtyard," said Tania. "Come on, Nick. This way."

Sylva and I followed Tania and Wolf Nick down the stairs.

"Why are you helping him?" I asked. "He shot one of the Guardians of Florissant."

"I know he did," said Tania. "I also know that sometimes there is no way to make up for something we've done, no matter how hard we try. In any case, I'm glad to see you feeling better. Mariposa can check on you tomorrow morning."

"Don't you worry Mariposa will get eaten one of these days?" I asked.

"I do, but all good things—"

"—are wild and free, even if they cease to be," I dutifully finished, as we walked out into the courtyard. "I know."

"It's always a risk, life," said Tania.

Maybe in Florissant, it was. In the humid, fresh air, with the giant moon over the wall of trees, the fireflies all around us, and the symphony of crickets, cicadas, frogs, and all other nocturnal critters, I thought it was definitely a risk worth taking.

"Are we going back to the dance?" asked Sylva.

"You two are," said Tania. "Mustardseed's already there. I'm going to collect some fernseed."

"Now? In the dark?" I asked.

"It *has* to be in the dark," she said. "You have to get it on Midsummer Night if you want to use it for invisibility."

No invisibility cloaks on Florissant, reader. Or magic wands. Or fairies with wings. This was a different universe—wilder, for sure, but more down-to-earth and less flashy. You wanted invisibility? You had to go get the seeds yourself.

"Can we come?" asked Sylva. "Please? I've never collected seeds."

"Fernseed's one of the good ones," said Tania. "There are lots of good ones in the forest, of course."

"Is that a yes?" I asked.

"Oh, all right," said Tania. "We won't be long, anyway."

She turned to Wolf Nick and looked straight into his eyes.

"You're very sleepy, aren't you? Ready to take a long nap, I wager."

No one, I think, could resist those green eyes. Every shade of green on Florissant seemed to be in them, somehow. Wolf Nick blinked, yawned, sat, and finally lay down, his head leaning against his large paws.

"I don't get how Nick could kill a wolf in the forest," I said. "I thought Florissant was enchanted to protect the animals."

"He didn't kill her in the forest," said Tania. "Grimsby's mate strayed just far enough from the magical boundary to be shot—not Nick's finest moment, unfortunately."

"Do you think the curse can ever be broken?"

"If Grimsby forgives him, perhaps. But it is no easy feat, earning forgiveness from a wolf. It's hard enough to earn their respect."

We reached the gate now, and Tania glanced up at the moon and thought for a moment.

"It's getting late," she said. "How do you feel about taking a short cut? I can show you how to get there another day."

Neither Sylva nor I had any problem with that, so she handwaved us to a spot in the forest where we were surrounded by the droning of the cicadas, the croaking of frogs, and the occasional owl. The forest floor was dappled with moonlight, and Tania showed us where the fernseeds were as the fireflies floated all around us.

Reader, I don't want to sound corny, but for the first time I felt that the forest was alive, its heartbeat pulsing through everything. I'll never forget the feeling. The magic of Florissant flowed right through me, leaving me happy and whole as I watched Tania inspect the different fern leaves with Sylva.

"This is a good one," Tania was telling her. "Did you know that fern leaves are called megaphylls?"

Sylva loved the name.

"Now," continued Tania, "megaphyll is a word that starts with the letter M—which looks like this."

The fairy queen drew a golden M in the air, and Sylva gasped with delight.

"Now you know your first letter," said Tania, as the letter began to fade.

"M for megaphyll," cried Sylva, excitedly. "Can we do another one?"

"How about we collect a few seeds, then do a few letters?" suggested Tania.

"Okay!"

"We only want to take from adult leaves, and even then only a few," said Tania, putting the vial in Sylva's little hands. "The ferns need the rest of the seeds."

She tapped the fern leaf—oops, megaphyll—and the seeds were sucked into the little vial.

"Is the vial magical?" asked Sylva.

"Just a little vacuum spell," said Tania. "Otherwise, it would be pretty hard to get these in there. Here, Wynd—you do some also."

She handed me a little vial, and I collected a bunch while she and Sylva went over letters: "a" for alder, "b" for beech, "c" for cedar—and so on, with Tania magically drawing on air the first letter of every tree Sylva had learned to recognize so far.

"You'll have the alphabet down in no time," said Tania, pleasantly. "Soon, you'll be able to read."

"Books about trees?" asked Sylva.

"About anything," said Tania. "You can learn a lot from the Old One, but you can also learn a lot from books."

Sylva was so excited at her prospects that she hugged Tania.

"Listen, Sylva," said Tania, kneeling down so that she was eye-level with my sister, "I loved your mother. She was my good—my truest—friend."

"Like Mariposa and Mustardseed?" asked Sylva.

"Not exactly," said Tania. "Mariposa and Mustardseed were part of my court, but your mother was not. I met your mother when I traveled to India, a long time ago, and we became best friends. She came to visit Florissant and stayed to protect it when I left."

"Why did you leave?" asked Sylva.

"I left because I was placed under a spell, and forgot I was a fairy."

"Who would put a spell like that on you?" asked Sylva, frowning.

"He's someone I hope I never see again," said Tania. "Fingers crossed."

"It'll take more than *that* to keep me away from Florissant, as you well know," said a man's voice behind us—quiet, like the murmur of water in a stream. Needless to say, the three of us swung around, startled.

A man's shape stood out against the moonlight: he was tall and lean, with shoulder-length wild, wavy hair. He had, somehow, come quite close to us without making a sound, the way a deer glides by unnoticed through the trees.

"Who's that?" whispered Sylva.

Tania's green orbs were blazing, and she took a moment before she answered.

"Oberon."

Chapter 7

OBERON

"THAT'S OBERON?" I whispered, stunned. "*The* Oberon?"

"And on Midsummer Night, no less," said Tania, under her breath.

"Ill-met by moonlight, proud Titania," he said, stepping forward into a moonlit spot.

Reader, Oberon was nothing like I had imagined. His bright eyes were dark brown, like forest acorns, and his walnut-brown hair seemed the embodiment of wildness itself, with its disobedient, ear-length waves blowing in the soft summer breeze (it was longer than Tania's, obviously, and slightly longer than mine). I'm honestly not sure what he was wearing: his pants looked as if they were made from a variety of leaves stitched together, and he was bare-chested, though he seemed to have some sort of long cape trailing behind him. Not sure what the cape was made of, either, but in the moonlight it seemed to have been stitched together with flowers, pine cones, twine, and grass.

"I go by Tania now," she said, flatly. "Tania Greenwood."

"Funny you should call yourself that, because much of the green wood has disappeared," he said. "What has happened to Florissant?"

"The humans happened," she said. "While you and I were away—"

"*Away*? I wasn't away," he said, though his voice was still quiet. "You locked me inside a tree!"

"Because you used one of your potions on me," she countered, holding her ground. "How could you?"

"It was meant to teach you a lesson," he said. "I was going to revoke the love potion in a few days. If you hadn't prepared a counter-spell and stuck me in a tree, I *would* have."

"I'm glad I prepared the counter-spell," retorted Tania. "The only thing I'm sorry for is that the storm toppled the tree. I had counted on you being in there for a lot longer."

Oberon's jaw hardened. In spite of his apparent resentment, however, he didn't strike me as malicious. He looked weary, exhausted even. Even in such a state, however, he was also beautiful and unearthly, with long eye lashes adorning the dark embers of his eyes. If this all sounds a bit poetic to you, it's because I had an *instacrush* on him. There was something mysterious I found incredibly attractive. Like Tania, he *was* the forest, with all its mischief and moodiness.

"How did you free yourself from the love potion?" he asked.

"Four-leaf clover," said Tania. "You know it breaks the magic of potions."

"You wouldn't have known that without your memory," he said, suspiciously. "Who helped you?"

"Rasayana," she said—and, surprisingly, she turned to Sylva and me. "You might as well know it. Your mother released me from the spell. One day, I was coming back from teaching my Shakespeare class, when I found an envelope in my office. I opened it, and there it was, a four-leaf clover. Thanks to your mother, I remembered who I was."

Rasayana. I suddenly recognized the name. A faint memory of seeing my mother laughing with a friend came to me—together with a flash of the most incredible green eyes. I had admired them as a child. They had been Tania's, for sure.

"I thought magic didn't work outside of Florissant," I said.

"Magic spells don't," said Tania. "Potions are different. Their influence reaches beyond the forest, and their antidotes work outside the forest also. Rasayana knew this."

Rasayana again. The name was back in our lives, and I felt a sense of joy and relief at having found something so precious.

"It was supposed to be a prank—a joke," continued Oberon. "How was I supposed to know the first thing you'd run into would be a copy of *The Collected Works of Shakespeare* someone had tossed in the woods? I intended you to fall in love with a porcupine, or a skunk, or a chipmunk."

"And thanks to your little *joke*, I became a Shakespeare professor."

"You should thank me, then," said Oberon. "Because of me, you're the most educated fairy there ever was."

"Do you know what it was like, to remember all of a sudden that I was the fairy queen?"

"And do you know what it was like, to be the fairy king and be forced to spend years and years inside a tree?"

As good as Shakespeare was, reader, he apparently missed these details.

"I hope it was educational," said Tania, with detectable irony in her voice. "In any case, you're no longer the fairy king, any more than I'm the fairy queen."

Oberon felt his head, and his expression turned to one of shock.

"The trees?" he asked.

She nodded. "Look, let's just agree to keep out of each other's way. I won't go anywhere near your cave, and you can stay away from Florissant Academy."

"Ah, yes," he said, scornfully. "I walked past your so-called Academy. Very clever use of reclaimed wood, but an otherwise futile endeavor."

"If we want the forest to be here in a hundred years, we have to help our youngest fairies to protect it. They need to understand the fairy kingdom *and* the human kingdom," said Tania. "This is why the Academy teaches human as well as fairy disciplines. These kids have to be versed in both, Oberon, to go back out there and help preserve the last fairy strongholds in the world."

"You'd wish that on them?" he asked. "They will be in a world that doesn't understand them, that doesn't value them—they will be without their magic, and they will age."

"I've aged," said Tania. "So have you."

"I know," he said, patting his cheeks. "I can feel wrinkles and sagging skin, and it's all your fault."

"None of us can stay young forever anymore," said Tania. "The more the human world encroaches on us, the more we'll age like the humans."

Oberon looked absolutely shocked and appalled.

"Is it possible?" he asked, his hook nose and wide eyes suddenly giving him the appearance of an owl. "Have things come to this?"

"The world has changed on us, Oberon," said Tania. "We lived in the heart of the fairy world, and we never saw the edges of that world disappearing."

"And now Florissant is also disappearing," he muttered, sadly.

Their gazes met. I can tell you it was incredible, the meeting of the dark woods with the green fire—but it was abruptly interrupted by the sound of a car pulling up to the edge of the forest.

"Am I hearing a car?" asked Tania.

"Those demon boxes that don't stop?" said Oberon, alarmed. "One almost hit me when I was walking back to Florissant."

"This can't be good," said Tania. "I hope they're not hunters."

"Hunters?" repeated Oberon, stunned. "On Florissant?"

"We have to be careful," said Tania, leading the way. "It sounds as if the car is at the edge of the forest. I have very little magic there."

"And I have no magic at all right now—thanks to you," said Oberon. "Imagine my surprise when I finally got out and discovered I was no longer in the forest."

"It *used* to be forest," said Tania.

"Yes, I know it *used* to be forest," said Oberon, irritated. "It *used* to be Florissant—the source of my magic as well as yours."

"My magic was always stronger than yours," said Tania, dismissively. "Admit it. You were a second-rate king. You were a second-rate everything."

"Now that is low, even for you," he said, so quietly he almost growled.

"Did you guys ever actually like each other?" I asked. I was getting tired of all the arguing.

"If you must know, we adored each other," said Oberon. "I will never forget the first time I chanced upon her on one of my forest rounds. She was dancing with her fairies, and it was glorious! Her long hair shone in the moonlight, and her eyes—like green stars."

"It was never going to work out," said Tania, though I could see that his words had affected her a little. "I was already queen of the forest when we met."

"And I was already king," he said. "But Florissant was large enough for the two of us."

"Apparently, it wasn't—not even back then. Imagine now."

And she stepped in front of him, blocking his way.

"Go home, Oberon," she said. "Go back to your cave and regain your strength. I'll handle this."

"I don't doubt you can," he said, and he was oddly sincere even if he was also annoyed. "But I have a right to investigate as much as you do. If Florissant has become so much smaller, it only means we'll have to work together."

"You should have thought of that before you used a potion on me."

"If you must know," he said, "I agree with you. It was incredibly foolish, and I've no excuse but my own narcissism."

Tania crossed her arms and surveyed him with suspicion.

"I'm being sincere," he insisted. "I've had a long and solitary confinement to think the whole thing over. You'd be amazed what forced reflection time can do."

"Look," I whispered (I was a few steps ahead), "someone's getting out of the car."

As quietly as we could, we made our way to the last line of trees. It was easy to see the vehicle—a shiny black Mercedes—because the engine and headlights were still on. As we peered from behind the trees, we saw that the man was a little older than Tania and Oberon—in his fifties, maybe?—and had a full head of gray hair. Something about him, his sharp chin or angular face, had a definite unfriendliness about it. Even his hair was thick and harsh, somehow (don't ask me how hair can be harsh—it just *can*). He was pounding a sign into the earth, a sign that said, "Future Site—Welt Development."

"Well, at least it's not hunters," said Tania. Oberon sniffed the air, and then squinted. His dark-rimmed eyes suddenly reminded me of a fox's, or coyote's, wild and sly as they assessed the situation at hand.

"Definitely foe," he said.

"Let's find out what's going on," said Tania, marching out from behind the trees and walking toward the car.

"Stay here," said Oberon, getting ready to stand up and run after Tania.

"I don't take orders from you," I said. "Or from anyone."

Oberon stared at me in disbelief. Clearly, he wasn't used to fairy folk talking to him that way.

"Is your sister always like that?" he asked Sylva.

Sylva nodded.

"Then tell her to do me a *favor* and stay here with you," he said. He bolted to catch up with Tania, who was already close to the man's car now.

"Excuse me!" she was saying to the man. "Can I help you?"

"You scared me, ma'am," the man said, dramatically putting his hand on his heart. "What are you sneaking around the dark woods for?"

"I'm not sneaking around," said Tania. "I live here."

"Live here?" he repeated. "You're not the one running that school, are you?"

"That's me," she said. "I'm Tania Greenwood."

She stretched out her hand, but he didn't shake it.

"Is *he* with you?" asked the man, surveying Oberon with unease. I can only imagine what the ex-king of fairies—a shirtless man with a wild mane of hair and clothes made out of nature's discards—must have looked like to someone who owned a Mercedes and dressed in expensive brand clothes.

"Let's just say you are in *our* forest," said Oberon, completely oblivious to the man's disapproving stare. "Explain yourself."

"I'm here on a business capacity," said the man. "This land's gonna be developed."

"Developed?" asked Tania, looking baffled. "Developed into *what*?"

"Anything," he said, shrugging. "I plan to sell the timber first, of course."

That's when I hated that man. Sylva's sapling was in the forest, happily bathed in moonlight and looking up at the stars. It could, maybe, survive all the odds nature pitched against it, but it could never survive the assault of a bulldozer.

"They're not timber," said Tania, her green eyes flashing with anger. "They're trees."

"Just a matter of perspective," he said, with a cruel smile.

"You can't cut down the trees!" cried Sylva, running out before I could stop her.

It was weird, reader, but the way the man looked at Sylva and me—I had scrambled after Sylva, of course—gave me the impression he knew who we were. I didn't like it one bit.

"Trees are profitable, young lady," he told Sylva, his cold blue eyes indicating a hostility that his smile tried to mask. Poor Sylva nervously clutched the border of her shirt, and her eyes filled up with tears.

"Not when you cut them down," I said. "Trees actually give us more when they're alive: they prevent flooding, give us oxygen, provide shelter for animals, and fertilize the soil."

"Is that from a book report you prepared for school?" he asked, in the kind of patronizing tone that was infuriating.

"It's common knowledge, actually," I retorted.

"Well, like I said, it's all a matter of perspective," he said, shrugging. "From my perspective, I'll be creating jobs."

"You could create other jobs—ones that don't need cutting down this forest," I said.

"You can't stop progress," said the man. "If it's not me, it'll be someone else."

"Cutting down a forest isn't progress," I replied. "It's just a quick way for you to buy a few more fancy cars."

Reader, the man stared at me with such contempt that, for a second or two, I wondered if I had gone too far. Then I decided I hadn't. I hated bullies. I was going to stand up to him, no matter what.

"You oughta teach her some manners," said the man, turning to Tania and straightening his tie with irritation.

"If you can speak your mind, so can she," said Tania.

"I don't know what kind of education you're giving these kids at that schools of yours, Mrs. Greenwood—"

"It's *Dr.* Greenwood," said Tania, "and you never said your name."

"It's Gunther Welt," he said. "I own Welt Industries."

"But you do not own this forest," said Tania. "The sign you just posted is illegal, given that ownership of Florissant has been under dispute for years, and that no verdict has been reached."

"I have reason to believe the dispute will end soon," said Mr. Welt. "There's a new judge on the case."

"Then I'll see you in court."

The man's face was pink with anger as he went back inside the car and slammed the door, driving away before he could even buckle up.

Tania sighed. Oberon turned to me and smiled approvingly.

"What is your name?" he asked.

"Wynd."

"Do you want to work for me, Wynd? I lost my minion a while back."

"I'll die before I become anyone's minion," I said.

Oberon laughed and clapped.

"I *like* her!" he told Tania. "I see the resemblance, too."

He turned to me again. "How is your mother? Usually, she and the fairy queen are inseparable."

"She's dead," I said. "She was murdered."

"Years ago," added Sylva, shyly.

"Here in Florissant?" he asked, in disbelief. "In *our* Florissant?"

"We weren't here to call it ours," said Tania, quietly. "We just . . . weren't here."

A flash of shame crossed Oberon's dark chestnut eyes.

"Who murdered her?" he asked us.

"I don't know," I said. "I can't remember. My sister and I grew up in the human foster care system."

"How sorry I am to hear about all this," he said, with a sympathy so sincere it surprised me. "I intend to find out what happened."

I was just wondering whether Oberon had left spies in the forest when a crow came out of nowhere and landed on his shoulder.

"Took your sweet time, didn't you?" said the former fairy king, and the crow cawed in reply. "A lady friend, you say? All right, that *is* important. I forgive you."

"Don't send Caster to spy on me, Oberon," warned Tania.

"I won't, Titania—Tania," said Oberon. "If I want to see anything, I shall come myself."

And he walked into the darkness of the forest—soundlessly, like deer at dusk—with Caster still on his shoulder.

"Oberon doesn't seem so bad," I ventured.

Tania said nothing. I wondered what she was thinking. Sometimes it was hard to tell. Her eyes were like that: at times, you could see everything in there, and at other times there was a green wall that let nothing through.

"What are you going to do about that sign?" I asked.

Tania turned to the "Future Site—Welt Development" sign and squinted for a few seconds. The sign burned to ashes that quickly scattered in the evening breeze.

"There," she said, pleased with herself. "Now, tell me something: did your mother leave you anything besides those acorns?"

"Not that I know of. Why?"

"I don't want to talk about it here," said Tania. "It's too close to the human world. Let's get deeper into the forest."

I let Tania and Sylva walk ahead of me. I noticed that Sylva, unlike me, seemed to know exactly where to step so she wouldn't trip. She also seemed to know or sense the location of fallen logs and tangled roots, so I stepped exactly where she stepped, hoping that the trees wouldn't trip me as I walked. They didn't.

"We're far enough now," said Tania, as we neared a small waterfall with a pool of water that glittered in the moonlight. "This has always been one of my favorite spots."

Sylva sat down on a stone and put her feet in the water, giggling as a bunch of frogs relocated from a half-sunken branch. I sat on a fallen log, and Tania sat next to me.

"Long ago, when the forests of England began to disappear," said Tania, after a while, "I decided that we needed to move the fairy kingdom from the Old World to the New World."

"You decided to relocate to Georgia?" I asked, amazed.

"Yes," she said. "The forests here were magnificent, and I discovered thousands of acres that were privately owned, given as a gift to a nobleman who had rendered outstanding service to the English monarchy. Naturally, no one *owns* a forest—might as well try to own the wind—but it was important to move to *this* stretch of land because *this* particular person was keen to keep the forest from being logged or used for hunting."

"Why?" I asked. "Who was he?"

"He was a mischief fairy, able to use his magic in the human world. He became quite famous and rich, but never lost his ties to the forest—until he cut down one of its trees, and as a punishment lost his magic."

"Why would he cut down a tree if he knew that?" I asked.

"I don't know," confessed Tania. "I asked him about it, and he said he wasn't in his right state of mind. I always suspected Oberon of being behind it."

"Oberon?" I asked. "Why?"

"Mischief fairies always serve the fairy king," explained Tania. "Oberon never forgave him for running off, and no one knows how to make magical potions like Oberon."

"He doesn't seem that petty," I said.

"He used a love potion on me, Wynd, to teach me a lesson."

"Maybe he's changed."

"No one changes."

"*You* changed, didn't you?"

Tania hesitated for a moment. "Well, yes—but only because *I* wanted to."

"Maybe *he* wanted to," I said, shrugging. "What did you two fight over, anyway?"

"Two mighty forces always clash, sooner or later," she said, evasively.

"You mean it wasn't over a changeling boy?" I asked, confused. Had Shakespeare also got *that* wrong?

"There are no changelings, Wynd," explained Tania. "Why would fairies want a human child? We've never stolen human children, because human children have nothing to offer us."

"What about the whole steal-a-beautiful-human-baby-and-leave-an-ugly-fairy-in-its-place thing?" I insisted.

"Human beings must have come up with that," said Tania, shrugging.

"Then what did you fight over?"

"Over who loved the other more."

I stared at Tania. I couldn't believe it.

"That's it?" I asked.

"That's it," she said. "Incredibly self-indulgent and irresponsible, considering the amount of damage we caused by casting spells over each other and leaving Florissant unattended."

She fell into a silent gloominess, with the kind of distant gaze that suggested she was brooding over the past.

"You're not going to fight with Oberon again, are you?" asked Sylva, worriedly. She had been listening attentively, with her little feet still dipped in the water.

"I'll do my best not to," Tania promised, earnestly. "In any case, I'm not leaving Florissant."

This seemed to reassure Sylva, who now amused herself by splashing her feet in the water.

"So what happened to the mischief fairy?" I asked Tania.

"He got married. Had kids. He left it in his will that Florissant could not be divided or sold, and for many generations after he died it stayed that way. Then one of his children went bankrupt and started selling bits and pieces of the forest. The bit that we're in now was bought in the 1800s, by a rich woman who was a conservationist. The same story repeats itself here: initially, her descendants continued her mission, until the last one decided he'd rather make a ton of money auctioning it. That's when your mother bought it. I can only imagine how much gold she had to create with alchemy magic in order to outbid all the timber and development companies."

"No wonder she was murdered," I said, feeling incredibly sad—not only for all the forest that had been lost, but for the noble and courageous actions of my mother. The sense of her as hero and martyr made me agitated, feverish. I wanted to be like her. I wanted to fight for something as precious as Florissant.

"If Mom bought Florissant, how come everyone's fighting over it?" asked Sylva, who had stopped splashing her feet the moment Tania had mentioned mom.

"The deed to Florissant has disappeared, and the sale documents have been stolen. The people involved in the transaction have all died some way or another, and there is no actual record of it. Nothing—in print or in electronic format."

"That's weird," I said. "Sounds like someone got rid of all the evidence."

"That's why there is a dispute," she replied. "The state is claiming ownership in order to auction it, and Welt seems pretty confident he can get his hands on it when that happens."

"We can't let that happen," I said. "We have to find evidence that she bought it. Maybe that deed is hidden somewhere."

"I was rather hoping she would have left it with you," said Tania. "I've been meaning to tell you this: you and Sylva are the legal owners of Florissant."

I felt uneasy about this. It was a lot of responsibility. I glanced at Sylva, to see how she felt. She looked confused. Like a true fairy, she thought she belonged to the trees, not the other way around.

"I thought no one owned a forest," she said.

"In the fairy realm, no one does," said Tania. "Not even Oberon and I would presume to think we were the owners of the forest. The forest is alive, and greater than all of us. We *serve* the forest."

"But in the human world," I continued, "it belongs to the two of us?"

"Yes. Humans think they can own everything."

I started thinking this could be good news: if we found the deed, we could save Florissant.

"Before you get too excited," said Tania, reading my expression, "remember that it's probably been destroyed already. The two of you were my last hope of using the deed to save this place."

"Even if we didn't find the deed," I said, "couldn't we outbid Welt if there's an auction? Aren't there any alchemy fairies who can make gold, like my mother?"

"I wish. Your mother was the last alchemy fairy I know of."

"And there's no gold in the forest?" I asked. "You always hear stories about fairies and gold."

"There *is* gold in Florissant, but it turns into tin the moment it leaves the forest," said Tania. "That's why alchemy fairies are special: the gold they create *remains* gold, even in the human world."

"This is so frustrating," I said. "Can't you summon a storm—or something—and get rid of Welt?"

"*Get rid* of him?" asked Tania, crossing her arms and watching me with interest. "You mean, *kill* him?"

"Okay, so when you say it like that, it sounds a bit . . ."

"Vicious?"

"Exaggerated."

"Wynd, you are new to Florissant, so listen very carefully to what I'm about to tell you," said Tania, and I immediately braced myself. "There are two things fairies must never do: they must never cut down a tree, and they must never—ever—use their magic to kill any creature of the forest."

"He's not a creature of the forest," I said. "Who came up with all these rules, anyway? The people who do bad things never play by the rules."

"Magic is a way of being, not a superpower to use against others," said Tania.

"Well, maybe it should be."

I was dizzy and nauseous now. I felt as if I were coming apart, somehow.

"Don't be mad, Wynd," said Sylva, lightly touching my elbow and gazing at me with her large, dark eyes. "You're a good person."

"I really don't think I am," I said, my whole body shaking.

"You *are*," insisted Sylva. "You take spiders outside and put worms back in the grass when they're in the driveway. You speak up for trees."

Thank goodness for Sylva. I suddenly felt like myself again. I couldn't understand what had taken hold of me. Why had I been so angry? I had felt as if I could have raised a storm and destroyed everything.

Then I remembered I was a wind fairy.

"Did I almost just turn into wind?" I said, leaning against a tree for support.

"You were on your way, I think," said Tania. "Are you all right?"

"I feel awful," I said, sitting down on a rock. Sylva watched sympathetically as I waited for the forest to stop spinning. It finally did.

"Now do you see why I don't want to be a wind fairy?" I told Tania.

"But as you do not get to choose, you might as well become acquainted with who you are," said Tania.

"Moody? Crazy?"

"I was going to say free," said Tania.

"No wonder most of us scatter by the time we're fifteen," I muttered, frustrated.

"You are not going to scatter," said Sylva, simply. "You promised."

"I did," I said, putting my arm around Sylva's shoulder. "I'll learn how to control myself better—don't worry."

"I'm not worried," said Sylva. "Are you worried, Tania?"

"Worry is useless," said Tania. "Resolve is better. And you know what's best of all?"

"No idea," I said.

Tania smiled mischievously. "Dancing."

She waved her hand, and the three of us were suddenly in the courtyard, with lively music and laughter coming from the dining hall.

"You can't be serious," I said.

"One more thing you should know about fairies," said Tania. "We are *always* serious about dancing."

And she went inside.

Chapter 8

OF FAIRIES AND MONSTERS

JUST IN CASE you're wondering, Ms. Williams didn't just disappear from our lives. But before I tell you about her, let me tell you about dancing.

Dancing is super important in the fairy world. Apparently, fairies are hard-wired to dance. They dance as much as they possibly can. Any special occasion is an occasion to dance. They have even been known to dance on non-special occasions.

They always dance in a circle.

Even the fairies who are playing instruments (fiddles, drums, fifes, and anything else) are tapping their feet and moving their bodies. In other words, they're *kind of* dancing.

If you're anything like me (someone who believes that dancing is for a select few who can move to music without looking ridiculous), you're in for a surprise: when fairy music plays, *everyone* dances well. Don't ask me how the logistics work. All I know is that everyone knows what to do with their feet. It's like *Riverdance* without the perfection and the fake grinning.

Fairy music, by the way, can only be played on fairy instruments, which have to be made with materials from a fairy forest. There were about six people on instruments, including Cobweb on the fiddle. All the other instruments were played by students, which was impressive because the music was totally awesome.

Here's everyone Sylva and I met that night:

1. Peaseblossom: lovely person! She was wearing a yellow gown made of (surprise!) real flowers. She had a smile on her

face the entire time. She told me she is originally from Asia, but didn't say what country. Maybe that was before there were countries. I assumed Tania met Peaseblossom during one of her wanderings, the way she had met my mother.

2. Pretty much every student. Couldn't believe how nice everyone was. There were kids from all over the country, though most were from Georgia. In the few breaks for cold apple cider, everyone wanted to know our story. They were genuinely interested, too—and *no one* had cell phones on them. Turns out the only working phones in the Academy are in Tania's office, the infirmary, the kitchen, and the large living room downstairs. Since there are no utility posts anywhere in the forest, I can only marvel at how Tania keeps these landlines functioning.

Okay, so as usual I'm getting off topic. But one more thing: when we finally got back to our room, and Sylva finally stopped twirling with joy, we talked about mom. Sylva repeated the name Rasayana several times, as if the word alone were magical.

"I can't believe Mom was from India," she said.

"I wonder how long ago that was, though," I said. "Tania was saying that fairies never used to age when the world was covered in forests. So she could have met Mom hundreds of years ago."

"I'll ask Giniana and Old One," said Sylva. "I bet they know about her."

"Ask them if they know anything about the deed also," I said.

"You think Mom hid it in the forest?" she asked.

"She could have," I said. "It could also have been stolen or destroyed."

"I hope not," she said, her eyes filling up with tears. "If we don't find it, will they cut down all the trees?"

"They might," I said, trying not to sound all doom-and-gloom, but not managing very well. "They don't think of trees like you do."

A fat tear rolled down Sylva's cheek, and then another.

"But look," I said, trying to cheer her up, "Tania's not going to give up like that, and neither are we."

"I like it so much here," she said, wiping all the new tears that kept coming. A sympathetic leaf on the wall stretched itself and touched Sylva's shoulder.

"Thanks," she said, blowing her nose on it. Another leaf, tapping her on the other shoulder, apparently offered to let her wipe her tears with it.

"I like it here also," I said. "And Oberon's kind of *hot*."

"Hotter than Nick?" she asked, wide-eyed.

"You tell me," I said. "What does Oberon have that Nick doesn't? And it's not magic. Or that cape."

She thought hard for a moment—then her face suddenly lit up.

"Guyliner!" she cried, excitedly.

I laughed, relieved to see her perk up. Ever since she had seen a picture of Johnny Depp in *Pirates of the Caribbean*, Sylva had become a fan of the look. I actually had a feeling that Oberon's dark-rimmed eyes were naturally that way, like those of a creature of the forest. I had already noticed that, at any time, his posture or expression might evoke one animal, and then all of a sudden another. And, at one point, when he leaned against a tree, he kind of looked like one, though he was still clearly Oberon. Maybe that was his magic. Maybe he could be himself and all of these other things, all at the same time.

And, reader, he smelled like the forest after rain.

In any case (I'm digressing again), all that mattered just then was that our conversation had turned happy again. By the time we went to bed, with the window open and the stars flickering out there, Sylva seemed to have forgotten all about the sinister Welt and his schemes.

The next morning, when I woke up, Sylva was gone—and Cobweb was peering at me. I jumped out of bed, my heart racing.

"Just so you know, I knocked," she said. "You didn't hear me, though."

"Where's Sylva?" I asked.

Which brings me to Ms. Williams. Bet you thought I'd never get there.

"The person from Social Services is here," said Cobweb. "She's in Tania's office. Sylva's there, too."

"Okay—thanks."

I went to the sink to wash my face, and when I looked in the mirror, Cobweb was no longer there.

Five minutes later, I was in Tania's office. I was momentarily surprised to see that the office was covered with walls of moss, flowers, and plants, and that the books were stacked between branches—then I remembered that I had only been in there once, before the magic had taken effect. On that first night, it had seemed like a normal office. That's probably the way Ms. Williams was seeing it.

"*The Great Book of Forest Quotes and Poems*," she was saying, as Tania showed her a volume. "Interesting."

"Read one for me," said Sylva, excitedly.

Ms. Williams had always had a soft spot for Sylva, so she obliged and leafed through the volume (no doubt looking for a short passage, since some of them were pretty long).

"Ah—here's one," she said, clearing her throat. "*I am a forest, and a night of dark trees: but he who is not afraid of my darkness, will find banks full of roses under my cypresses.*"

"Nietzsche," observed Tania.

"You got it," said Ms. Williams, impressed. I think she was also secretly relieved that Tania had said Nietzsche's name first, so she wouldn't have to take a shot at pronouncing so many consonants.

"Read another one," begged Sylva.

"I'll let Dr. Greenwood read one," said Ms. Williams, and Tania gracefully took the book from her, but didn't open it.

"I have a favorite one," said Tania.

And this, our life, exempt from public haunt,
Finds tongues in trees, books in the running brooks,
Sermons in stones, and good in everything.

Sylva jumped up, clapping. "You didn't even have to look at it!"

"I know it by heart," said Tania.

"Is it Shakespeare?" I asked (I hadn't wanted to interrupt before, and had been standing quietly by the door).

"It sure is," said Tania, pleasantly. "The man, as you know, has a way with words."

"Good morning, Wynd," said Ms. Williams, as I approached to give her a hug. "It's so nice to see you again."

I was happy to see her, too. It seemed so long since the last time we'd met.

"Read one for me, Wynd," pleaded Sylva, taking the book from Tania and shoving it in my hands.

"Okay," I said, opening the book up to a random page. "This one is from 'The Woods of Westermain,' by a guy called George Meredith."

"Good choice," said Tania.

"It's super long, so I'll read just the first stanza," I said. I knew poems were divided into stanzas, not paragraphs, and I saw this as a chance to impress. It worked, and I took that as my cue to begin:

Enter these enchanted woods,
You who dare.
Nothing harms beneath the leaves
More than waves a swimmer cleaves.
Toss your heart up with the lark,
Foot at peace with mouse and worm,
Fair you fare.
Only at a dread of dark
Quaver, and they quit their form:
Thousand eyeballs under hoods
Have you by the hair.
Enter these enchanted woods,
You who dare.

"Brava!" said Tania, as Ms. Williams and Sylva clapped. "You have a great speaking voice, Wynd."

"Thanks," I said, feeling the brief high of being flattered. "I always wanted to be in a play, but I've never auditioned for one."

"Read another one," cried Sylva.

"Maybe just a short one," I said, seeing that Ms. Williams definitely wanted to talk about more serious things. "Here's one: *I came into England with Oak, Ash and Thorn, and when Oak, Ash and Thorn are gone I shall go too.*"

"That's sad," said Sylva, and I suddenly regretted my choice. It hadn't occurred to me that a quote could remind Sylva of the danger Florissant was in.

"Kipling," said Tania. "'Puck of Pook's Hill.' Don't worry, Sylva," she added, reassuringly. "I have it on good authority that Puck is alive and well."

Sylva was probably more worried about oak, ash, and thorn than about Puck, but I figured I probably shouldn't bring that up in front of Ms. Williams.

"The three of you have important things to talk about," continued Tania, "so I'll leave you to it. Why don't you all come down to the kitchen afterward? Breakfast hours will be over by then, but I'm sure we can at least get a snack."

"Sounds lovely," said Ms. Williams. "Thank you."

Tania closed the door behind her, and Ms. Williams lost no time in asking us how we had ended up in a boarding school so many miles from our last foster parents.

"I was worried sick until I received Dr. Greenwood's call," she added.

I tried to retell the story, leaving out the magical acorns and saying instead that we had run away and hitched a ride with a kindly older woman. I also left out Florissant's guardian wolves. I mostly focused on how our foster parents' insistence on separating Sylva from her sapling had led to Sylva not eating. Ms. Williams could have never imagined, from my account, how close Sylva had been to dying.

"I've been eating a lot since I got here, though," said Sylva, happily going along with my story. "I love it here!"

"I see that," said Ms. Williams, pleased. "Dr. Greenwood has told me most of the students here are orphans, and that the school has a large endowment that covers student tuition and board. She's told me that she would be happy for you to enroll here."

"Can we?" cried Sylva. "Please?"

"You're treated well here?" she asked, turning to me for confirmation.

I nodded. "As far as we're concerned, we're home."

I said "as far as we're concerned" because I didn't want to say we *were* home. It would have raised too many questions. I glanced nervously at Sylva, hoping she wouldn't reveal 1) that we had been born in Florissant, 2) that we were fairies, and 3) that Tania Greenwood was the fairy queen—well, *former* fairy queen.

Sylvia, who could read me (at least) like a book, understood perfectly and said nothing. But she nodded enthusiastically.

"That works out well for everyone, then," said Ms. Williams. "I'll let your foster parents know. They were the ones who first called and said you had run away."

"They were cruel and horrible," I said. "They shouldn't be foster parents."

"I'll take that into consideration," said Ms. Williams. Somehow, she didn't sound as if she'd take them off her list. Maybe she thought there might be kids who would benefit from their "style." Maybe she thought we were ungrateful. Maybe she was too hungry to think clearly—I certainly was by now.

"Can we do the rest in the kitchen?" I asked. "I haven't had anything to eat yet."

"I'm not going to say no to a snack," said Ms. Williams, with a more relaxed expression. "Lead the way. This place is a little confusing."

She sneezed, and gave Calumet, who was snoozing in a pool of sunlight on the floor, a disapproving glance.

"Lots of cats here," she said, sniffing. "I'm allergic."

We went down the spiral staircase, after Sylva.

"Dr. Greenwood says she thinks that Sylva can learn to read here," said Ms. Williams, tentatively. "What do you think? There is no special needs teacher here for her."

"I don't think she'll need that here," I said. "Tania plans to teach her between now and the beginning of classes in August."

"If classes only begin in August, and there's no summer term, what do the kids do all summer?" she asked.

"Art, music, and dance," I said. "Oh, and there's lots of outdoor education."

"Like summer camp," she said, approvingly. "It's an alternative education, for sure. Dr. Greenwood tells me that she hires additional teachers just for the school year, and that during the summer the school runs with a few permanent teachers."

"Yeah, I've met them," I said. "They're all nice."

Except for Cobweb—maybe.

"They are all qualified, too. I can't think of any reasons not to let you stay here."

We were in the living room, and I wondered why she had stopped. To my surprise, Oberon was sleeping in one of the couches, with Trego nestled on his stomach. I noticed that the light was just right to accent the green hue of his olive skin.

"Who's this?" she asked.

I had to think fast. Having some random, unannounced guy sleeping on a couch could raise all kinds of red flags for Ms. Williams. On top of that, I imaged what Oberon must look like to her. I'm not even talking about the issue of guyliner here. The fairy king had leaves decorating the waves of his dark hair, and had covered himself with his cloak full of acorns, ferns, butterfly wings, and flowers. At least she couldn't see he wasn't wearing a shirt.

Sylva looked up at me, beaming, and mouthed the word "guyliner."

"That's the new theater teacher," I said. "He was touring in a production of *Midsummer Night's Dream*. He just got here last night, and his room isn't ready."

"I see he's still wearing his costume," she said, looking puzzled.

I secretly thanked our stars that Caster wasn't there with him, and decided I *had* to get us out of there before Oberon woke up.

"He looks really tired," I noted, saying the first thing that popped into my head. "We probably shouldn't wake him."

I was hoping to rush things along, but Oberon stirred—and then opened his eyes just as Ms. Williams was staring down at him.

"Well, good morrow," he said, pleasantly, and was about to sit up when he realized Trego on his stomach. "What in the forest's name . . . a feline bedfellow?"

"That's Trego," I said, gently plucking the complaining cat from Oberon and putting him on another couch. "I guess he likes you."

"Every creature likes me," said Oberon, getting up and, with a grand gesture, sweeping his cape backward. Ms. Williams seemed impressed.

"We meet again, Wynd and Sylva," said Oberon, with a courteous nod. "And who is this lovely lady?"

"This is Ms. Williams in charge of our case," I said. "She's taking a tour of Florissant Academy, and making sure it's a suitable place for us."

"I see," he said, turning to her with interest and offering his hand. As she went to shake it, he held it and kissed it. Reader, he had a *lot* of charm. Anyone else doing it would have looked stupid, but not him.

"I hear you're the new theater teacher," she said, trying to regain her composure.

"Theater?" he repeated, glancing at me and taking note of my nodding. "Ah—yes. Theater."

"I was telling her you got in from a production of *Midsummer Night's Dream*," I said, hoping he'd play along.

"What role were you playing?" asked Ms. Williams. "Puck?"

"Puck?" he repeated, so insulted he took a step back. "Oberon's minion and imp?"

That was it, I thought. *It's all over. We'll never be able to stay here now.*

"There you are," said Tania, rushing toward Ms. Williams. "I was just coming to get you! I see you've met Mr. . . . . Ron Obe."

"Interesting last name," said Ms. Williams. "Is it an artistic name?"

"It's Nigerian," said Oberon.

Wow. That was so random I almost started laughing.

"Ron," began Tania, barely able to hide her irritation, "don't you think you should—?"

"Have some breakfast? Thank you. I was thinking the same thing."

"He's welcome to join us," said Ms. Williams. "Unless you object, Dr. Greenwood."

"I promise to be on my best behavior," said Oberon, with a taunting smile.

Tania was about to retort, when she checked herself. She had self-control—I'll give her that.

"Let's go, then," she said, ushering Ms. Williams on with a forced smile. "This way."

We finally moved out of the living room, crossed the courtyard, and entered the kitchen, where, unable to see the growing walls, she commented on the light-filled space and welcoming environment.

Oh—before I forget: Mustardseed dropped everything she was carrying when she saw Oberon walk in.

"Hello, Ms. Seed," he said, assisting her as she put broken pieces of china back on her tray. "How are you this fine morning?"

"Mr. Ron Obe will be joining us for breakfast," said Tania, flatly.

"And he is famished," said Oberon. "Feels as if he hasn't eaten in years."

We all sat down. There was sweet tea, juice, and little round buns with raisins and jam.

"Ladies first," said Tania, passing the tray around to Ms. Williams and us. Oberon looked on, nervously, as the quantity of buns diminished. When the tray finally got to him, he put the remaining five buns on his plate.

"I have another batch in the oven," said Mustardseed.

"Good, because it seems Mr. Obe has the appetite of an ogre," said Tania, under her breath.

"It takes a lot of energy to be the fairy king," said Oberon.

"So *that's* the role you were playing," said Ms. Williams, approvingly.

"Yes, he was the tyrant of the forest," said Tania, and Oberon nearly choked on a large piece of bun he was eating. "It must be exhausting playing that role."

Here we go again, I thought. I was thinking of how to intervene, when the kitchen door opened, and Cobweb came in. I had been hoping for a distraction, but wasn't sure if Cobweb counted as a distraction or a disaster.

"What is it, Cob—Ms. Web?" asked Tania.

"Looks like the police want to tow her car," said Cobweb, gesturing to Ms. Williams. "It's on the shoulder by the main road, and they think it might be abandoned."

"I should have parked it in the dirt road, like you suggested, but it's a new car, and I didn't want to drive in the gravel," said Ms. Williams, so nervous that she barely registered Cobweb's unusual appearance. "I better go and take care of it."

"I can go with you," offered Cobweb.

"I'll take her," said Tania, and I wondered if she, too, was worried about Cobweb spilling the beans on how crunchy and delicious moths were.

Sylva and I gave Ms. Williams a hug, and then she left with Tania.

"How have you been, Cobweb?" asked Oberon. "Still hoping to eat Mariposa?"

"What's *he* doing here?" Cobweb asked Mustardseed.

"Eating us out of house and home," she replied, crossing her arms and watching him with disapproval.

Oberon was unfazed. "Your queen is the one responsible for my monstrous appetite."

And he grabbed another two buns. As he began to eat the first one, Caster flew in through the window and perched himself on Oberon's shoulder, cooing and clicking.

"That's all we needed," muttered Cobweb, sourly, as the bird rattled on.

"Caster," said Oberon, with a slightly peeved expression, "I would *not* have gotten into an argument with Ms. Williams and spoiled everything. I'm in perfect control over my moods, thank you very much."

Caster replied with a long sequence of clicks, coos, and soft caws.

"Yes, I know you told me not to come here," said Oberon, "but the cave hasn't been lived in for a long time. It's dreary, and lonely."

Caster's reply was enigmatic. I had no idea if he agreed or disagreed with Oberon.

"Is Caster a crow all the time?" I asked. "Or is he like Mariposa?"

"He's completely crow," said Oberon. "Aren't you, Caster?"

Caster was.

"Will he come to my shoulder?" asked Sylva, hopefully.

"What do you say, Caster?" asked Oberon. "Do you want to humor the tree child?"

Caster did not, and Sylva was disappointed. She reached out her hand to touch his shiny black feathers, but quickly changed her mind when he threatened to give it a good peck.

"If he decides to like you, tree child, it will be on his terms," said Oberon.

"At least he doesn't hate you, like the trees hate me," I told Sylva.

"Trees can change their minds," said Oberon. "If they decide to like you, of course, it will be on their terms as well. Still, I can tell you there is nothing braver and more determined than a tree. We fairies could not have created the Underworld without them."

"Fairies created the Underworld?" I asked. I had heard of the Underworld before, but never in that context.

"Before there were fairies," explained Oberon, "there was no Underworld as a separate space. The creatures that are now in the Underworld used to live in this world, long before there were any forests. You can call these creatures what you will. I tend to think of them as giant beings from an ancient world. They inhabited most of the Earth before the time of the forest."

"Monsters," muttered Sylva, wide-eyed.

"Precisely," said Oberon. "When the fairies started appearing, these beings resented them. You see, now they had to share the world."

"But where did the fairies come from?" I asked.

"From the trees," said Oberon. "The fairies came *with* the trees, to be more precise. The world became a giant forest. It was beautiful beyond words."

"Then what happened?" I asked.

"Then the monsters began to kill the fairies and cut down the trees," continued Oberon. "So the fairies and the trees used their joint magic to create a separate realm and banish them."

"The Underworld," I said.

"Yes. Contrary to what some humans think, the Underworld is not full of dead souls. It's full of living—and very angry—creatures."

"So what keeps them there?" I asked.

"The roots of the trees," said Oberon. "Not just any trees, of course. Trees from old-growth forests such as Florissant."

"But there are hardly any old-growth forests left," I said.

"Unfortunately, that's true," said Oberon. "But there are still a few pockets of them in the world, which is also where you find remnants of magic. All of these places used to be part of Florissant—which, incidentally, is also the oldest fairy word for *forest*."

"Hang on," I said, trying to put all the pieces of Oberon's remarkable story together. "What happens to the Underworld when people cut down the forest?"

"Whenever a chunk of old forest disappears," explained Oberon, "the creatures of the Underworld directly beneath it are released. They've been imprisoned for so long, however, that most of them turn into disembodied, toxic magic."

"Like toxic energy?" I asked. It made sense. I had felt it many times.

"Exactly! The world is full of it. In some places, it manifests as hatred, and in others as the desire to own nature or destroy it. It can take many forms, all of them destructive."

"So let's say there's an old-growth forest, and half of it gets cut down. What happens with the other half?" I asked.

"The remaining trees set up a new perimeter to guard what's left of the Underworld. Not a very good situation, as I'm sure you can see: the more these old forests are cut, the worse the world gets."

"And the worse the world gets, the more people want to cut down the trees," I said.

Oberon nodded. "It's a pretty vicious cycle—and one that magic cannot fix."

"Maybe if people out there knew how important trees are to the fairies," ventured Sylva, innocently, "they wouldn't cut down these old forests."

"Maybe, if they could remember," said Oberon.

"Remember?" I asked, confused. "Remember what?"

"That they used to be fairies," said Oberon. "We in the fairy kingdom use the term *human* to denote fairies who forgot they were fairies and lost their magic. It started out as one or two people, and grew—until they became most of the world."

"Do you think the toxic magic from the Underworld caused all the forgetting?" I asked.

Oberon thought about it for a second. "It could have."

And he stuffed another bun in his mouth.

Chapter 9

PUCK

JUST AS OBERON was swallowing his last morsel, Nick walked in.

"Hi Nick," said Mustardseed, leaving us at the table and walking toward him. "Want some breakfast?"

"Some sweet tea would be awesome," he said, with a grateful smile. "Where's Tania?"

"She'll be back in a few minutes," said Mustardseed. "Have a seat."

"Who's the peasant?" Oberon whispered to me. I almost started laughing—but Oberon was dead serious. He surveyed Nick with suspicion, and I suddenly realized it was because he saw Nick as a rival.

"I'm Nick," said Nick, pleasantly stretching out his hand. "Handyman."

"Oberon," replied Oberon, reluctantly shaking Nick's hand. "King."

"From what I hear, it's *ex*-king," said Nick, sitting down. "Back from exile?"

"From a period of intense meditation," retorted Oberon. "You should try it."

"Meditation doesn't suit me," said Nick. "I'm too much of a hands-on guy."

"It changed me," said Oberon. "I'm a different Oberon."

"For better or worse?" asked Nick.

"That remains to be seen, I suppose."

I should mention here that the four of us—me, plus Sylva, Mustardseed, and Cobweb—were watching this little exchange, waiting to see if Oberon would turn Nick into a toad or something like that. Mustardseed and Cobweb looked worried enough to suggest that Oberon might have done something like that in the past.

"What's he saying?" asked Nick, as Caster cawed loudly—and rather rudely—every time Nick took a sip of tea.

"It's better if you don't know," said Oberon. "On second thought, it's rather amusing. He's saying—"

"I'm back!" said Tania, walking through the door and heading straight for the refrigerator. "I need to drink something—it's already hot out."

"Did they tow the car?" I asked.

"They were about to," said Tania. "Thankfully, we were right by the edge of the forest, so I could use some magic."

"Let me guess: the tow truck wouldn't start," said Mustardseed.

"How convenient," said Oberon. "Of course, when one has magic, one has no need of these hands-on types in the vicinity."

"I see the two of you have met," said Tania. "I'm glad. Nick has been indispensable around here, Oberon."

Oberon didn't seem pleased by the comment. In fact, for a moment I could have sworn he became *greener*.

"I smell wet fur," he said, sniffing and turning to Nick. "Have you been a dog lately?"

"A wolf," he replied.

Caster cawed softly in Oberon's ear now.

"I see," said Oberon, nodding. "That would explain it."

"Is he your pet crow?" asked Nick, surveying Caster.

"He's a wild crow," said Oberon, and Caster puffed up with pride.

"If he's so wild, what's he doing on your shoulder?" retorted Nick.

"I'm wild, too," said Oberon. "Tania and I are the wildest creatures in all of Florissant, which makes sense, since we were fairy monarchs."

"I can see Tania as a queen," retorted Nick. "But who'd want *you* as king?"

Oberon stood up. He looked fierce: his hair seemed alive, his eyes were bright, and his whole posture made me think of a powerful stag about to charge. I wondered if Nick would have been able to defend himself, even as a wolf.

"We're not doing this," said Tania, quickly pulling Nick away and breaking eye contact between the two. "We have more important things to think about. I need to go into town to speak to the lawyer who's handling the Florissant case. Nick, you said you'd take me?"

"Yeah—of course," said Nick. "Anything for you, Tania."

Oberon rolled his eyes.

"Let's go, then," said Tania. "Come on."

"I'm coming as well," said Oberon. "Florissant is also my forest, and I have the right to know what's going on."

"Can we come, too?" I asked. "We haven't seen the town."

"It's small—nothing to see," said Nick. "Just a little town square, a few shops, movie theater, waffle house—"

"Sounds awesome," I said, and Sylva nodded in agreement, though it was only because she was a little trouper. Secretly, I'm sure she would have much rather been exploring the forest. I, on the other hand, wanted to see if Oberon and Nick would kill each other. At the very least, I wanted to see if Oberon would turn Nick into *something*.

"All right," said Tania. "You can come."

"It'll be tight," said Nick, looking reluctant.

"We can fit five, Nick," said Tania, in a decisive tone.

Oberon flashed a victorious smile at Nick.

"Little but fierce," said Oberon. "That's the queen for you."

But his excitement was short-lived when Tania announced he shouldn't go dressed as he was.

"Why in the forest's name not?" he asked.

"You need to at least put on a shirt," she said.

"You can borrow one of my t-shirts," said Nick. "I have a bag of clothes in the car, for when I go to the gym. It'll probably be a little large for you, because I have more muscle mass."

"It'll probably be short, also," retorted Oberon, "since I'm so much taller than you."

Nick was about to say something—not something very nice, obviously—when Tania gestured impatiently.

"I'll summon a shirt for him," she said. A hand wave later, Oberon was wearing a plain white t-shirt.

"You want me to wear this rag?" he asked, in disbelief. "It is not worthy of a king."

"I don't see either of us wearing a crown," said Tania.

Oberon sighed, and waved his hand. The word "Royal" appeared on the t-shirt.

"I wear the crown in my heart," he said.

"I see your magic is back," said Tania. "Can you use it to lose the cape?"

"No, no, and no."

"People are not going to respond well to some weird guy in a cape," said Nick.

"It's a *cloak*," said Oberon, cocooning himself within the cape—cloak—by folding his arms like a bat. Tania gave out an exasperated sigh and turned to Mustardseed and Cobweb.

"Ladies," she said, "we'll be back for dinner and the stargazing field trip afterward. We'll have lunch in town, so don't worry about us."

"Where are your other two ladies?" asked Oberon. "Are they still with you?"

"If you mean Mariposa and Peaseblossom, yes," said Tania. "I'm sure they won't be happy to see you, any more than I was."

"Caster's happy to see me," said Oberon, as we walked out of the kitchen. "He's a true friend."

"He just pooped on your shoulder," said Tania.

Caster decided this was a good moment to fly off. Annoyed, Oberon waved his hand over his shoulder, and the blob of poop disappeared.

"That settles it," he said, wretchedly. "I need better minions. Wynd?"

"No," I said.

"What about you, Sylva?"

"I don't know what a minion is," said Sylva.

"Probably not a good idea, then," he said. "Tree fairies don't make good minions. Wynd fairies, on the other hand, could be excellent minions—if one could get them to stick around."

"Wynd isn't leaving," said Sylva, earnestly. "She promised me."

"Did she?" said Oberon. "I say good for her. I'm glad the two of you are friends. There's nothing like a friend—even one who poops on your shoulder."

"A second ago you said he was a minion," I said.

"Yes, but that's the sort of thing one says when one's upset," retorted Oberon. "Poop on the shoulder does that, you know."

Sylva giggled. She liked Oberon. I did, too—a lot more than I did Shakespeare's.

"You're not like I expected," I said. "You're meaner in Shakespeare. You're kind of a bully in *A Midsummer Night's Dream*."

"Do you mean to say that I've had that reputation for over four hundred years?"

"Pretty much," I said. "You should read the play."

"Very annoying, this Shakespeare fellow," said Oberon. "I can't believe Tania dedicated herself to him all these years."

"Lots of people do," I said, "and without being under a magic spell."

"That's baffling," he said. "Where can I find a copy of this unflattering play?"

"Tania might have a copy," I said. "But we can probably find one in town also."

We scrambled to catch up to Tania and Nick, who were considerably ahead of us by now.

"That pace of hers is maddening," complained Oberon. "Only an ostrich could keep up."

But we finally reached the entrance door of Florissant Academy—and only a few steps behind Tania and Nick.

"Do we get boots?" I asked, seeing that we were all barefoot—all except for Nick, who was wearing tennis shoes.

"Just regular shoes today," she said, waving beige loafers for herself, green Mary Janes for Sylva, and flat yellow sneakers for me.

"Don't you wear shoes, Oberon?" I asked, seeing he was still barefoot.

"Never," replied Oberon. "I like my feet to feel the earth."

"Like me!" cried Sylva, happily, and Oberon returned a playful wink.

"There's not much earth in the town," said Tania. "As a grown man without shoes, you might not be able to get into places."

Letting out a sigh of frustration, Oberon waved a pair of shoes (made of leaves and mushrooms woven together) into existence. Sylva thought they were *really* cool, but Tania was not impressed.

"Just you watch, tree child," said Oberon. "Next thing, Queen Greenwood here is going to say I can't go into the town with my glorious hair."

A fiery green glance from Tania indicated that Oberon had managed to annoy her.

"I *was* going to say you should brush it," said Tania. "But forget it. We don't have time to argue. I'll wave us to Nick's car, because we're so late already."

A moment later, we were in Nick's old SUV, which was parked at the edge of the forest, where a dirt road dead-ended into the trees. That dirt road would take us to the "real" road going to town.

Oberon found himself in the back seat, squeezed between Sylva and me.

"Good heavens," he said, nervously. "This is a death trap."

"Wear your seat belt, and you'll be fine," said Tania.

It took Oberon forever to understand the logistics of the seatbelt. In the end, Sylva and I had to help him, and he fidgeted uncomfortably the entire time he was in the car.

Things got interesting when, not too long after, we drove past a high school soccer field.

"Where are we?" asked Oberon, suddenly. "Is that . . . ? Stop the box!"

"Oberon, I can't be late," warned Tania.

"I'll walk the rest of the way," he said. "Stop the box, I say!"

Nick pulled into the parking lot, and Oberon struggled fiercely to unhook himself from the seat belt.

"Here," I said, clicking on the buckle and opening the door. "I'll come with you."

"I'm coming, too!" cried Sylva, getting out with us.

"Meet us at the waffle house," said Tania. "It's about a mile or two from here. And don't forget: you're not in the forest anymore."

"As if I could forget," Oberon said, under his breath.

The car drove away, and he turned his attention to the soccer field.

"That way," he said, marching with determination.

"What's going on?" I asked, as we neared the tall chain-link fence that surrounded the field. "Did you see something?"

"*Someone*," he said. "What is this place?"

"It's just a field where kids play soccer," I said. "Looks like it belongs to the high school. I guess there's some sort of soccer summer camp going on."

"Unbelievable," he said, putting his hands on his waist with indignation as he watched one of the players. "Unbelievable."

The player he was watching, by the way, was a blondish high schooler who must have been eighteen or so. As we stood there, he scored a goal. Strangely, although everyone on his team clapped and cheered, he seemed not to care. He just ran back to his position, without so much as cracking a smile.

"At least he's miserable," said Oberon, with a great deal of satisfaction.

Sylva and I both turned to Oberon, expecting some kind of additional explanation, but all he said was "unbelievable" again—and then he made for the field entrance.

"You can't just go in there," I said. "They're having a practice."

"I have to wait?" he asked, in disbelief.

"Unless you want them to call security," I said.

"Unbelievable."

A few minutes later, the practice ended. We watched as the goal-scorer Oberon was so interested in sat down on the grass to take off his cleats. Several other players sat by him. The more they joked around, however, the more he seemed to intensify his effort *not* to have any fun. It was really strange.

When everyone else had left, Oberon walked along the perimeter of the fence, making for the entrance.

"What's going on?" I asked, as we rushed to keep up. "Who is he, anyway?"

"Puck. A mischief fairy if there ever was one."

"That's *him*?" I cried. "*That's* Puck?"

I must have been loud enough for Puck to hear us. Spotting us approaching, he jumped to his feet and took a few steps back.

"You little imp," growled the former fairy king, glaring. "Are you hiding in the human world now?"

"I can explain," he said, taking another step back.

"*What* can you explain?" asked Oberon. "That you betrayed me?"

"You were stuck inside a tree," he protested.

"And you were happy to have me there, or you would have done *something*," he snarled.

"I *was* happy, okay?" said Puck, standing his ground now. "I couldn't believe I was so lucky. You were a self-absorbed jerk, and I celebrated when Titania's counter-curse got you!"

"Why, you poor excuse for a minion—" began Oberon, raising his hand—and then realizing he had no magic.

"You're not king here," said Puck, triumphantly. "Why do you think *I'm* here? I knew someday you'd get out."

"How can you abandon the forest for the human world?" asked Oberon, a little more subdued now. "Don't you know what humans have been doing to the forest?"

"I have a good life here, okay?" said Puck. "No one makes me do stuff like you used to. I have friends, and I have parents I like."

"Parents?" repeated Oberon, incredulously. "You were born from a pine cone, Puck."

"I go by Robin now," he said, proudly. "I was adopted by the Goodfellows several years ago. I'm not going back to the forest to be your minion."

"I didn't consider you my minion, you fool," said Oberon, shaking his head. "I considered you my friend."

"You didn't treat me like a friend," complained Puck—I mean, Robin. "You bossed me around and took me for granted. I'm never going back."

Oberon regarded Robin for a moment. Robin quickly looked away.

"You lost your magic, didn't you?" said Oberon, with an accusatory squint. "That's why you're not going back."

"What? No! I have my magic."

"Prove it. You and I both know that mischief fairies retain their magic in the human world—so show us a trick."

"I'm not doing tricks for you," he said, and then turned to Sylva and me. "Who are they?"

But Oberon could not be so easily distracted from the topic at hand.

"What in the forest's name did you do to lose your magic?" he insisted. "Did you cut a tree down?"

Robin's cheeks reddened with shame.

"You cut down a *tree*?" asked Oberon, shocked. "Why? You knew the law of the forest. You knew what would happen."

"Not having magic was the only way to live in the human world without drawing attention to myself," said Robin, miserably. "It was the only way to get rid of *you*."

Oberon, distressed, took a step back.

"Was I so awful?" he asked.

An awkward moment of silence followed.

"Good heavens," he muttered, stunned. "I *was*, wasn't I?"

"Everything okay here?" someone asked. We swung around. The voice belonged to a plumpish, middle-aged man wearing a sheriff's outfit and sunglasses.

"Hi, Dad," said Robin, grabbing his belongings. "This is—uh—the costume designer for the show."

"Sheriff Andy Goodfellow," said the man, firmly shaking Oberon's hand. "I see you're wearing one of the costumes."

"The fool's, apparently," said Oberon.

"I didn't know there was a fool in *A Midsummer Night's Dream*," said Sheriff Goodfellow.

"They cut his part, unfortunately," added Robin, awkwardly.

"I see," said Sheriff Goodfellow. "Well, Robin, we better leave if you're going to make that dentist appointment."

"Okay, Dad," he said. "Let me just get some stuff I left on the bench."

Sheriff Goodfellow said his pleased-to-meet-yous and good-byes, and went back to the police car. Oberon watched him.

"He does seem like a good fellow," said the fairy ex-king.

"He is," said Robin. "Anyway, I hope you'll come see the play."

He ran to the bench and grabbed a soccer ball to take back to the car.

"What role are you playing?" asked Oberon. "Yourself?"

"No," said Robin. "I'm playing you."

And he ran off.

Chapter 10

THE ATTACK

OBERON WAITED FOR the car to drive away, and then slumped onto the grass. He seemed rattled by the encounter, depressed.

"Are you upset because they cut your part, Oberon?" asked Sylva, sympathetically.

Oberon shook his head. "It's not a part I'd want to play, anyway. What part would *you* want to play, if you were in *A Midsummer Night's Dream*?"

"That's easy," she said. "A tree."

Oberon smiled. Sylva had managed to cheer him up.

"How clever you are," he said. "You picked the best part."

"Can we go, then?" she asked. "It's hot here."

"Of course it is," said Oberon. "There aren't any trees."

He got up and looked around, hands on his waist.

"The forest is back *that* way," he said, "so we should probably go in *this* direction."

"Do you always know where the forest is?" asked Sylva.

"Yes," said Oberon. "I'm attracted to it."

"Like a magnet," I said. "Or the needle of a compass—if you know what that is."

"I *do* know what that is," said Oberon. "And it's a very good comparison. The forest *is* my north."

Sylva skipped ahead of us, touching every tree she went by, and we walked behind her. I say "walked," but I'm not sure that's what Oberon was doing, because he seemed completely incapable of going in a straight line. He meandered to one side and another—to the point where I became worried someone would stop him for drunk *walking.*

"Can't you walk in a straight line?" I asked.

"Why would anyone want to do *that*?" he asked, baffled.

"Exactly," cried Sylva, who was about as good at walking straight ahead as he was.

"It's faster," I said, not wanting to say he gave the impression of being drunk.

"But it's the detours and the wanderings that make a journey interesting," said Oberon. "Besides, this surface is uncomfortable to walk on."

"That's what shoes are for," I said.

"You say that because you are a wind fairy, and wind fairies are comfortable going anywhere—just like the wind. You do not feel the pull of the earth."

I feel the pull of the sky, I wanted to say—but I didn't. Oberon already knew that.

"It's ghastly," he complained, gesturing to the pavement. "It's hard and hot. I can't believe they took down trees for *this*. I say, there was a magnificent magnolia right here—Briffin—and over there a yellow poplar—Pinko—and over that way an imposing loblolly pine called Lyrid. How I mourn their loss," he added, his large brown eyes as sad as a deer's.

"At least we're in luck," I said, pointing to a table near the entrance of the school that had a "Library Summer Sale" sign scribbled by hand. "I bet they have what we want."

Jackpot! *A Midsummer Night's Dream*, for all of fifty cents.

"I have exact change," I told the librarian, hoping that my reaching for money would distract her from Oberon. It didn't. We left quickly.

For the next several minutes, as we kept walking in the direction of downtown, Oberon flipped through the pages of the play.

"I don't appear until Act 2," he complained. "Am I not the main character?"

"You're one of them," I offered.

"What was that playwright thinking?" he said, shaking his head. "Next, you'll tell me Nick has a part in this, too."

"Actually," I began—but Oberon had already moved on.

"I don't suppose there'd be a way to change the writing," he said. "You know, have it take place in Florissant, with me being the hero."

I thought for a moment. "We could rewrite it," I suggested. "But probably no one would perform it."

"*We* could perform it," he said, his eyes flashing with mischief. "What a lot of fun we'd have, putting on a foolish pageant like that."

"Nick would want to be in it," I said, teasingly. "And he's an actor, so he'd want to play the hero."

"He'd better not even try, or I'll turn him into a . . . donkey," said Oberon, sourly.

I smiled to myself. Oberon was glorious, moody, powerful—and vulnerable. He was the forest. I knew that.

"We'd need to include Caster," added Oberon, thoughtfully. "He'll be in a foul mood if we leave him out, and we'll never hear the end of it. You know how crows like to talk."

"Would there be a tree part for me?" asked Sylva.

"Absolutely," said Oberon. "We could have you play the Old One, if you wanted."

"I'd rather play myself," said Sylva. "Could we do it in the forest?"

"Where else, but outdoors under the moonlight?" said Oberon.

"I don't think anyone would want to watch our version," I said. "People like the original version."

"The one in which I'm a jerk?"

"Yeah, that one," I said. "They're used to it. I know I always wanted to play Puck."

"Let me get this straight: you don't want to *be* my minion, but you want to *play* my minion?"

"You just said he was your friend."

"You have an annoyingly accurate memory," said Oberon—but he was smiling. "So I did."

"Can we be your friends too, Oberon?" asked Sylva.

"My dear tree child, you and your sister already are. Let's toast to it."

He raised an imaginary glass. "To friendship."

"What are we drinking?" I asked.

"A goblet of magic dew. I don't suppose there's any place around here that serves some?"

"They must serve coffee at the waffle house," I said. "That's the human version of magic dew, by the way."

"I have heard of coffee, and am most eager to try it," said Oberon. "Is it true that it has magical properties?"

"I think you'll have to decide that for yourself," I said.

When we finally found the waffle house, a block away from the main square of the town, Oberon called the server over (you can imagine how thrilled she was to be called "my good woman") and asked for the "magical drink."

"He means coffee," I said. "One for him and one for me, please. Sylva, what would you like?"

"Water," she said. "My roots are thirsty."

"Y'all want anything to eat?" asked the server—Dottie, according to her name tag.

"A large tray of fruits with our magic dew," said Oberon.

Dottie stared at him, trying to figure out if he was for real.

"Just three bowls of fruit," I said. "Some toast and jam as well, please."

Dottie wrote it down and left, but not before taking another good look at us.

"I find humans so hard to understand," said Oberon. "Tell me, tree child, what is it they really want?"

Sylva shrugged. "No idea."

"What about you, Wynd?" he asked. "What do human beings want?"

"Undivided attention."

"That's it?" asked Oberon.

I nodded. "I've put some thought into this."

Oberon took a look around the waffle house.

"That can't be right," he said. "No one in here is giving or receiving undivided attention. They're all looking at those little black rectangles instead."

"Exactly," I said. "No one does it, but everyone wants it."

"Do you want that, too?" he asked.

"Nope," I said. "Neither Sylva nor I were ever under the spell of the black rectangles."

"So what *do* the two of you long for?"

"Tons of morning sunlight and rain in the afternoon," said Sylva, excitedly.

"What about you, Wynd?"

"I long for Sylva to get what she wants."

"And after that?"

I long to fly.

"I long to stay in Florissant—forever," I said. It was also true.

"That makes two of us, then," said Oberon.

"Three," added Sylva.

"Then let's make a pact," said Oberon. "From now on it is our goal and intention to protect Florissant for all time."

He placed his hand, palm down, on the table, and Sylva and I added ours. I wanted to say we were like the three musketeers, but I was pretty sure Oberon wouldn't understand the reference, so I decided against it. There was another reason, also: I had seen, since our entrance in the waffle house, several customers sending unfriendly glances in our direction—in particular, four rough-looking guys who were sitting on a booth had now stood up and were coming toward our table.

"Y'all from that school in the forest?" one of them asked, without so much as a "hello" or "how're y'all?"

"I'm far too old to go to school," replied Oberon. "You, on the other hand, could benefit from being taught a thing or two. For example, one generally opens with a greeting before—"

"You're not welcome in this town," said the man. He was the tallest of the bunch, with a considerable amount of stubble and brownish hair that was hidden under a camo hunting cap.

"And why not?" asked Oberon.

Everyone in the waffle house had stopped messing with their black rectangles now. Like me, they were watching and anticipating trouble.

"Something wrong with that forest," said the man. "People've died there. Decent sort. Gone there to hunt and never come back."

"There are wolves in that forest, too," added one of the other men. "They shouldn't be there."

"And why not?" asked Oberon, innocently.

"Them's dangerous."

"So are people," retorted Oberon.

"There shouldn't be any of them wolves in this part of Georgia," said the third man.

"Maybe they moved here after you killed all the other ones," said Oberon.

The first man slammed his fist on the table. Everything rattled. The waffle house was silent.

And I was mad. I hated bullies. So much. The anger within me had been building and building—and now it had to go somewhere.

"We're not afraid of you," I said, boldly. "You can slam our table until you break your hand—we're not leaving 'til we're done."

"We'll see about that," said the man, and he reached out to grab my arm. Oberon held his wrist.

"Do not presume to touch her, you *oaf!*" growled the former fairy king. "She is a creature of the forest, under my protection."

As he twisted the man's wrist behind him, Oberon's eyes had the expression of a wolf's, focused and ready for attack. If I had been that man, I would have been afraid. The other three men were, I think, but they finally rallied each other, and were about to lunge at Oberon when the door of the waffle house opened.

"Hey!" cried Nick. "What are y'all doing?"

"Stay out of it, Hintern," said one of the men. "We can handle it."

"You know these sorry fellows?" Oberon asked Nick.

"He's gonna break my wrist," whined the man.

Nick rushed over to Oberon.

"I suggest you let go," Nick whispered. "Things will get a *lot* worse if you hurt him."

Somewhat reluctantly, Oberon let go of the man's wrist.

"You okay, Starveling?" asked Nick.

"What do you care?" said Starveling, trying not to whimper. "You're no longer one of us."

"Yeah, where you been all this time?" asked another. "You done turned into a hermit."

"Been busy, Snug," said Nick. "Why don't we all sit down and have a cup of coffee together?"

"We don't want nothin' to do with you these days," said another one. "We hear you gone work for that school woman."

"I need the money, Flute," said Nick. "I'm a good handyman. And I like being out there."

"That forest ain't nothing but trouble," said the fourth man. "Ever since the judge ordered the mill to stop, we all lost our jobs."

"Come on, Snout," said Nick. "It's an old-growth forest. It takes forever for a forest to get like that. You can't cut down a forest to build a car wash or a strip mall."

"You saying you prefer them trees over us?"

"That's not what I meant, Snout," began Nick. "I was just trying to say that—"

"Come on, boys," said Starveling. "Leave him be. Let's get outta here."

They walked past him, and Flute purposely bumped against Nick's shoulder to stress the point that they were no longer friends. Snout slammed the waffle house door behind him.

"They're simple men," said Nick, sitting down with us. "They're just angry."

"Why are you making excuses for them?" I asked.

"I grew up with them," said Nick. "I understand where they're coming from."

"You don't speak like them," observed Oberon.

"I try not to," said Nick. "I'm not likely to impress a former Shakespeare professor if I do, right?"

"Stop trying to impress her," said Oberon, narrowing his eyes with irritation. "She's a queen. She'll want to be with a king."

"She'll want to be with the better person," said Nick. "You know, the one that treats her right."

"Maybe she won't want to be with either of you," I ventured. "Maybe she'll want to do her own thing."

Oberon and Nick seemed considerably worried at this new possibility, but Dottie arrived with our order, and Oberon's attention promptly turned to the "magic dew" cup he was about to try for the first time.

"Want some coffee, Nick?" she asked.

"That'd be awesome, Dottie," said Nick. "I sure could use some."

Dottie left, and Oberon expectantly took a sip from his mug.

"Ugh," he said, making an effort to swallow. "This is revolting."

"Try a few more sips," said Nick. "You get used to it."

"Why would I want to get used to it?" asked Oberon, pushing the mug aside. "Maybe that's why those men were so angry. I noticed they had been drinking this foul nectar."

"Speaking of them, what could you *possibly* have done—besides being yourself—to make them so angry?" asked Nick.

"Actually, it was Wynd," said Oberon. "She has a temper."

"I'm still angry, actually," I said. "I have this thing where I get really intense."

"I know a solution," said Oberon. "Every time you get upset from now on, remember what I'm about to tell you."

He leaned over into my ear.

"Remember the forest," he whispered.

Reader, there was magic in that whisper. A wave of calm came over me—the calm of the dappled forest floor and its golden leaves. The knot in my chest dissolved; I could breathe again. And think.

"Can't you make a potion to make the town like us?" I asked.

"No, no, no, no, no," said Oberon. "Those tend to backfire—trust me on this one."

"What about a potion that makes everyone realize they're descended from fairies, and that they need to protect the forest?" I insisted.

"Not sure that is a good idea," said Nick. "Imagine everyone in this town calling their relatives and friends in other parts of the state and saying they've discovered they're descended from magical beings. It would cause a great big mess."

But Oberon did not seem as willing to discard the idea as Nick.

"There could be a potion to help them remember, subconsciously, that they loved the forest at one point," he said, thoughtfully. "Unfortunately, subconscious memory revival potions require an ingredient I don't possess."

"Which is?" I asked.

"Mischief from a mischief fairy. Creating such a potion would suck the last little drop of mischief from that fairy. It's a rather cruel thing to do—like leaving a tree fairy without earth—so I have never done it. If I had known Puck—Robin—would do what he did, I might have considered it. It's too late now, in any case."

"Maybe Tania can think of something to make these people see us in a better light," said Nick.

"Speaking of the queen," said Oberon, "where is she?"

"She said she'll call me when she needs a ride back," said Nick. "Said she's going to spend the afternoon in the Public Library, to look for newspaper articles. I think she's hoping she can find something mentioning that Florissant was purchased by a private individual."

"Mom?" asked Sylva.

"Yes," said Nick. "If Tania can dig up any kind of record, she may be able to sway the judge."

So we got back in Nick's car, and began the drive back to Florissant. This time, Oberon rode in front.

"I'm surprised you were okay leaving Tania back there, actually," said Nick.

"Why?" asked Oberon.

"She says you were always overprotective."

"There used to be many more dangers in the forest when it was vast," said Oberon. "Goblins, dark elves, kelpies, banshees, the occasional giant—and so on."

"Where did they all go?" asked Sylva.

"I haven't a clue," said Oberon. "As Florissant shrank, only the fairies and the animals remained."

"You must like Florissant a lot better now, then," said Nick.

"Not at all," said Oberon. "I much preferred it when all of its inhabitants were present—even the ones I considered a nuisance. That Florissant was whole, complete, diverse."

"Like an ecosystem, where everyone has a role to play," I said.

"Exactly," said Oberon. "It was thrilling, but dangerous also—this is why I was overprotective of Tania."

"She says she did just fine before she met you."

"Of course she did," said Oberon. "She has a ridiculous amount of magic."

"Not in the human world, though," said Nick.

"Which is why I've given Caster instructions to keep an eye—two, actually—on her."

"She told you not to send Caster to spy on her," said Nick, outraged.

"He's not *spying*," said Oberon, matter-of-factly. "He's *protecting* her."

"She'll be furious."

"I don't care," said Oberon. "The human world is the most dangerous world there is."

"I think we can agree on that," was all Nick said, and we drove silently the rest of the way. Sylva dozed off, and I also felt sleepy. We finally pulled into the dirt road: it ended abruptly in the trees, as if the forest had swallowed the rest of it.

"That's as far as we can go with a car, obviously," said Nick.

"This is where that man was putting up his sign the other day," observed Oberon. "It looks different by day."

"The Academy is over that way," said Nick. "I'll be back with Tania later."

After he drove off, Oberon announced his intention to take a nap in his cave.

"It's far too hot to do anything else but sleep," he added. "But I shall stop by the Academy later, to torment Tania."

"Where's your cave, Oberon?" asked Sylva.

"In the deepest part of the woods."

"Near the Old One?" asked Sylva.

"Indeed," said Oberon. "You could say we're neighbors, though we're not exactly talking to each other at the moment."

"Did you also forget TreeSpeak?" asked Sylva.

"Regrettably," said Oberon. "I have the feeling the trees will only let us remember when—if—they find us worthy again."

"I can be your translator until you remember," offered Sylva.

"Awfully nice of you to offer, tree child," said Oberon. "Maybe you can put in a good word for me."

"I can do that," said Sylva, helpfully. "I've already done that for Wynd."

"Did it work?" he asked.

"Well," said Sylva, thinking it through, "they didn't kill her."

They tried, though, I thought.

"Then they must really like you," said Oberon. "I'm counting on you, tree child, to repair diplomatic relations between trees and fairy folk."

"Okay!" said Sylva, beaming with pride.

Until our arrival in Florissant, everyone (even well-meaning people) had treated her as if she were stupid. Now she had something to offer, and it made her happy. It made *me* happy. In Florissant, Sylva was beginning to *bloom* (yeah, I know—corny plant metaphor and cliché).

Upon reaching the Academy, we parted ways with Oberon and went in. Lunch was nearly over, but Mustardseed said she still had some cold bean soup. I wasn't sure I wanted to eat anything after fruit and toast, but the cold soup (sprinkled with edible flowers, by the way) was so refreshing and tasty that I had a whole bowl. So did Sylva. We sat, surrounded by other students, telling them what had happened in town with Oberon.

"Is Oberon like the rumors about him?" asked a twelve-year-old music fairy called Sonoro.

"Is he creepy?" asked Mathemagus, a fourteen-year-old math genius who could summon—and then solve—floating equations.

"Is it true that he turns into a killer stag when he's angry?" asked Aimsir, a weather fairy who looked as if she were around sixteen or seventeen.

"It's not a stag, it's a wolf—a wolf with red eyes and enormous fangs," said Etoile, a star fairy (by the way, I later discovered that star fairies never ever get directions wrong, and can figure out where they are and where they should be headed even in the worst fog, snow, or rain).

"He's not creepy, actually," I said. "We like him."

And the conversation moved on to what animal Tania turned into when she was angry. As before, there was a great deal of debate over it, and neither Mustardseed, Cobweb, or Peaseblossom (Mariposa wasn't there) were willing to lay our burning doubts to rest.

"We don't want to spoil it," said Mustardseed.

"You may see it for yourselves someday," said Peaseblossom.

"It's fearful, though," added Cobweb. Coming from Cobweb, that meant a lot.

I knew, of course, what *I'd* turn into if I got mad: a great, blowing storm. But what if I felt happy? Would I become a pleasant breeze? If I were sad, would I morph into a barely noticeable murmur of wind? I wanted to know more about my *wind-being*—and, since there were no other wind fairies I could ask, I decided my best bet was (yes, you guessed it) the library.

Most of the other students had planned outdoor activities (nearby waterfall-wading, berry-picking, mushroom-picking, and so on), and tried talking me out of spending the afternoon browsing through the book trees. As much as I thought it'd be fun to go into the forest, I really wanted some answers. The library it was, and the forest would have to wait.

"What about you, Sylva?" I asked. "What are you going to do until dinner?"

"I think I'm going to hang out with Giniana," said Sylva. "Maybe I'll go into the forest afterward."

I sensed she wanted to visit her sapling—and possibly the Old One.

"If you go into the forest, see if someone will go with you," I said. "If you end up going alone, at least let someone know where you're headed, okay?"

"Okay!"

So I went to the library. Once again, I stood in the avenue of trees, and once again I thought this indoor forest was awesome.

"Library," I said, after a moment, "can you show me books about wind and wind fairies?"

Nothing happened, and I felt pretty stupid. But then something occurred to me.

"Library," I said, "could you *please* show me books about wind and wind fairies?"

A sign post emerged from the floor: "This way to books about wind and wind fairies." I followed the sign, and walked some before I found another sign that said, "Up this tree for books about wind and wind fairies."

"Thanks so much, library," I said, climbing up the ladder onto the first branch. I had a feeling I would discover something major about being a wind fairy.

And I did. The first book on the branch had no title, but the moment I opened it, the hand-written lines caught my attention:

Faeries, come take me out of this dull world,
For I would ride with you upon the wind,
Run on the top of the disheveled tide,
And dance upon the mountains like a flame.
— W.B. Yeats, "The Land of Heart's Desire"

I was hooked! Somehow, this W. B. Yeats person had managed to express exactly how I felt.

It turns out the entire book was a diary written by a wind fairy. From the first few entries, I discovered that she had been born in Ireland in the late nineteenth century, and claimed to have used her wind magic to keep her sea-side village and all its sailors safe from disastrous tempests and extreme weather.

My heart beat fast as I read. I was feverish with excitement to learn that there *had* been others like me who hadn't drifted away for good. The wind fairy—Gaoth was her name, a name she had given herself, because it meant "wind" in Irish—had kept an extensive diary. She hoped the book would help another wind fairy: "you do not have to be a victim of your nature," she said, in one of her first entries, and then, "I learned how to control my *windkind*. You can, too."

Then came the warning: "Do not try the harder exercises before the easier ones. Doing so could prompt you to lose yourself prematurely. To this day, I believe my patience was the reason I was able to master my nature, while so many other wind fairies lost themselves before their time." I froze. I wasn't patient. Not a good sign.

I kept reading.

"Controlling wind essence has to do with goal and focus," she said, in another entry. "In my case, protecting my village—especially my father and brothers, who were sailors—was my single goal. Because of the intensity of my desire to keep them safe, I was willing to focus, to wait—to learn, so that I could achieve my goal."

So what if I wasn't naturally patient? I could learn to be. There was hope, after all. The world wasn't as unfair as I had believed.

I was still smiling when I realized Sylva was coming toward me.

"Hey," I said, pleasantly surprised. "I thought you were going into the forest."

"I already went," she said. "That was hours ago."

"Oh, yeah—I keep forgetting time feels different in here," I said. "What are you up to?"

"Oberon's back. He dozed off waiting for Tania, so I decorated his hair with wild flowers. Want to see?"

"Wouldn't miss it," I said, closing the book and climbing down the rope ladder.

"Did you find anything interesting?" asked Sylva, as we left the library (no checkout of any kind, apparently—I just walked out with the book). "It's almost dinner time."

I told her everything I had read so far, and Sylva listened attentively, the way she always did.

"So this fairy never turned into wind and disappeared?" she asked. I could see her latching onto the hope—the possibility—that she wouldn't have to lose me.

"Never," I said. "The writing is really good, too. I can't believe that was the first book I found. How lucky is *that*?"

Sylva agreed that it was super lucky. "Maybe the library is enchanted, like the rest of Florissant. Maybe you always find the book you're supposed to read."

"Maybe," I said. "I guess your mentor is a tree, and mine is a book."

"I actually have two mentors now," she said, cheerfully. "The Old One and Aynia."

I stopped dead on my tracks. "Who's Aynia?"

"The tree fairy inside the Old One."

"But Tania said all the tree fairies were gone," I said.

"They're gone because they've been inside the trees for a long time and don't want to come out," explained Sylva. "But Aynia came out, so that she could be my mentor."

"So Aynia is a tree fairy, like you, and the Old One is like your sapling," I said, trying to understand.

"Uh-huh," said Sylva. "So now I have two mentors."

I wasn't sure how I felt about that. I might be able to handle one mentor who didn't like me. But two?

"Okay," I said. "Just make sure you tell Tania about her."

We stopped by our bedroom to leave the book, and then headed downstairs to the courtyard. There was a crowd of students whispering around the sleeping Oberon, whose mane of hair had dandelions, daisies, dewberries, dayflowers, and daylilies (Sylva told me she was practicing the letter D).

"Have you all had your fill of admiring me?" he asked, unexpectedly, still with his eyes closed. "When I open my eyes, I shall turn into the most terrifying creature you have ever set eyes upon. One, two—"

The students scattered, screaming, and Oberon opened his eyes and chuckled.

"Three," he said. "I had forgotten how much fun it is to be around youngsters."

"You were taking a nap, so I decorated your hair," said Sylva.

Oberon waved his hand, and summoned a mirror ornamented by vines.

"You have done a masterful job," he said, pleased. "I look beautiful."

I smiled. Only Oberon could say something like that and get away with it sounding perfectly normal.

"Now," he continued, getting up, "I've been waiting here for Tania. Has she come? I'm eager to hear how her day went."

"I haven't seen her," I said.

"Mustardseed said she's not back yet," said Sylva.

"Not back yet?" asked Oberon, frowning. "The sun's nearly setting."

As if right on cue, the heavy front door opened, and Nick came in, looking worried.

"Hey, y'all," he said, rushing toward us. "Anyone heard from Tania?"

"She has not contacted you?" asked Oberon, alarmed. "Something must have happened."

Just then, Caster flew in over the courtyard and landed on Giniana's lowest branch, cawing miserably.

"I'm guessing it's bad news?" asked Nick.

"Tania's in grave danger," announced Oberon. "She's been attacked. Caster says she's somewhere near the edge of the forest, by the dirt road."

Without waiting another second, he waved his hand and disappeared.

"Caster, how do we get there?" I cried.

The crow flew off, inviting us to follow him.

"Sylva, tell Mariposa and the other fairies what happened," I said. "We'll need their help."

And I ran off with Nick before Sylva could say anything.

I'm a fast runner, reader. I know it has to do with being a wind fairy. For a few minutes, I was running faster than Nick, keeping one eye on Caster and the other on the ground. Then the sun set—and, all of a sudden, Wolf Nick caught up with me and leapt ahead. It was another full moon night.

I forced myself to run faster, though my lungs burned and my heart seemed about to burst. I heard gunshots. Then I arrived at the edge of the forest.

Reader, I'm going to try to narrate what happened next as best as I can, but keep in mind that everything went down incredibly fast. What I remember is this:

There were two men and a pickup truck parked by the dirt road. One man was Welt. He was carrying a gun and shooting at Oberon. I had never seen the other man before. He had a rifle, and his target was Wolf Nick.

Oberon had turned into some creature that had the horns of a stag, the piercing gaze of a wolf, the claws of an eagle, and a body that seemed to be made of leaves, fluid in movement the way a school of fish or flock of birds is. Now that I think about it, I wonder if the horns weren't more like tree branches, and the claws more like twigs with razor-sharp thorns. In any case, his eyes were orbs of brown fire, and he was about as tall as three men stacked on top of each other. I really wish my description could do him justice, because, reader, he was scary as he positioned himself between Tania and her attackers.

Tania was bleeding severely, but was still alive, and some random dog—shaggy, thin, and really tall—was by her side.

So I rushed to help Tania. Nick had been wounded but had managed to bite the arm of the man who had shot him, causing him to drop the rifle. Welt shot at Oberon several times, and then his gun was out of bullets.

That's when the Guardians of Florissant arrived. They lined up in front of Oberon and snarled in a way that was so terrifying I would have run for my life without a second thought. Welt, however, made for the rifle the other man had dropped. He was going to shoot everyone and everything there.

He made me so mad, that guy. I couldn't believe his nerve. I'm not sure exactly what happened at that moment, but I think I pushed him. Kind of. Actually, it was more like my hands turned into a whirlwind that hurled him several feet away—far enough from the rifle that he couldn't reach it. I felt very nauseous after this, and everything that happened next was a bit of a blur. Grimsby took a step forward, but Oberon—now back to his usual shape, and bleeding from several places on his chest—called out after them.

"Do not step over the boundary of the forest!" he cried, his voice hoarse with effort.

Grimsby stayed put, and the others followed his lead and kept their positions. Then Welt and the other man scrambled into the pickup truck and raced off, leaving a trail of dust to settle under the moonlight.

Chapter 11

THE DEAL

BEFORE THE DUST from the pickup truck had settled, Mariposa materialized out of nowhere. Her brown eyes nearly popped out when she realized the extent of damage before her: I was throwing up, Nick had turned back into a guy with a wounded shoulder, Tania had a ton of blood coming out of her right side, and Oberon was bleeding from pretty much everywhere in his chest.

"The queen," whispered Oberon. "Take care of the queen first."

Mariposa waved us all out of there—random dog included—and into the infirmary, where she promptly gave Tania a vial of healing water to drink, and then grabbed another one from the shelf to wash the wound with. A bullet popped out—the skin healed—Tania breathed a sigh of relief—and Mariposa offered her a third vial of healing water.

"You lost a ton of blood," she said. "Drink this."

"Give it to *them*," said Tania, gesturing to Oberon and Nick. "I'm regaining my strength already."

"I can wait," said Nick. "Oberon's in a lot more trouble."

Nick had assessed the situation correctly. Oberon was losing a lot of blood. How he was still standing—covered in sweat, and with bloodshot eyes—was beyond me.

"I'm perfectly fine," said Oberon, and then nearly collapsed. I had to prop him on one side, and Tania on the other.

"I don't have enough healing water to treat all of this," announced Mariposa, helplessly.

"I know what to do," said Tania. "Take care of Nick."

Tania waved her hand and we re-appeared inside a cave—Oberon's cave. Reader, this place was incredible. There was a waterfall in the back of the cave, and the resulting pool of water was emerald green. I could see the newly darkened sky, and even a few stars, from holes in the ceiling of the cave. There were fireflies happily flitting about, illuminating the mushrooms, flowers, ferns, and moss that seemed to be everywhere.

Tania and I struggled to place Oberon next to the waterfall (he had passed out, I think), and I stood by as she found a large, hollow gourd and filled it with water.

"Iron bullets," she said, pouring the water over his chest. "Lethal to most fairies."

But Oberon wasn't most fairies. As Tania continued pouring over him, he groaned, and his skin foamed a little—and then the bullets popped out. He breathed a deep sigh of relief, and his skin began to heal. Even the blood that was on the ground fizzed and steamed, and then disappeared, as if called back to its rightful owner.

And then, Oberon opened his great brown eyes.

"My queen," he said, gazing up at her, "are you well?"

At that moment, I realized that Oberon longed for Tania the way the forest longs for rain.

"Yes, I'm well—thanks to you," said Tania, with no small amount of gratitude in her voice. "I'm happy to say I think you'll also make a full recovery."

"I could recover faster if you kissed me."

Tania smiled—and then checked herself.

"Come on, Wynd," she said. "Help me get him to his hammock."

Oberon's hammock was more like a large cocoon made of leaves and twine and every soft material from the forest. It looked unbelievably comfortable and cozy.

"How did that horrible man get to you?" asked Oberon, once he had lain down. "And who was that other fellow? I thought you said you would be at the library the whole time."

"I did," said Tania. "I stayed there until about five-thirty, when the library closed."

"Did you find what you were looking for?" he asked.

Tania shook her head. "Someone went through a lot of trouble to hide old records—and now we know who it is."

"How does Welt have so much power?" asked Oberon.

"From what I've discovered, he's invested so much money in the town that it's practically his," said Tania. "He's hailed as a local hero. No one breathes a negative word about him. Our lawyer has received a bunch of death threats just for taking on our case. In fact, that's why I got shot."

"What do you mean?"

"When I left the library, I needed some fresh air and decided to walk back to Florissant. I knew I'd have to go pretty close to the timber mill, but I decided it was close enough to Florissant that I'd at least have some magic on me if anything happened."

"How could you go near the mill?" asked Oberon. "You know what seeing cut trees does to our kind."

"I know," said Tania. "It's heartbreaking. But I had a very strong feeling I should walk home that way. That part of the mill was pretty deserted, and I kept as close as I could to the woods. That's when I ran into Welt. He and the other man had tied our lawyer to a tree and beaten him. I think they were going to kill him, Oberon."

"Who was the man with Welt?" asked Oberon.

"I think he is the owner of the mill, and Welt's business partner," said Tania "The lawyer told me his name is Bob DuBois. How ironic, that a man with such a name should own a timber mill."

I must have looked confused here, because Tania then explained that the word "bois" means "wood" in French.

"Let me guess what happened next," said Oberon. "You decided to save the lawyer."

"Yes," said Tania. "I only had a little magic, so I could only wave us a few feet away. It was enough to hide us for a few seconds, and for the lawyer to be able to escape."

"Yet you were shot," said Oberon. "How?"

"I stayed behind to save the dog," said Tania. "You know, the wolfhound that you saw with me. I heard DuBois yelling at her and kicking her for not pursuing us, saying he had paid a fortune to buy a purebred wolfhound that was tamer than a little lap dog."

"And that's when you decided the dog needed a new home?" asked Oberon.

"Right then and there," said Tania. "I've always been partial to mutts, but I like any dog. I had to do something."

"I can't blame you," said Oberon. "You did the right thing, even though you could have been killed."

"Actually," said Tania, with a mischievous smile, "I rattled them a bit before I got shot. I did a little rage thing."

"White eagle with flaming green eyes?" asked Oberon.

"Yes—that one."

"Not your most fearful one—but not bad, considering you weren't even within the magical boundary."

"Were you shot by the guy with the rifle?" I asked Tania.

"No," she replied. "Welt shot me—and trust me when I say I was not happy to realize his gun had iron bullets. Thankfully, the dog helped me. If I hadn't had her to lean on, I wouldn't have been able to get to Florissant."

"How would Welt have known about iron bullets?" I asked. "Do you think he was the one who killed mom?"

"Two good questions," said Tania. She was about to say something else when Caster flew in, making a lot of noise, and then landed a few feet away from Oberon.

"Where the blazes were you when all of this was happening, Caster?" asked Oberon, angrily. "You were supposed to keep watch."

Caster cawed softly, ashamedly.

"You were with a lady friend?" repeated Oberon, exasperated.

Caster cawed loudly in protest.

"Yes, I realize it's mating season," said Oberon. "But still. The queen comes first."

Caster did not seem to agree.

"Leave him, Oberon," said Tania. "All's well that ends well."

Oberon said nothing more on the subject, though he still gave Caster the side-eye once or twice.

"The rifle stayed on the ground," I said. "Maybe we should go and get it. It could be proof against them."

"What proof could it be?" asked Tania. "The rifle is probably registered to him, and he would just tell the police he dropped it near the woods when he was chased by wolves."

"There *has* to be a way to prove they attacked you, though," I said.

"How?" asked Tania. "We don't have any visible wounds. The most we could do is accuse them of criminal intimidation and assault. To be honest, I think our lawyer will be leaving town very soon—if he hasn't done so already."

Oberon thought for a moment.

"We need to hold a Council," he said.

"I agree," said Tania.

"You do?"

"Yes."

"Caster, announce to everyone that there will be a Council," said Oberon.

"And Caster," said Tania, just as the crow was about to fly off, "thank you."

Caster clucked twice and then flew out of the cave.

"I better go back to the Academy," said Tania. "Nick has probably turned back into a wolf—and we just happen to have a tame wolfhound on the premises. It could mean trouble."

"Stay," said Oberon, grasping her hand. "The others can take care of it."

"We also need to destroy that rifle," said Tania. "Even if it's not proof of anything, I don't want it anywhere near our forest animals."

"Do your turn-into-ash gaze from *within* the forest," said Oberon. "Please promise me you will not leave the perimeter of the forest again—at least for tonight."

"For tonight, I promise," said Tania.

Oberon drew her closer. It was clear he intended to kiss her—and equally clear that she had no objection.

"Hey—I'm right here," I reminded them. "Get a room."

"This *is* my room," said Oberon.

"And that's my cue," said Tania, standing up with her cheeks red.

"You plan to leave me here, in my condition?" asked Oberon. He attempted a cough, but Tania saw right through it.

"Wynd can keep you company until you fall asleep," she said.

I was about to protest—I *really* wanted to go back to the Academy, talk to Sylva, get dinner, etc.—but Tania had already waved herself out of there.

"Minion, fetch me my book," said Oberon, lazily pointing to the copy of *A Midsummer Night's Dream* we had purchased earlier, and which he had decorated with a book cover made of leaves.

"I'm not your minion."

Oberon seemed amused. "Being called a minion really annoys you, doesn't it?"

"Yeah—it does. I'll leave if you keep calling me that."

"I won't call you my minion if you read to me," offered Oberon. "I must confess I'm having a rather hard time with this play. There are so many characters. And the language is so . . ."

"Flowery?"

"Precisely. Why would anyone write like that?"

"When you look at a really elaborate pattern in the forest, or see a flower with many layers of petals, you think it's pretty, don't you?"

"More than pretty. Beautiful."

"It's the same way with the language. If you can figure out the patterns in the language, and the images and stuff, you can discover that it's really beautiful."

"I see, I see," said Oberon. "Very interesting. Here, have some light."

He waved his hand, and a candle holder with a burning candle materialized next to me. I started reading from the beginning of Act 2. I read the conversation between Puck and the nameless fairy, wondering the whole time how Oberon would react to Puck's character, as well as the fact that he had so many lines. I decided to stop just as Puck announced Oberon was coming.

"What do you think?" I asked. "It's not that difficult, right?"

A light snore caught my ear: Shakespeare had put the fairy king to sleep. It was so delicious an irony I couldn't stop smiling.

I carefully placed the play on the hammock next to him, blew out the candle, and tiptoed out of the cave. I turned back to check on something. Yup. You'd have to know the cave was there to even spot how to get in.

Reader, the night was lovely: the leaves swayed gently back and forth, and the moon was a bright diamond against an indigo sky. I took a deep breath. I was happy. In spite of all that had just taken place, I felt that I belonged somewhere. I belonged in Florissant—and

I had done my bit to defend it, like Tania and Oberon and Nick and the Guardians.

And I would do more. I would use my wind powers to protect Sylva and the forest, the way Gaoth had used hers to protect her family and her village.

As I stood there, mentally plotting my course of action, a moth fluttered toward me—and then suddenly turned into Mariposa.

"Oh, man—you scared me," I said.

"I prefer flutter travel to handwaving," said Mariposa. "How are you feeling? Do you need stabilizing salts?"

"I'm okay now, actually," I said. "I feel much better."

"You *windified* your hands, but you are handling it very well," said Mariposa, approvingly. "How is Oberon?"

"Asleep."

"That is a good sign," she said. "He will recover quickly in the cave. It's where his power is greatest."

"Is that waterfall in there healing water?" I asked.

"Yes. There are several sources of it scattered throughout the forest. That is one of them."

How cool, to live in a cave with healing water flowing right through it. It was the stuff of fairy tales. Or maybe just fairies.

"I will check on him. Do you want me to handwave you back to Florissant?" she asked.

"I'd like to walk back, actually."

"Florissant's that way, then," she said, pointing. "In any case, Majesty wanted me to give you these," she added, giving me a pouch of acorns. "These are Giniana's. If you get lost or tired, you can eat one. You'll be transported right back to the courtyard."

"Thanks," I said. "See you later."

Once Mariposa went in the cave, I went in the opposite direction she had shown me. I knew I wanted to go somewhere else *before* I walked back to Florissant.

You might think it was stupid of me to go anywhere near the Old One again, but I couldn't shake the feeling that I had to face her—without Tania or Sylva protecting me. Don't ask me why, but I somehow sensed she was at the heart of everything—past, present, and future.

So I headed to the thickest, darkest part of the forest. It was probably a mile—tops—from Oberon's cave, but it struck me as a completely different place. It *felt* old. Dangerous. I sensed I was being watched, and a hollow feeling in my stomach made me want to bolt back to the entrance of Oberon's cave, with its moonlight and moss and fireflies.

I kept going, though. I could already discern the Old One's roots—thin at first, and then thick as the tentacles of a giant octopus. As I treaded carefully, trying not to step on the roots themselves, I held on to one of the cracked acorns, just in case.

I caught a glimpse of Sylva's sapling from the corner of my eye. I couldn't believe how much it had grown. It looked like a small magnolia tree now. No way it could have grown so quickly on its own. Magic *had* to have something to do with it. Maybe old magic was especially powerful. I was just wondering how old the Old One might be, when I heard a voice. Someone else, besides me, was in that darkest and deepest part of the forest.

I knew that voice. It was Robin's.

"Come on," he was saying. "Just take away *all* of my magic. You've punished me enough!"

I must have not been quiet enough, because he turned around, startled—and I saw that he had been crying.

"Sorry," I said. "I didn't mean to interrupt. I was just in the area."

"She's not answering me, anyway," he said, stepping away from the massive trunk. "Not even in TreeSpeak."

"I thought you had lost all of your magic," I said.

"The trees left *some* magic in me," he said, miserably. "That's why half the school burned down."

"What? When did that happen?"

"A few hours ago," he said. "We were rehearsing *A Midsummer Night's Dream* when a fire broke out. The school theater burned down to ashes, the drama teacher resigned—it's a mess."

"Was anyone hurt?"

"Thankfully, no—but it could happen next time."

"What do you mean, *next time*?"

"I used to be a mischief fairy," he said. "When I cut down a tree to escape Oberon, the trees cursed me by leaving some mischief magic in me—magic I can't control. Whenever I'm happy, I release that mischief."

"But you never seem happy," I said.

"Because I try to keep myself miserable," he said. "Every time I get happy, something bad happens. Our kitchen flooded, lightning hit our roof, and my dad hit his car—all in moments when I was feeling happy. I've been keeping track. I know it's the curse, and I don't know what to do. I'm afraid of hurting my family, other people—all because Oberon was a jerk and I wanted to run away from him."

"I get that he was a jerk," I said, "but you didn't have to cut down a tree. You could have found a different way."

"I was desperate," said Robin. "You don't know what Oberon is like."

"*Was* like," I said. "He's not like that anymore."

"Yeah, right," said Robin, nervously running one hand through his slick blond hair. "He just wants you to think that."

"He's had a change of heart," I said. "If you're willing to be wrong about him, you could get what you want."

"What do you mean?" he asked, suspiciously.

"I think he'd like to make it up to you," I said. "Tania says he's really good at making potions. Maybe he could help."

"You think he'd do that?" asked Robin, a glimmer of hope in his eyes.

"I could ask him," I said. "I mean, the punishment for cutting down a tree is losing your magic. He's not even going against the law of the forest if he helps you get rid of whatever magic you still have left."

"I guess you're not afraid of him," said Robin, impressed.

"I'm not afraid of anyone."

Not strictly true, but close. The only person I was afraid of was myself, but he didn't need to know that.

"Anyway," I continued, "there's a Council in the forest tomorrow. You could probably catch Oberon afterward."

"A Council?" he said, raising his eyebrows in surprise. "That's really serious. What's happened?"

"I don't know if I'm allowed to say," I replied. "I guess you can find out tomorrow."

"Fair enough," he said, though he looked disappointed. "I'm not a creature of Florissant anymore, I guess."

"You're not an enemy, either," I said. "The wolves aren't after you."

"I always liked Grimsby," said Robin, nostalgically. "He and I used to have fun racing each other."

I tried to imagine what Robin might have looked like when he was still a fairy. Did he dress like Oberon? Did he have little horns on his head? He seemed so human now, with his jeans and t-shirt, that I wondered how he could have ever had the wild eyes of Tania and Oberon.

"Do you miss the forest?" I asked.

"Less and less, the longer I live in the human world," he said. "I still dream about it, but I don't feel the call like I used to."

How sad. I hope I never stop missing the forest.

"I'll come tomorrow, then," he said. "See you."

"You're going the wrong way," I said, though I wasn't sure how I knew it. I just did.

He stopped, surprised.

"The dirt road is *that* way," I said.

He hadn't just lost most of his magic: he had also lost most of his sense of Florissant.

"Thanks," he said, embarrassed.

"Will you be able to get home okay?" I asked.

"I still have *some* Puck in me," he joked. "I'll make it."

He vanished through the forest, and I waited a few more moments. Now that I'd said I wasn't afraid of anyone, I had to make good on it.

"Aynia!" I cried. "Could you come out, please? I'd like to meet and propose a deal."

I don't know what, exactly, I was expecting. But out walks a woman who is *seriously* old. Somehow, though, she was beautiful too. Her perfectly white hair went all the way to her waist, and she was wearing a white dress and a white and silver robe over it. She had slightly pointed ears, and her blue eyes—darker than most—were bright and sharp. Her wrinkles gave her a ton of dignity and authority. She was an ancient sentinel of the forest, just like the Old One was—and was equally intimidating.

Oh, and did I mention that she had large, nearly-transparent wings? They weren't like a butterfly's, or like a dragonfly's, either: they reminded me more of the petals of a magnolia flower.

"Since you said *please*," she said. Her voice was low, melodious—not at all how I had imagined it.

"I didn't think you'd actually come out," I confessed. "Thank you."

"Please *and* thank you," she remarked. "I didn't think the young ones were still polite."

And I didn't think trees could be sarcastic. It caught me off guard. Then I remembered she wasn't exactly a tree, any more than Sylva was.

Sylva. The reason I was there. My mind became sharp again.

"I know you probably don't like wind fairies," I said. "If you help me, though, you might have a way to get rid of me."

"Explain."

"Before I do," I said, tentatively, "I'd like to know if I'm right about something. That man from Welt Development—the one who shot Tania and Oberon—is he the one who murdered my mom?"

"Yes."

I already suspected it, of course. But it was hard hearing it, reader. Really hard.

"Who is he?" I asked.

"The King of the Underworld."

"Then how come he's not in the Underworld, where he belongs?" I asked.

"We are the ones who decided he belongs there. Perhaps this was *our* mistake, thinking he could be fully contained."

"What do you mean?"

"Look," she said, walking toward a smaller tree that a vine had completely wrapped around it. "This tree is choking."

In one decisive pull, Aynia somehow managed to uproot the entire vine, leaving the tree intact.

"Was that a weed?" I asked, stupidly.

"From our perspective, yes," she said. "Yet nature gives it the same chance it does everything else. I sometimes wonder if I have the right to pull it out."

"But the tree would die if you didn't," I said.

She sighed before she continued. "There are so many competing interests in the world. Sometimes I am weary of having to choose."

"Our interests are the same," I said, "but you choose to hate me because I'm a wind fairy."

"Not because you are a wind fairy," she said. "Because you are Sylva's sister. Tree fairies do not generally have siblings. This is so they can devote their full attention to their mentor."

"You hate me because I'm *competition*?" I asked, in disbelief.

"If you want your sister to become a strong tree fairy, she needs to devote herself to the Old One and me, not you."

"That should be her call to make," I said.

"You are both too young to understand," she said. "You do not know what it is like to wait centuries for the unlikely possibility of a new tree child in Florissant, and then realize that her fate is in jeopardy because she has a sister."

A sister who loves her, I wanted to say. But what would have been the point? I knew she had made up her mind about me. About everything. Those thoughts had solidified over the centuries, like the hardening of a trunk, and they would break before budging.

"I think it's Gunther Welt, not me, who's jeopardizing everything," I replied. "How comes he looks human?"

"Evil always reappears, sooner or later, with a new face."

She continued walking, pulling out weeds here and there. As she walked past the Old One's roots, TreeSpeak lines lit up, following her, communicating with her. I wondered what they talked about.

"Are you and the Old One strong enough to open a crack to the Underworld?" I asked.

"Not a large passage, and not for long—but yes."

"If you do that, I'll turn into wind and push him in," I said. "You can close the crack before he can get out."

"He won't go in without resisting. You will have to get in with him, and then you'll be trapped."

"Exactly. You get rid of him *and* me."

She surveyed me for several seconds.

"You are not a typical wind child," she said. "You have formed a very strong attachment—and to a tree child, no less. If we are to make a deal, you must understand the terms. You will die in the Underworld. Does that not frighten you?"

"It's less scary to me than the idea that this place could be gone. Sylva needs Florissant."

"Florissant," she muttered, looking around. "It has been so long since I was out here."

She let her hand trail over a fallen and half-decayed trunk, and at her touch all kinds of little flowers and mushrooms sprouted.

"You look different from Tania," I observed. "More like a fairy, somehow."

"It is because I am one of the old ones."

"Are all of the other old ones gone?" I asked.

But she seemed to have little interest in answering my questions, so I finally went back to what mattered.

"If I make a one-way trip to the Underworld, will you take care of Sylva after I'm gone?"

"Yes."

"Then we have a deal."

She came toward me and took my hand in her thin one. It shocked me, how strong and painful her grip was. I quickly pulled mine away, trying not to wince.

"The Old One and I accept the deal," she said, walking back into the massive trunk of the Old One, and blending with it until I could no longer make her out.

I stared at my hand. The small outline of a magnolia flower shone brightly on my palm for several seconds before it faded completely.

I had been marked, reader. My fate was sealed.

Chapter 12

COUNCIL

RECAP: I'VE MADE a deal with an ancient tree and tree fairy who are possessive over Sylva. I know it sounds like a really bad decision—and that's exactly what I was thinking as I headed back to the Academy. My thoughts were so intense, and so confused, that they were eventually as tiring as my steps.

But I finally made it back to Florissant Academy. Its lights were comforting and inviting, and I opened the heavy entrance door hoping that I wasn't too late for dinner, because *something* smelled really good.

As I crossed the courtyard, Sylva jumped down from Giniana's lowest branch and ran toward me.

"I was worried," she said. "Where were you?"

"I was in Oberon's cave, and then I decided to walk back," I said. "Everything okay here?"

"Nick's gone back to being a wolf," she said, pointing to sleeping Wolf Nick, who had been partially hidden from my view by Giniana's trunk. "Tania says this is the last night of the month he'll turn into a wolf."

"And where's Tania?" I asked.

"In the kitchen," said Sylva. "Quince is there, too."

"Who's Quince?"

"The wolfhound she rescued," explained Sylva.

"That's a weird name for a dog."

"She told Tania that was her name. She was born under a quince tree."

"Is she nice?"

"Super. She's in the kitchen. Tania made her a nice plate."

"Have you eaten yet?" I asked.

"No—I was waiting for you," said Sylva. "Let's go—I'm hungry."

She grabbed my hand and we went inside the kitchen, where Tania was sitting, surrounded by students, telling them some horror story. Even Quince, tall and shaggy, was sitting down and paying attention—though I think what she was actually paying attention to was the floor, in case someone accidentally (or not accidentally) dropped a morsel she could snatch up. She was a lean thing with clever eyes, and I was happy she had a home where she was treated like family. The kids all seemed to be thrilled she was there. I wondered if the cats felt the same.

But back to Tania and her story.

"And then," she was saying, "he wandered the world, and ended up in Georgia."

"In Georgia?" cried Jamarcus, a student who was an earth fairy (really good at making anything grow).

"Yes," said Tania, laughing, "where he's been doing horrible and sinister things ever since."

"If he's human, shouldn't he go to prison?" cried McKenzie, a color fairy (sees emotions in color, and knows exactly what color and color combination you need to feel better at any given moment).

"He should, if people recognized the horrible things he's been doing," said Tania. She noticed me now. "Everything okay, Wynd? You took forever to come back."

"I wanted to walk, to clear my head," I said. "It's a nice night."

"A perfect night for stargazing," said Tania, pleasantly. "We are meeting on the roof at nine-thirty, so come and join us if you want a good view."

Sylva and I grabbed plates and served ourselves slices of lentil loaf with house mustard sauce, collards, and roasted potatoes. We sat down before we realized we forgot the watermelon juice, so Sylva got back up to get it.

In the meantime, Tania had started telling everyone about the good old days when kelpies roamed the woods and *ate* people. The littlest fairy in the Academy, a five-year-old called Sono, was listening with wide eyes. Now, reader, before you blame Tania for not telling age-appropriate stories, you should know that fairies do not understand this concept. They simply don't think of stories the way we do, and they absolutely will not dumb down a story or remove the scary parts so that their listeners feel comfortable. Even the youngest fairies can tolerate stories with darkness and death as well as color and light.

One more thing: all fairy stories, as far as I can tell, focus on great joys, great crimes, great mistakes, great jokes played on others, and great courage. And, no matter what, they contain great magic. Tania always says this is why she loves Shakespeare also.

"That kelpie was a handful," she said, with a nostalgic chuckle. "We started finding all these guts by the water, which he'd spit out after he had dragged them under and devoured them."

"*Was* a handful?" I asked, very much hoping all of this was in the past.

"He's gone, with the rest of the magical creatures of the forest," said Tania.

"Is he coming back?" asked Sono, worriedly.

"I don't know," said Tania. "I guess we should always be careful, or *it could be our guts they find by the water!*"

She grabbed little Sono, who squealed and laughed. Then the conversation turned to the stargazing, so the little guy lost interest, got off her lap, and wandered off to Peaseblossom, who gave him a bowl of flower petals and asked him to separate them by color, so that she could make flower garlands later. He did that for a little while, and then asked Peaseblossom if he could leave. When she said yes, he gave her a good-night kiss and skipped out of the kitchen.

"Dream fairies always want to go to bed early," she said, sitting down at our table now and showing us a beautiful garland she was working on.

"So they just sleep a lot?" I asked.

"And have good dreams," said Peaseblossom. "No matter how many kelpie stories they hear, they'll sleep peacefully and dream of something nice. They can send good dreams to other people, too, but he's far too young to do that. They're kind of like the good-luck fairies, who can send good luck to people."

"Are there any good-luck fairies here at the school?" I asked.

"Not yet," said Peaseblossom. "If there were, you'd know. They're very popular. Everyone wants to be the friend of a good-luck fairy."

Too bad. I could have used a dose of good luck.

"Are you done?" asked Mustardseed, as Sylva and I finished eating. "The two of you have clean-up shift with me tonight."

See, reader? If I had been a good-luck fairy, it wouldn't have been a clean-up night. It'd *never* be a clean-up night.

But, really, it wasn't so bad. Tania decided to stay and help, and we were done before nine-thirty.

"Are either of you coming to stargazing?" asked Tania.

"I am," said Sylva. "I love stars."

"I think I'm going back to my room," I said. "I'm super tired from walking back. I should have eaten the acorn Mariposa gave me."

I *did* want to go back to my room, reader, but not because I was tired. I *was* tired, but my head was racing, and I desperately wanted to go back to Gaoth's book for guidance.

"Sure," said Tania. "Tuck in with a good book and relax."

Wondering if she could read my thoughts (and deciding it had just been a coincidence), I went back to my room, though not before talking to Celynnog, who settled for petting when I told him (nicely) I couldn't see his treasure trove.

The moment I got to my room, I changed into my pajamas (green stripes with stitched pink and yellow flowers—as usual, exactly what I would have wanted to wear) and crawled into bed. Gaoth's book was already under the pillow, and I quickly pulled it out and began reading it. I immediately felt better. I knew this person, somehow: her voice, her sense of humor, and her heartfelt honesty.

I already knew that wind fairies could not fly like the wind without risk of losing their bodily form forever. But what I learned that night, as I lay in bed, was that the longest anyone had ever managed was five minutes.

Five minutes. That wasn't long.

My heart sank as I considered whether I'd have enough time to push Welt into the Underworld. How exactly did a wind fairy keep track of time? Checking a watch wasn't a possibility when you were in wind form and had a monster on your *windified* hands.

I must have been on that depressing thought when I fell asleep. At some point, Sylva came back in, kissed me good night, put on her pajamas (brown and green with stitched acorns), and climbed into her bed. It's funny, reader, but since she had planted her sapling on forest soil, she didn't need to bury her feet in the earth or sleep outside as much. She felt home anywhere in Florissant.

The next day, when I woke up, Sylva was already out in the forest. This was not surprising. During the summers, she always woke up with the crack of dawn. I wondered if she was with Aynia and the Old One.

I sat up and yawned. Then I remembered Council. It was today, and I had no idea when. Could I have missed it already? I ran out, still in pajamas, and headed for Tania's office. No one else seemed to be up yet. I had no idea what time it was.

The door of Tania's office was open. Turns out Oberon was in there, and he and Tania were chatting when I knocked on the door.

"Good morning, Wynd," said Oberon, pleasantly. "Come on in."

"Have a seat," added Tania. "Oberon and I were discussing what to do about the Council."

Oh, good. At least I hadn't missed it.

"Since we have called a Council to inform the creatures of Florissant that the King of the Underworld has returned, it also falls on us to propose *something*," said Oberon. "That's our problem: we have nothing."

"Perhaps we should tell them we are unsure how to handle the situation," suggested Tania.

"We can't give them bad news *and* say we're at a loss," said Oberon. "We have to think of something brilliant in the next two hours."

"I have an idea," I said, sitting down. "Did you know half the high school burned down yesterday?"

"While we were getting shot?" asked Oberon.

"I think so, yeah."

"Were there casualties?" asked Tania.

"No, but the drama teacher resigned, and they don't have where to perform their summer camp production of *A Midsummer Night's Dream* now."

"That is unfortunate," said Oberon. "But what does it have to do with our impending fiasco at Council?"

"Hear me out," I said. "If we staged *A Midsummer Night's Dream* here in the forest, Tania could call a bunch of city leaders and investors to pitch something about how profitable saving the forest could be. There are a bunch of places that offer people the chance to view wildlife, walk on trails, have a picnic, and—"

"Leave their trash behind?" asked Oberon.

"Yeah, I know people are bad about that," I replied, "but if people here thought the forest could become an attraction, they might be more motivated to save it."

"How could we turn *our* home into a place with trails and wooden steps and signs—all just to make it easier for these human fools to get about? Next thing you know, there will be handrails all over the forest. I hate the idea."

"The whole thing could be on our terms, though," said Tania. "And it could safeguard what's left of Florissant."

"In any case, all these people from town would be curious enough to come here," I said.

"And why in the forest's name would we *want* them all here?" asked Oberon.

"Because, if they were all here, it would be easy for you to unleash your potion on them—you know, the one that makes them subconsciously remember they were fairies once."

"But I've told you, Wynd, that I could not do such a potion without mischief from a mischief fairy."

"But here's the thing," I said, "Robin wants you to take his mischief away."

"But hasn't he already lost his magic?" asked Oberon.

"Not all of it," I said. "The trees left some mischief in him he can't control, and it's wreaking havoc with his life. He says it's what caused the fire at the school."

I watched Oberon's and Tania's stunned expressions with a sense of triumph. I mean, how often does it happen that you have just the right information at just the right time? You have to enjoy these moments, reader.

"Anyway," I continued, since they were speechless—a first, especially for Oberon—"Robin thinks you won't do it, because you hate him."

"I don't hate him," said Oberon—and, then, softer, "I never hated him. And, in spite of what everyone may think of me, I have never retaliated against a mischief fairy."

I gave Tania my *See?-I-told-you-he-wasn't-that-petty* look. We'd probably never know who was responsible for that first mischief fairy cutting down a tree—my money was on Welt—but at least I had been right about Oberon. He loved everything in the forest too fiercely to do that.

"So you'll make the potion?" Tania asked, tentatively—probably from feeling guilty of having suspected him all these years.

"I will."

"Then we have everything we need to present at Council," said Tania, recovering her usual spunk. "We can propose preparing the forest for a human tour, culminating in the performance of *A Midsummer Night's Dream*. The tour and the performance will just be a way to lure Welt into the forest, send him back to the Underworld, and ensure the survival of Florissant by releasing the potion on the audience."

"Can we use one potion for all those people?" I asked.

"It has to be a gaseous potion," explained Tania.

"I was afraid of that," said Oberon, unenthusiastically. "Those are incredibly hard to make accurately."

"But you can do it," said Tania. "If the town is on our side, Oberon, it'll be much harder for Welt and DuBois to destroy Florissant. If we're lucky, the wind could even blow the potion all the way to town."

"Very well," said Oberon. "I can prepare the forest for the tour and the performance, but I won't allow handrails on Florissant—ever. And we restrict human movement to one or two lanes. Barely discernible, and uneven. None of that clean and tidy stuff with the hard walking surface."

"How do you feel about wooden steps on some of the steeper places?" asked Tania.

"I prefer stone, but reclaimed wood from the forest floor is acceptable," he said.

"Then the two of us are in agreement once again," said Tania. "It has been a while since that's happened."

A surprised—and then flirtatious—smile crept onto Oberon's face. "Is that so, my queen? How about we celebrate by—"

"Before you start flirting again," I said, "we need to figure out what to do with Welt and DuBois."

"Well, we're not inviting them to the performance—that's for sure," said Tania.

"But we could lure them to the forest, and send Welt back to the Underworld," I said.

"Ah, so you figured out who he is," said Tania, uneasily.

"He's the one who killed my mother," I said. "I'm sure, even though I can't remember his face and there's no proof."

"There is, actually," said Oberon, waving his hand so that he was suddenly wearing a pair of white cotton gloves. "One moment, please."

He rummaged inside his cape and pulled out a bullet.

"Do you see this?" he said. "Take a good look."

"An iron bullet?" I asked.

"Yes, but not one of the ones Welt used to shoot us," said Oberon. "This is a larger one—an older one. Caster found it."

I waited. I think I knew where he was going, but I didn't—couldn't— say anything. My heart was racing so fast I couldn't even breathe.

"This is the bullet that killed your mother," he said, quietly.

I stared at the iron shell. It had changed *everything*.

"It's made of iron from the Underworld," said Oberon, holding it out of my reach. "Even touching it can harm a fairy."

"How . . . how did Caster get a hold of it?" I asked, my voice shaky.

Oberon hesitated. "Are you certain you want to know?"

"Yes."

"The bullet went through her," he explained. "Caster saw the whole thing and noted where it fell. They have a remarkable memory, crows."

I had always wanted to get to the bottom of my mother's murder, but knowing the details made me feel worse. It didn't bring any kind of relief. Now all I thought about was the bullet going right through her.

"When were you going to tell me?" I asked.

"It's not an easy subject to bring up," said Oberon. "It seemed the right time now."

He inserted the bullet back into his cape and waved the gloves away.

"I'm sorry, Wynd," said Tania, putting her hand on my shoulder. "Is there anything I can do to make you feel better?"

"You can help me send Welt back to the Underworld," I said.

"I doubt he'd set foot in the forest after trying to kill us," said Tania, helplessly. "Even if he did come, how would we get him back to the Underworld? We'd need the help of the trees—well, *one* tree in particular. *That* tree."

"The Old One's on board," I said. "She'll help us. I already spoke to Aynia."

"Just so we're clear," said Oberon, cautiously, "when you refer to Aynia, you *are* talking about the Old One's tree fairy?"

"Yup."

"How did you get her to come out of the tree?" asked Tania. "And how did you convince her to help?"

"I know what she cares about the most."

"Sylva," they said at the same time.

"The Old One will use her roots to create a crack to the Underworld," I said. "I agreed to use wind magic to push Welt in."

"What makes you think Welt will be willing to risk coming into the forest?" asked Tania.

"I'm going to work on him," I said. "I have an idea I'll explain later."

"You'll be putting yourself at great risk," said Tania, worriedly. "Magic from the Underworld is very different from fairy magic. Most fairy magic requires the forest. Underworld magic doesn't. Monsters can be monsters anywhere."

"Yes—Welt can discard his human shape at any time," added Oberon.

"So can I," I said, pretending not to notice the worry on their faces. "Trust me: it'll be worth it."

They seemed impressed by my confidence. Even I was.

"It's strange, though," said Tania. "Wynd, did Aynia make you promise anything in return for her help?"

"No," I said, trying my best to sound legit.

"Be careful how you deal with her," warned Tania. "She's very cunning."

"I know she doesn't like me," I said, evasively. "I think she's doing it just for Sylva."

"Maybe," said Tania, looking unconvinced. "Still, don't commit to anything, okay? Come talk to us first."

"Okay. I will," I said, with my best *you-don't-have-to-worry-I'm-a-responsible-fifteen-year-old* face.

"How about some breakfast before Council, then?" said Tania. "I think I smell pancakes."

"Is that what that heavenly odor is?" asked Oberon. "I'm famished. Haven't eaten anything since last night but berries and nuts I picked on the way here."

"Who says you're invited?" said Tania. "You're an embarrassment at the table."

"Speaking of embarrassments," said Oberon, "you know that Caster will have to be in charge of releasing the gaseous potion, don't you?"

"So?"

"I worry. He's not reliable this time of year. The only thing he thinks about is his lady friend."

"It'll take a while to put the performance together, anyway," said Tania.

"He'll probably have a nest full of fledglings by then, and it'll be even worse," said Oberon. "I'll have to impress upon him the importance of the task."

"Tell him the fate of Florissant will hang—literally—upon his beak," said Tania, with a smile.

The two of them were in high spirits now. It was so unusual for them to be getting along that I decided I'd leave them to it for a while and go change before breakfast.

"Don't take too long, though," Tania called after me. "Council is always the fourth hour after sunrise."

"I hope Caster told everyone," said Oberon. "I hope we're not the only ones there."

They chuckled, and I heard the word "minion" at least one time before I was finally out of earshot.

By the way, reader: if this were a chapter about anything other than Council, I'd probably spend quite a bit of time talking about how good Mustardseed's pancakes were. But Council is Council— the most important event in the forest—so I'll let you imagine how mouthwatering breakfast was and skip to the part that actually furthers the plot.

When a Council is called, every creature of the forest is invited. Not all attend, but there are representatives from each type of animal family. For example, there's a squirrel representative (yes, you heard right) that represents squirrels and flying squirrels. And there's a ferret that represents all ferrets, pine martens, weasels, beavers, and badgers, because the pine martens never bother to attend, and the beavers are always too busy, and the weasels are too nervous. It's all quite complex and detailed, and I actually found some of it kind of boring when Tania explained what animal represented what family and so on.

"You'll learn it all eventually," said Oberon, and then mentioned a few instances in which an oversight or other had nearly resulted in a Wood Wide War.

"Where is Council, actually?" I asked, as the three of us—together with Cobweb, Mariposa, and Peaseblossom—walked out of the Academy together.

"You have three guesses," said Tania. "One: in the glade. Two: in Oberon's cave. Three: in front of the Old One."

"That one," I said.

"You seem terribly certain," said Oberon. "Why couldn't it be in my cave?"

"Too many animals, and there'd be a lot of pooping in there."

"Good heavens, you're right," said Oberon. "Thank goodness I never suggested it."

"The glade might be nice," I continued, "but it would exclude the Old One, and it's risky to expose all the animals to an open view."

"Good reasoning," said Tania. "The Old One also carries the votes of all the trees."

"And who does Aynia vote for?"

"She and Old One vote as one."

Made sense. Maybe one day, Sylva and her tree would vote as one, too, if Sylva ever became the new Old One.

"I always love walking to Council," said Mariposa. "You can see the animals going in the same direction, animals that might usually be rivals . . . gives you a real sense of the importance of the event."

"Kind of like the water truce in *Jungle Book*," I said, but only Tania really got what I was saying. I guess we were the only readers of the group.

"I always get nervous when I have to cast a vote," said Peaseblossom. "Sometimes it's hard to hear all the tiny voices of plants and flowers clearly. It takes a lot of concentration, and I'm usually exhausted afterward."

"Take the afternoon off," said Tania.

"Thank you, Majesty," said Peaseblossom. "A nap with some wildflowers should recharge me."

"That's exactly why I told the arachnids they had to have their own representative," said Cobweb. "I used to get horrible headaches after Council. The arachnids always alternate between whispering and shouting. It used to drive me mad. I'd have to spin myself into a cocoon and stay there for days to recover."

"What about you, Mariposa?" I asked. "Are you the moth representative?"

"No," she said. "But I know who is. Actually, it's a bit awkward, really, seeing him again in this context. I think we were, shall we say, romantically involved at one point—at least I *think* it was him."

"I know exactly what that feels like, Mariposa," said Cobweb. "Council can be a bit of an embarrassment to those of us who change shape."

"Thank goodness I only deal with plants and flowers," said Peaseblossom.

What can I say, reader? The world of fairies had its share of the bizarre. For me, the strangest of all was an ancient magnolia tree that was obsessed with my younger sister and had marked my hand so I wouldn't back out of a shady deal. As you can see, the whole situation was weighing on my mind.

Speaking of *that* magnolia tree . . . there she was, dressed for the special occasion in amazing white flowers. And Sylva, predictably, was standing near her, between a black bear and a fox (Sylva and the fox seemed to be having an animated conversation—the bear seemed only marginally interested). Behind Sylva stood Aynia, quietly, watching the arrival of all the animals. I noticed she fixed her eyes on me for a moment—and the invisible scar in my hand burned for that moment, as if to remind me to not even *think* of pulling out of our agreement.

"Welcome," said Aynia, turning her attention to Tania and Oberon. "I will speak and vote on behalf of TreeKind."

"Very well," said Tania. "We welcome you and TreeKind to Council."

"Wynd! Come sit here," cried Sylva, somehow carving space for me to sit next to her and the fox.

"Hi there," I said, not sure if I was greeting her or the other two—or all of them.

"Bear and fox didn't want to be next to the snake, or the stinging insects," said Sylva.

"Good thinking."

"Look!" said Sylva. "The Guardians of Florissant are here."

The wolves trotted into position, creating a circle around the gathering. I wonder what the rabbits and the deer thought about that. If they were uncomfortable about it, however, they didn't show it. Today they would trust in Council, just as they would trust in Nature once Council was over.

Oberon and Tania walked to the center of the circle. Oberon rummaged inside his cape, pulled out a horn (made from discarded snail shells, maybe?), and blew. The sound was unearthly, strange—nothing that could have been uttered by a creature of the forest.

Council was now in session, apparently.

As Tania began to address all the animals and explain why they were there, Caster flew hurriedly in and landed on Oberon's shoulder. He cawed softly, and Oberon gave him the side-eye, as if to say, "you're late, minion!"—but I could tell he was happy to see his crow friend shifting about on his shoulder.

Tania told them about the King of the Underworld and the threat he posed, and the gathering became noticeably quiet—so quiet that I could hear the bear breathing, as well as the incessant murmur of the InsectKind representatives. Tania outlined (more or less) our plan to defeat Welt and asked if the animals were willing to have strangers rehearsing in the forest.

"For everyone's safety, we ask that you stay out of the humans' way, as far away as you can," she added. Then she asked if Aynia and the Old

One were still willing to open a crack to the Underworld. TreeSpeak lines lit up on the massive trunk.

"We are," said Aynia. "Are Tania and Oberon willing to defend Florissant with their lives, should something go wrong?"

"We are," they said, in unison.

They looked good together, Tania and Oberon—they seemed so strong, and evoked so much confidence, that I believed we really could stand up to Welt.

"Are all in agreement with our plan?" Tania asked. "Step forward and cast your vote."

Peaseblossom was the first to step forward. "On behalf of all Plant and FlowerKind, yes."

Caster then cawed loudly—"yes" on behalf of all corvids, I guessed. An eagle, cardinal, and mockingbird also cast their votes, together with three tiny hummingbirds and one loud mallard. Then came a bee swarm, a large mosquito, gnats, moths, and butterflies. The different mammals in attendance followed: the bear, the fox, the stag and the doe, a group of restless raccoons, and so on. Reader, it was kind of adorable to watch. The toads, tortoises, and salamanders—and even two snakes in attendance—all cast votes (I'm guessing the snakes said yessss). Oberon even bent close to the ground to listen to an earthworm and a snail, and also walked to where the stinging insects were, in order to ask what their vote was.

"There is one last group," said Tania. "How do the Guardians of Florissant vote?"

Grimsby started howling, and the rest of the wolves joined. Tania smiled.

"All the creatures of the forest have voted," she said.

It was a *yes*.

Chapter 13

Gunther Welt

WHEN THE ANIMALS started leaving, I noticed that Robin had been watching, crouching from a branch on a nearby tree. I couldn't tell how long he had been there, but something about his posture reminded me of a faun's or other magical woodland creature's. I wondered if he had dressed like Oberon in his previous life as minion, and if his combed blond hair had been a wild mane like the fairy king's. Most importantly, however, I speculated as to whether Oberon let him wear a cape, and guessed that the answer was *no*.

"I'm going to see the fox babies," said Sylva, excitedly. "Papa Fox invited me."

"Fox babies are called kits," I said, mindlessly. "Wait—you're not staying with Aynia?"

"Nuh-uh. I already learned a lot about trees lately," said Sylva, innocently. "I also want to learn about stars, and animals, and flowers."

"Sounds good to me," I said. "Have fun and be polite to Mamma Fox."

"Okay!"

Reader, don't ask me how the fox "talked" to Sylva. In Florissant, animals could understand and be understood by fairies. We simply *knew* what an animal was trying to communicate. It wasn't guesswork, either, or stuff we made up. It was all strangely accurate. It's as if we all had some kind of telepathy going. I had felt it for the first time the night we'd arrived in Florissant, when I'd had the distinct impression the fireflies in the courtyard were welcoming me.

I briefly scanned for Aynia and caught her watching Sylva leave with Papa Fox. There was a lot of competition for Sylva's attention these days. I thought I detected a sigh of resignation—tree children will be tree children—before she turned away and withdrew into the Old One.

So I turned back to Robin, who had already climbed down the tree and was coming toward me.

"Hey!" I said. "You came."

"I used to love Council," he said. "One time, I put a bunch of stinging insects in Oberon's horn."

Oberon happened to be standing right behind Robin—he had approached, quietly as a deer, from behind.

"I remember," said the former fairy king. "I blew out two unhappy scorpions and a livid hornet."

"Oberon!" said Robin, swinging around. "I didn't hear you."

"You must be slipping," said Oberon. "You used to surprise *me*."

"Those were different days," said Robin.

"I hear you want to leave them behind completely."

"That's right," said Robin. "Can you help me, for old time's sake?"

"I'm sorry about the way things ended between us," said Oberon, his acorn-eyes simple and honest. "I'm sorry for all the times I was unreasonably vain, self-centered, and insensitive."

"That was most of the time," said Robin. "But you were never cruel—I'll give you that."

This seemed enough for Oberon, but Caster wasn't so eager to be reconciled: he flapped his wings at Robin and cawed loudly.

"Caster still doesn't like you," observed Oberon.

"That makes two of us," said Robin.

"Caster, why don't you take the rest of the day off?" said Oberon. "This is a busy time for you, and you have done a lot of service lately."

Caster clucked appreciatively, and then flew off.

"You never gave *me* the day off," complained Robin.

"Precisely because I was unreasonably vain, self-centered, and insensitive. But I have already apologized for that."

"But I haven't told you whether I accept your apology."

"Well, do you?"

"I do, if you remove whatever mischief the trees left in me—for good."

"Come with me, then."

I decided to let Oberon and Robin walk by themselves to the cave. I was more interested in finding out why Tania was inspecting the trunk of the Old One so carefully.

"What are you looking at?" I asked.

"I've been foolishly hoping to find the way in," she said.

"There's a way in?" I asked, amazed.

"Yes, but it's by invitation only," she said. "Even if I were still queen, I would not be able to go in uninvited—such is the power of trees."

I knew about the power of trees, reader. In particular, *that* tree.

"I was rather hoping Aynia would have remained behind," continued Tania. "It has been a long time since the two of us talked, and we did not part on the friendliest of terms."

"What do you mean?" I asked.

"When Oberon and I started fighting, there was great debate among the trees about what should be done. Some of them wanted to take my side, others wanted to take Oberon's—and Aynia wanted a new ruler of the fairies."

"Who?"

"Herself."

Wow. That was big. Not sure a friendship could recover from *that*—if there had been a friendship in the first place.

"I don't blame her," said Tania, with a sigh of resignation. "Oberon and I threw the forest into turmoil."

"But my mother didn't abandon you *or* try to become queen," I said, hoping this would irritate Aynia and the Old One.

"You're right—she didn't," said Tania, with a sad smile. "But your mother was special. Our bond of friendship was very strong."

I didn't know how to say this to Tania, but I wanted to honor that bond. If my mother had found her worthy, it was good enough for me.

"What about Oberon and Robin?" I asked. "Were they like that too?"

"I don't know if they had the same kind of friendship," said Tania, thoughtfully. "Maybe they did. Or maybe Robin was just Oberon's—"

"Minion?" I asked.

"Exactly," said Tania, with a chuckle. "It's hard to tell. But it's always sad when a relationship breaks beyond repair."

"I thought nothing was beyond repair."

"Perhaps nothing is," said Tania. "But there's certainly no magic that can repair a broken heart. Only time can do that."

"You know that's a total cliché, right?" I asked, smiling.

"It's a cliché because it's true," said Tania, unfazed. "Now, come on—let's stop all this philosophy and get back to the Academy. We have a *lot* to do today."

I was about to ask if I she'd handwave us back, when we heard screaming—definitely Robin—and saw TreeSpeak lines on the Old One's trunk.

"Why is Robin screaming?" I asked, uneasily.

Tania's frown indicated she knew the answer. She turned to the Old One.

"You are making it hard for Oberon to remove the last traces of magic from him," growled Tania. "Do not interfere."

To our surprise, Aynia walked out of the tree.

"We do not forgive those who cut down trees," she said, simply. "The Puck will suffer if Oberon tries to remove our curse."

"You are too harsh," said Tania, appalled.

"If I am harsh, it is because I have seen so much," said Aynia.

"Have you not seen the power of forgiveness?" asked Tania.

"You are interested in forgiveness because you yourself are in need of it."

"*Everyone* is in need of it," said Tania, passionately. "Forgiveness is like the gentle rain that the forest yearns for. It's precious. It's more precious than a crown."

"You say that because you have lost yours."

"Through my own foolishness, yes. But I hope I am not so foolish as to have lost the ability to forgive."

"Forgiveness encourages mistakes," said Aynia, "and nature does not tolerate them."

"Nonsense," said Tania, impatiently. "Mistakes can lead to something new. The magic within Robin can help us turn the humans in our favor."

"What a convenient coincidence," said Aynia, dryly.

"Coincidences are part of the wider fabric of magic," insisted Tania. "You have to admit there have been quite a few lately."

I could tell Tania's statement had caught Aynia off guard, even though the sly old fairy recovered fast.

"Are you suggesting the forest is behind such coincidences?" she asked.

"The forest can see things we can't," said Tania. "Are you willing to claim you know more than Florissant itself?"

Robin stopped screaming now, and the TreeSpeak lines vanished.

"Because Oberon needs the ingredient for the potion, we are willing to let the Puck go," said Aynia, dryly. She turned her back on Tania and made to walk inside the Old One.

"I will endeavor to be worthier," Tania called after her. "You should endeavor to be more forgiving."

Aynia shot a dismissive glance back at Tania and disappeared inside her tree.

"We better check on Robin," said Tania, worriedly. "It didn't sound good."

She waved her hand, and in the blink of an eye we were outside the entrance of Oberon's cave. As we rushed in, Oberon was helping Robin get up. Poor kid was all pale and sweaty from convulsing on the floor.

"Here, drink," said Oberon, handing him a cup of water from the waterfall. "I am sorry it was so painful."

"It was the trees," said Tania. "They were holding onto his magic, while you were trying to pull it out."

"What made them stop?" asked Oberon.

"Tania gave them an awesome speech about forgiveness," I said.

"Can't really take credit for it," said Tania. "Most of it was from Shakespeare."

"From *A Midsummer Night's Dream*?" I asked.

"*Merchant of Venice*," she said. "And I don't think Aynia bought it."

"Trees are not poetic," said Oberon. "To convince them, you have to speak in terms of earth, or sap—or something along those lines."

"I did," said Tania. "That's why they let "the Puck," as they call him, go."

"I hate that name," said Robin. "I never want to be Puck again."

"But you may have to be, for a little while longer."

That was Nick talking. I hadn't seen him in the courtyard of the Academy, so I had assumed he had just turned back into a human being and gone home. My assumption was right, too: he looked like he'd had a shower and changed.

"Who said you could come in here?" said Oberon, with mild outrage. "How do you even know this place?"

"I'm part wolf," said Nick, with a grimace. "I traced Tania's scent here."

"So now you're a stalker, too," said Oberon, disapprovingly.

"You took a big risk coming here, Nick," said Tania. "You could have run into Grimsby."

"I think he only attacks me when I'm a wolf," said Nick.

Tania had an *I-wouldn't-be-so-sure* expression on her face, but she let the matter drop.

"What did you mean, I might have to be Puck again?" Robin asked.

"Someone from the school called me and asked me to sub as the drama camp teacher," he said. "Because of the fire, a large group of students quit. The kids who were playing Titania and Puck were in that group."

"What?" cried Robin. "What are we supposed to do now?"

"I suggest you play Puck instead of playing Oberon, and let Tania and Oberon play themselves," said Nick.

"But I've already learned most of my part," protested Robin.

"It was never your part to play," said Oberon. "Don't you want to play yourself, one last time?"

"It could help us save the forest," said Tania. "I know you love Florissant as much as we do."

Robin held out against Tania's and Oberon's gaze for all of two or three seconds.

"Okay. Fine," he said, finally. "It'll be a way to thank the forest and say good-bye."

"Fantastic," said Nick. "If the three of you can learn your lines within a month, we can pull it off."

"There's more at stake here than a production of *Midsummer Night's Dream*," said Tania. "Oberon, do you have everything you need for the gaseous potion now?"

"I have the most important ingredient, courtesy of Robin here," said Oberon, showing them a little glass vial with a green gas inside.

"What a relief," said Robin. "That little bit of mischief was driving me crazy."

"I envy you," said Nick. "Perhaps one day I'll be rid of my burden, too."

Tania and Oberon exchanged confused glances. How could magic be a burden? But I understood Nick and Robin. In some ways, I was still trying to figure out if magic would make me free or simply be the end of me.

"Let's go, then," said Tania. "Wynd, you need to put the next part of the plan in motion. Nick, can you give us a ride into town?"

"Sure," said Nick. "Where do you need to go?"

"Wynd needs to go to Welt's office," said Tania. "I'll explain on the way. We also need to stop by the school so I can talk to the principal. There are a lot of details to sort out if the play will take place in the forest."

"I suppose I'll remain here, and work on the potion," said Oberon, half-heartedly.

"And start learning your lines," said Tania. "Shakespeare gave you some good ones."

"Uncanny how he keeps coming into our lives," mumbled Oberon. "The man is veritably impossible to get rid of."

So we left Oberon to his mumblings, and took Nick's car to town. We dropped Robin off first, in time for his first class of the day.

"I have another break later," he told me. "Want to meet?"

"Maybe tomorrow," I said. "There's a ton of stuff going down today."

"Okay," he said. "Careful with Welt. If he's King of the Underworld, he's a monster on the inside."

"And I'm a hurricane."

Robin gave me a weird smile. Was it admiration? I wasn't used to getting these kinds of looks, and I can't say I minded completely.

"We'll be back to talk to the headmistress when Wynd is done," Tania told him. "Maybe we'll see you."

"Okay—bye," he said, and we drove away.

"Robin has a crush on you," said Tania, after a few moments.

I always hate it when people say the obvious.

"I'm not interested," I said, calmly.

"Really? Why not?" asked Tania, looking at me through the passenger seat's vanity mirror.

"I want to be free," I said.

"Like the Queen song?" asked Nick.

"Yeah. Like that."

"Can't you be free if he likes you?" asked Tania.

"Maybe, but not if *I* like him."

"Ah, so *that's* your worry."

"You can never be completely free when you like someone," I said.

"Maybe," said Tania, giving up on the mirror and looking out the window instead. "But maybe total freedom is also an illusion. Even the wind isn't totally free. It's at the mercy of all kinds of atmospheric forces and so on. And, when you like someone, it can also give you strength. Love is the most powerful magic there is. And *before* you say it's a cliché, remember that love is what helped you and Sylva survive and get to Florissant."

True. I'd never love anyone as much as I loved Sylva. Or the wind. But that was very different from a crush, or even a *like*.

"I just can't think about anything else right now," I said. "I have to concentrate."

"I hate to say this, but are you sure Welt will even see you?" asked Nick. "I've heard it's hard to get an appointment with him."

"He'll see me."

They dropped me off two blocks away and drove around the corner to wait for me. My heart beat fast as I walked past the antique store, the insurance agency, and the Chamber of Commerce building before I reached the storefront with *Welt Development* on it. I took a deep breath and went in and up the stairs to the main office. A male receptionist in his twenties, with pale skin and oily hair, stared at me as if asking to see Mr. Welt were the most unreasonable thing I could do.

"Uh, he is all booked up for today," he said, after clicking his mouse a few times and pretending to look at the schedule.

"I think he'll make time for me," I said. "I'm pretty sure he'll drop whatever he's doing and invite me in."

"And why's that?" asked the receptionist, in a condescending tone.

"Because I know he's the King of the Underworld."

"Uh, yeah—sure."

"Just tell him I said that, and see what happens," I dared him.

The young man hesitated, then got up and knocked on Welt's door.

"What?" I heard Welt bark from inside.

"There's someone here saying you're the King of the Underworld," said the young man, nervously.

Two seconds later, Welt himself walked out. You should have seen his expression when he saw me (hint: a *lot* of hostility). The pale receptionist promptly sat down and started compulsively clicking the mouse.

"You have some nerve," Welt told me.

"I could tell you the same thing," I retorted.

"Did *they* send you?" he asked.

"Tania and Oberon? They have no idea I know."

And I walked into his office. Just like that. He followed me in, closed the door, and stood there with his arms on his waist.

"What else do you know?" he asked.

"I know you killed my mother."

I had expected him to turn pale, but he laughed instead. For a moment, a flash of red darted from his eyes, and his teeth sharpened. Unnerved, I quickly averted my gaze, and realized his fingers were longer than usual—too long to belong to human hands. They hadn't been noticeable in the forest, at night, but they really stood out now. These were bony claws, reader, hiding under human skin.

"Look," he said, sitting down on his desk, "the real culprits of your mother's death are Tania Greenwood and Oberon."

"What do you mean?" I asked. "How could they be responsible?"

"Your mother pleaded and pleaded with them to either reconcile or part ways, but they didn't do either. They were consumed by their little fight. I bet Tania didn't tell you that you and your sister are the legal heirs to Florissant, did she?"

"Actually, she did. But she said no one can find the deed."

"That's because she probably destroyed it herself."

"No way," I said, shaking my head with conviction. "She's been looking for it for a long time."

"That's what she *told* you," said Welt. "Did she mention that your mother also left you a fortune in gold? She didn't, did she? She's playing you."

"I don't believe you," I said, stubbornly.

"You don't think Tania Greenwood is capable of stealing your fortune?"

"No."

"Then let me tell you what really happened," said Welt. "She came to *me* and proposed a deal."

This was an unexpected turn of events.

"What kind of deal?" I asked, tentatively.

"Once the judge turns Florissant over to the state, she'll purchase it herself."

"Why would she do that?" I asked, my confidence trickling away.

"Because then Florissant will be in *her* name, and not yours and your sister's. Do you think the fairy queen really wants to have two of her students own the entire place? If you do, you're pretty naïve."

I must have looked confused and vulnerable, because he smiled with a kind of cruel satisfaction.

"Now, if you want," he continued, "I can disregard your previous rudeness to me, as well your reckless accusations, and resolve all of this to both of our satisfactions."

"How?" I asked, in a more subdued tone. "Do you have the deed?"

"No," he said. "Like I said, that deed must be long gone. But if you help me get rid of Tania and Oberon, I will make a deal with you, and hand the forest over to you and your sister after they're gone."

"You're just saying that," I said, visibly shaken. "I'd need some kind of written proof."

"It's not exactly something I could put in a contract, but I *could* draw up a document saying I drop any and all claims to Florissant. Would that do it?"

"I don't think I can let them down," I said, full of indecisive anguish. "I mean, they're working really hard on a way to save the forest."

"What way?" he asked, and the red fire unwillingly flashed out of his eyes again.

"They're staging a one-night production of *A Midsummer Night's Dream* in the forest, and inviting a bunch of investors and important town people to convince them to protect the forest. They want to turn Florissant into some sort of forest experience with trails and stuff, and they think there's a good chance it could work."

"Then that's the night I want you to get rid of them," he said. "You can hide in the forest and shoot them both."

"No way," I said, horrified. "Besides, I'd get arrested."

"I'll get you the best lawyers. You'll only do a little time."

"Forget it," I said, getting up. "I can't do this."

"Hang on," he said, as I rushed to the door. "There's still a way you can help me *and* get Florissant."

I had my hand on the door handle already, but still I stopped and turned around.

"How?" I asked.

He opened a drawer, and gave me a vial filled with a dark, dirty-looking liquid.

"Give this to the wolves the night of the performance," he said. "We can't have them patrolling the forest."

"Will it kill them?" I asked.

"It'll just give them a good night's sleep."

I knew he was lying, yet I let him place the vial in my hands. As his fingers brushed against my own, I cringed: they were unusually hot and sweaty, as if the entire man were burning up from the inside.

"I'll only do this if I have the document you promised," I said.

"When is the performance?" he asked.

"In about a month. You'll see the exact date when they start advertising it."

"You'll have your document the day before," he said. "Come and pick it up here."

"Okay."

"Once you walk out that door, the deal is set," he warned, as I turned around to leave. "Don't back out."

Or what? You'll kill me and Sylva, the way you killed our mom?

"I won't back out," I said. Then I walked out of his office, went down the stairs, and left the building.

I had never auditioned for a play, reader, but I had just given the performance of a lifetime.

Chapter 14

Sylva's Question

WHEN WE GOT back to Florissant, the entire school—Quince included—went on a picnic together. Hot as the day was, it was pleasant in the forest, and the spot Peaseblossom picked—by a quiet stream with flat rock islands scattered in the middle—was like a postcard. The ground on the bank was covered in a carpet of tiny ferns and moss (with a few wildflowers scattered here and there), and the sloping branches of trees served as canopy and much-welcomed shade.

"Great choice," said Tania, approvingly. "This was Rasayana's favorite spot in the entire forest."

I wondered how many times my mother had sat there with Sylva and me. The dance of sunlight over moving water was endlessly relaxing, and I could understand how someone might want to sit there for hours, just soaking it all in. I stuck my feet in the water—cold!—and ate the roasted mushroom sandwich (with mustard) that Mustardseed had packed, inside a cloth napkin, for each student. It was a simple lunch, but delicious, and those of us who were thirsty drank from the waterfall pool. I never thought water could taste so good.

When I was done, I got up and found a nice shady spot to chill in.

"I'll be over here," I announced, leaning on a comfortable moss-covered trunk.

I had nearly dozed off to the rustling canopy of leaves (and the sound of kids having fun), when I realized Aynia was sitting next to me. I sat up, my heart racing.

"Your sister is enjoying herself," she said, watching as Sylva played on the rock islands with some other kids. "She knows how to be a fairy child now, as well as a tree."

So Aynia had also noticed that Sylva had found both parts of herself in Florissant—big deal.

"You are wondering why I am here," said Aynia. "Because Sylva cares about you so much, I came to help you understand."

"Understand what?"

"Let me show you," she said, resting her hand on my shoulder.

My eyes suddenly went dark, but somehow I could still see the forest—though in a way I had never done before. I could make out the fine silver threads of fungi linking the roots of the trees, and the sap flowing through the trunks, and the entangled roots, and all the energy of everything spilling onto the energy of everything else. Life pumped through all with an intensity that was almost overwhelming. I could finally discern the forest as Aynia and the Old One saw it—maybe as Sylva saw it or was beginning to. The dark world of the earth was comforting, cozy, silent—and the world above the earth was exciting, loud, and filled with light.

"Do you understand now?" asked Aynia, removing her hand from my shoulder. My vision went back to normal, and I was relieved—even as I realized how much of the whole picture I no longer saw.

"It's incredible," I said.

"The forest is a world of relationships," said Aynia. "They are at the core of everything. Perhaps you can understand that this is a type of love, too."

"Tania told me love is the most powerful magic in the world," I said. "Do you think that's true?"

"It can be."

Enigmatic. Just like a tree.

"Do you know anything about a treasure my mother left behind?" I asked. Surely she would know if this was something Welt was making up or not. And trees tended not to lie.

"I know many things," she said, and got up—with incredible ease, I should add, for someone so ancient.

Next thing I knew, Sylva was sprinkling water on me.

"Hey!" I protested. "Cut it out."

She giggled and sat down next to me. I blinked. Had I been dreaming, or had Aynia really been there? All of a sudden, I couldn't tell for sure.

"Did you see Aynia?" I asked.

"This morning," said Sylva. "Why?"

"Has she ever answered anything you ask her?"

"She says the answers are all out there, but we haven't figured out the right questions."

"Tree reasoning," I said, shaking my head. "I can't make any sense of it."

This did not seem to bother Sylva in the least.

"Do you want to get in the water?" she asked.

"I don't feel like getting all wet."

"Our clothes dry as soon as we're out of the water," said Sylva. "Look!"

She had been dripping a few seconds earlier, but all her clothes were dry now. I even touched, just to make sure.

"Magic?" I asked.

"Drying spells," said Sylva, nodding.

"You're welcome," shouted Tania. She was lying in a shady spot, arms behind her head, watching the sky through the canopy of leaves. Quince was lying next to her, watching the commotion of kids in the water with calm interest.

"That dog is so funny," I said. "She's Tania's shadow."

"If you're not getting in the water, can I decorate your hair?" asked Sylva.

"Okay."

"Come with me, then," she said. "We need to pick flowers."

"Sylva—no—come on," I pleaded, as she pulled my hand. "I want to take a nap."

"You won't regret it," she said, and she was so insistent I had no choice but to get up. "Tania, come with us."

"All right. But only if you decorate my hair as well."

"Okay!"

We left the sounds of the picnic behind—kids splashing in the water, Cobweb strumming a guitar and singing some sort of fairy folksong (surreal, reader), Peaseblossom and Mustardseed playing a type of pinecone badminton—and wandered away. Quince trotted cheerfully next to Tania, not straying farther than two or three steps from her.

"Quince really likes you, Tania," I said. "Do you think DuBois got her just so he could hunt the wolves here?"

"Probably," said Tania. "Nick tells me he's an avid hunter. He has several hunting dogs. Quince was probably just one of them. Anyway, Nick says DuBois lives in a lavish mansion, with a ton of trophies of all the animals he's killed. He hasn't killed a wolf yet, though, so I'm sure that's what Quince was meant to help him do."

I should mention, reader, that whenever Tania said her name, Quince wagged her thin, shaggy tail. Adorable.

"Has she met any of the wolves here?" I asked.

"She saw Wolf Nick in the infirmary that night we were all shot," said Tania. "I had just come back from Oberon's cave when Nick turned back into a wolf."

"And what happened?"

"Quince freaked out and bolted out of the infirmary."

"And Wolf Nick?"

"I put him under a sleeping spell. But Quince still wouldn't go anywhere near him."

I liked the idea of a wolfhound that refused to go anywhere near wolves. No one could tell her to be something she didn't want to be. There was something admirable about that, something that resonated with me.

"I wanted to thank you for what you did today," said Tania, unexpectedly. "You came up with a plan to save Florissant, and you faced Welt without any of us there to give you support."

"I think it worked," I said. "He really hates you and Oberon."

"I'm not surprised," said Tania. "Speaking of Oberon, have you realized that Sylva is headed for his cave?"

I hadn't. I had been thinking about wolfhounds and free will, instead of paying attention to where we were going.

"If I didn't know better," said Tania, "I'd say she's leading us there deliberately."

"Why would she be doing that?" I asked.

"I don't know," said Tania. "Shall we find out?"

Tania was absolutely right. Sylva kept leading us on, collecting flowers here and there, until we "chanced" upon Oberon, sitting outside the cave with a young doe. Quince whined and stood behind

Tania, looking rather intimidated. We waited, barely moving, as the doe apparently "talked" to Oberon, while he listened attentively and nodded thoughtfully here and there. After a few moments, he whispered something in the doe's ear. She appreciated whatever he told her so much that she nuzzled him, and then happily trotted away into the forest.

"Hi, Oberon," said Sylva. "What were you doing?"

"I was listening to her troubles," said Oberon. "It's hard being a young doe."

"What did you tell her?" asked Sylva.

"A deer secret," said Oberon. "Not for the ears of tree children, I'm afraid. To what do I owe the pleasure of the visit?"

"I have a question for you," said Sylva, gesturing for him to bend down so she could whisper in his ear. Oberon obliged, and then seemed surprised at whatever she said. He whispered something back, and Sylva seemed satisfied. Tania and I watched the whole thing, baffled.

"Sylva, what's this all about?" I asked.

"Come on," she said, gesturing us to follow her inside.

Tania turned to Oberon, as if expecting some sort of clarification, but he shrugged—he seemed as confused as she was—and we all went in the cave after Sylva.

"Sorry for the mess," said Oberon, embarrassed. An entire wall of the cave had vials, tubes, scales, and spatulas he was using for the gaseous potion.

"Are you making progress on the potion?" asked Tania.

"I was, until I went outside for fresh air and was accosted by young Gertie the doe and afterward by a party of ladies—one of whom is a canine and has already taken over my hammock."

"Quince is feeling quite at home," said Tania, smiling to see the wolfhound wag her tail even as she dozed off.

"I noticed she's rather frightened of the forest animals," said Oberon. "As she does not seem to have a hunting bone in her body, she is very welcome in Florissant."

Quince was already half-asleep on the hammock now, so it's doubtful she heard Oberon's warm words.

"Sylva," I began, "what did you whisper to Oberon back there?"

"Your sister had a rather intriguing question," said Oberon, turning to Sylva. "Would you like to share now?"

"I asked if Aynia and the Old One can hear us inside the cave," said Sylva.

"And I said they can't," said Oberon.

"Is there something you want to tell us, Sylva?" asked Tania.

"I want to know why Wynd agreed to be trapped in the Underworld."

Tania and Oberon both turned to me, with a mixture of surprise and shock.

"How do you know about that, Sylva?" I asked, uneasily.

"I can hear everything my tree hears," she said. "I heard everything you and Aynia talked about."

I should have thought of that. I had forgotten there was always someone listening in the forest.

"It's the only way, Sylva," I said, lamely.

"Wynd!" said Tania, disapprovingly. "I warned you about Aynia."

"It was already too late," I said. "Look, I already made the deal. I just have to accept that my fate is set."

The three of them looked unconvinced. I had expected them to be sympathetic and thankful, and to appreciate beyond question my willingness to be a martyr.

"You don't believe in fate?" I asked.

"We live in the forest, Wynd," said Tania. "*Nothing* is written in stone here."

I sighed. This conversation was going to take a while.

Chapter 15

THE STORM

A MONTH GOES by *really* fast, reader. Einstein wasn't kidding when he said time is relative. Even in the forest, it can fly faster if you don't want it to. Time, I concluded, is the moodiest kind of mischief magic there is.

Let me explain: everyone in Florissant was incredibly busy. Tania had requested the help of former colleagues from her days as a professor, and they had helped her put together a business plan titled *Florissant Forest and Natural Wilderness Area*, which she then distributed to a bunch of people in town, including the mayor, investors, etc. To Oberon's complete annoyance, they were all interested in the idea and confirmed their attendance at the play. Grumbling a great deal about the human invasion of Florissant, the former fairy king nevertheless used his magic to carve a few paths through the forest and insert a few wooden steps here and there to make the paths easier to navigate.

And then there was the stage.

In collaboration with Nick ("collaboration" is probably not the right word, since the two fought over the entire process), Oberon created a stage made from reclaimed forest materials. But before you even think it was anything like Shakespeare's Globe, let me tell you it wasn't. Even though the idea of the thrust stage was the same, Oberon's stage wasn't even close to symmetrical (nothing in the forest was, he said), and the Old One's branches served as the roof, or canopy, instead of the "heavens" above Shakespeare's stage.

It looked like what Shakespeare might have built if he lived in Neverland.

Needless to say, Nick wasn't thrilled with it. He also wasn't happy with Oberon's approach to his lines. The former fairy king seemed to be under the impression that lines were *guidelines*, and that it was the *sentiment* behind them that counted, more than Shakespeare's words.

"You can't just say whatever you want, Oberon," cried Nick, losing it during one of the rehearsals.

"Why not? I'm the fairy king and I'm playing myself."

"People are going to be expecting Shakespeare."

"Well, blast that man and his bambic haymeter."

"It's iambic pentamer, Oberon," said Tania. "And Nick has a point."

Oberon approached Tania.

"It's bad enough these so-called rude mechanicals are stomping all over the plot, and that you are *cavorting* with one of them," he whispered. "Now I'm being told how to say my lines. I can't speak in meter."

"Because you haven't been practicing," she retorted.

"I might practice more if I didn't have to get that impossible potion ready *and* patrol the forest to maintain those ridiculous trails," he said. "Every time I turn around, the forest has swallowed them."

"Speaking of the forest," said Tania, "do you think I should cast an insect-repelling spell around the stage area? Mosquitoes aren't good about keeping promises—not even ones made at Council. It might be too tempting, having all these humans around."

"Let the mosquitoes eat them alive, for all I care."

And they would start arguing all over again.

"For crying out loud!" screamed Robin. "It's impossible to practice like this. What if this were a rehearsal with everyone else present? You'd be wasting everyone's time. And you can't talk about being the real fairy king and casting spells in front of everyone."

As you can see, reader, it was a challenge—and, as time ticked away, it got worse: Tania and Oberon were no longer talking to each other, Nick and Oberon were ready to kill each other, and Robin was about to quit.

And me, reader? I was practicing wind magic. Ignoring all the drama, I'd find a calm place in the forest (there were many), and practice Gaoth's exercises, one by one, until I could do them. I mastered the art of turning most of my body into wind for five seconds. I also learned how to turn my hands and arms into wind, and how to use them to push and blow objects. I became confident that I could do what Tania and Oberon had told me to do, which was to use *windified* arms to push Welt into the Underworld, without actually getting into the crack and becoming trapped.

"What about the Old One and Aynia?" I asked them. "They'll be really mad when they figure out I tricked them."

"Do not worry—we will deal with them *after*," said Oberon.

"They had no right to ask you to do that in the first place," said Tania. "Keep practicing."

So I did. And then I could do everything the book taught—except for the final exercise, which was to let all of myself become wind—first for two seconds, then five, then ten, and so on. According to Gaoth, if I mastered thirty seconds at a time, I could eventually string together several segments of thirty seconds. That's how I'd be able to remain wind for five minutes without losing my identity and form.

I couldn't bring myself to try it. Not even for two seconds. What if I lost myself to the wind? What if I never saw Sylva again? What if I ruined everything *before* sending Welt back to the Underworld? So I decided I had learned what I needed to in order to defend Florissant— and everything else could wait.

I felt pretty good about my decision until the day before the play. That was also the day Ms. Williams made an unannounced visit to the Academy, as well as the day a major storm swept through the region.

Neither Ms. Williams nor I knew about the storm, so she found herself stranded in Florissant under a tornado watch, and I found myself in a wind-swept forest, with the wind calling me in the kind of irresistible way only a wind fairy could understand.

Fly, it whispered. *Be free. Let yourself go.*

And I did.

I'm still not sure how to describe what it was like. It was the strangest, most liberating feeling I've ever had. But I was no longer entirely me. I was everything, and I was nothing. I was flying through the forest, weightless, observing everything. I wasn't *I*, but rather the wind.

Then I remembered Sylva. It wasn't so much that I remembered her, but that an image of her flickered in whatever mind I still had, and called me back.

Except I couldn't get back. I couldn't find myself. Even though I was flying over the Academy, I couldn't figure out how to stop being wind.

I panicked. I sensed I was a thousand fragments with only the thinnest connection, like worn out threads that are about to snap. One time, when I was a lot younger, Ms. Williams had bought me a balloon, and I had accidentally let go of it. I still remember watching, helplessly, as the balloon floated into the sky, beyond reach. This is how I felt at that moment—except that I was a hundred balloons all at once.

Sylva. Sylva. Sylva. Sylva.

The words helped. The more I repeated them, the closer I got to the ground. I was over the Academy courtyard now . . . and then I was on the ground, throwing up. My entire body was shaking, but it was *my* body. I was back to being Wynd.

At some point while I was throwing up, someone knelt next to me—Tania—and then I was in the infirmary, with Mariposa's busy eyebrows (and the rest of her) giving me a salt pebble to put under my tongue and a concoction to drink. I dutifully did both, and finally stopped shaking.

"Thank goodness," said Tania, relieved.

Then I realized Ms. Williams was also in the infirmary. She looked mystified.

"How did *I* get here?" she asked.

"What's the last thing you remember?" asked Tania, cautiously.

"We were in your office, Dr. Greenwood, and you were looking out the window, when all of sudden you saw something and disappeared right before my eyes."

She spoke slowly, thinking things through. Tania and Mariposa exchanged uneasy glances.

"Then I went to the courtyard," she continued, "and saw you with Wynd—she was vomiting—and I ran down there to see what was happening. I was just asking Wynd what was the matter when the three of us reappeared here."

"Did you, by chance, touch Wynd?" asked Tania.

"Her shoulder."

Tania cringed. Not only had Ms. Williams seen her handwaving, but had been accidentally transported to the infirmary herself. She had, reader, just experienced proof that magic was real.

"That's not possible," continued Ms. Williams, shaking her head. "That's *just* not possible."

And then, reader, Oberon appeared in the room—poof!—out of nowhere. With Caster on his shoulder, too.

"Caster said Wynd was in trouble," he said. "I handwaved myself here as quickly as I could—" and only then did he see Ms. Williams.

"Oh, dear," was all he managed to say.

There was an awkward silence in the room as Ms. Williams surveyed us with a mixture of suspicion and horror. I saw Oberon reach for something within his cape—and it was a good thing he did, because Ms. Williams bolted for the door. With the speed of an owl, he blocked her way and shoved a vial under her nose. She breathed in a swirl of turquoise smoke before Oberon closed the vial and put it back in his cape.

Then the strangest thing happened.

"Wynd, sweetheart, are you feeling better?" she asked, turning to me.

The corners of Oberon's mouth curled into a triumphant smile.

"Uh—yeah," I said. "Much better."

"What happened to you?" she asked.

I hesitated. I wasn't sure what parts I could tell Ms. Williams.

"Did the windstorm almost get you?" asked Oberon, carefully choosing his words.

I nodded. "I almost got lost."

"You poor thing," said Ms. Williams. "Thank goodness you're safe now. This tornado warning was completely unexpected, wasn't it?"

"It's beginning to rain, too," said Tania. "Why don't we go to the kitchen and have a snack? There's fruit juice and iced tea and coffee and toast with jam."

"Sounds lovely," said Ms. Williams, as Tania ushered her out the door. "Come on, Wynd—you need a snack after what you've been through."

I wasn't sure my stomach could handle anything yet—it didn't feel like it was all back together, to be honest—but I hopped off the bed and followed them. As I walked through the door, I glanced back, and saw Mariposa's relieved expression. More memorable, though, was Oberon's look of satisfaction.

"The potion works," he mouthed to me. "We are ready."

Chapter 16

DRESS REHEARSAL

THE RAIN STOPPED, Ms. Williams left, and I went back to my room, exhausted. And gloomy. I had nearly ruined everything. *And I had left Gaoth's book in the forest. It was probably soaked by now.*

I felt lonely. I wanted to talk to Sylva, hug her little body, and tell her I was still there for her. But she was probably in the forest. She loved everything about rain. My guess was, she was sitting under her tree, or by the Old One, with her feet stuck in the earth, happily breathing in the wet forest.

So I sat by the window, miserably, until the wind blew the clouds away and the sky turned blue again. A ray of sunshine fell on me and thawed my gloominess. I went downstairs. No sign of Tania or Oberon. I went out into the forest.

Every now and then, the light of the forest hits you just right for you to realize that the world is beautiful and perfect and glowing with all things good. At that moment, you bathe in the magic of the forest. At that moment, you see things you normally don't.

At that moment, reader, I saw my mother sitting under a ray of sunlight and smiling. She was so pretty, reader, with her white dress against her brown skin and black eyes and long dark hair.

"Wynd," she said, smiling. "Were you looking for this?"

She was pointing to Gaoth's book, jutting from the crevice of a trunk. It had miraculously escaped the worst of the rain and was only moderately damp and smudged.

"Mom," I said, trying to touch her hair and realizing there was nothing there but warmth and light.

"What's troubling you, my darling?"

"Mom, I don't want to be a wind fairy," I said.

"You cannot unwish yourself, my love," she said. "You will always be Wynd, no matter how hard you try not to be."

This wasn't quite what I had wanted to hear. Something like "life is unfair" would have been more up my alley at that moment.

"I don't understand why things happen the way they do," I moaned.

"Perhaps you should focus on a different question," she suggested. "Focus on what you *can* do, rather than on so many whys."

I wanted to ask *why* she couldn't give me any answers, but that would have only proved her point. Maybe I *did* have too many *whys* in my life. They were frustrating to no end, because I could never get to the bottom of them.

"There are things you will not understand from your side of the door, my darling," she said, sympathetically. "From my side, everything makes sense, because I can see the whole web of magic."

"Speaking of magic," I said, "I tried doing some new wind magic today, and it went really badly."

"Bad beginnings don't necessarily mean bad endings," she said, reassuringly. "The most unpromising seed can bloom beautifully, and a crooked tree can straighten and reach for the sky. I've seen countless miracles in the forest."

"It'll be a real miracle if I can pull off this thing tomorrow," I said. "I can do *some* things with wind magic, but I *never* feel like I can control it completely."

"Because magic has a life of its own, Wynd," she replied. "Even the most powerful fairies can't always control it."

"That's what I'm trying to say, Mom," I replied. "I think wind magic controls *me*, more than I control *it*."

"But just as you can't always control it, it also can never fully control *you*—or make you do something you don't really want to."

"That makes it even worse," I confessed. "What if it turns out I *do* want to turn into wind forever?"

"Would that really be so bad?"

"Yes! I promised Sylva I'd be there for her."

"Are you afraid you'll discover you love being wind more than you love Sylva?"

My heart skipped a beat at hearing my deepest secret voiced. It was out in the open now, unburied, free.

"It's *exactly* what I'm afraid of," I confessed.

She smiled—and that's the last thing about our conversation I remember, reader. No words of advice, no "everything will be all right" or anything like that. At some point my mother disappeared, like mist under sunlight—but I can't recall how long I was with her. I kept walking, clutching Gaoth's book, and somehow got to the thrust stage just in time for the dress rehearsal.

I stood there for a moment, taking it all in. The stage looked incredible: Peaseblossom had decorated it with flower garlands, leaf vines, and garlands of holly and acorns. Even some of the lower branches of the Old One had been decorated, and I wondered what she thought of *that*.

"Just in time for the dress rehearsal," said Robin. He was right behind me, and his outfit consisted of pants covered in leaves and other forest materials, as well as hair styled upward as if he had been a punk fairy. Something about his make-up, with its glittering hues of green and blue, made him look unearthly. I wondered if that's what he had looked like when he was still a magical creature.

"Cool costume," I said. I was about to ask if Oberon had designed it when Sylva came running toward me and hugged me as if she hadn't seen me in a long time. She even started crying.

"Sylva, you okay?" I asked. "Did something happen?"

"I thought you'd be gone," she said, "because of the storm."

"I'm right here," I said, making a quick decision not to tell her about my little episode for now. "You missed Ms. Williams back at the Academy. Were you having fun in the rain?"

"No!" she said, pitifully. "I wanted to get back to see you. The Old One wouldn't let me."

"Wouldn't *let* you?" I repeated. "What do you mean, wouldn't *let* you?"

"She said it was dangerous," said Sylva. "She kept me inside."

"Inside the Old One? You were inside the tree?" I asked.

"Yes," she said. "Where Aynia stays."

"It's not unheard of," said Robin. "Trees often protect fairies—and not just tree fairies, either. When the Dark Elves still roamed the forest, the trees were always on the side of good, and you could always count on them to help. One time, a beech tree called Soma hid me from the dead cavalcade."

"The *what*?"

"The Wild Hunt," he said. "Most of the trees hid animals, too—the Old One held a bunch of deer in there to keep them safe."

I honestly couldn't figure out what was more disturbing: the host-of-the-whatever going on a hunt, or trees that could hold living beings inside them.

"Don't look so surprised," said Robin. "Oberon was inside a tree for years."

"Exactly," I said, amazed that Robin seemed so chill about the whole thing. "He was imprisoned there."

"Because of a spell," said Robin. "A tree doesn't usually hold you against your will."

"The Old One just did that to Sylva!" I said.

"The Old One was protecting her," said Robin. "A heavy branch from some tree could have broken and fallen on Sylva, or flying debris could have hit her, or the stream could have flooded—I don't know."

I glanced in the direction of the Old One—there she was, with her poker face. I'd never find out if she had been trying to protect Sylva or hoping that, without Sylva around, I'd turn into wind and disappear forever.

"Anyway, we're about to start," said Robin, as Nick called everyone onto the stage. "Are you going to stay for the whole thing?"

"I want to," I said. "I bet these benches are really wet, though."

Robin lowered his voice. "They're not, actually. Tania cast a drying spell on them before all the parents arrived with their kids."

"Nobody thought it was strange that the benches were dry, after the rain we had?"

"Maybe for a second or two," said Robin. "Then they realized they had no cell reception, and they've been focusing on *that* ever since."

I looked around: most of the parents were, indeed, fiddling with their phones—even Sheriff Goodfellow.

"That's hilarious," I said, sitting down. "I guess no one noticed there aren't any utility poles, either?"

"Not a single person," he said. "They probably think the spotlights and stringlights are solar-powered."

"But we know they're *Tania*-powered," I said.

"Yeah, we know that," he said, smiling. "Thanks for staying."

"No problem. I love this play."

He looked disappointed. "I kind of thought you might be staying for other reasons."

I stared at him. I couldn't figure out whether to resent his persistence or feel sorry for him.

"No offense," I said, finally, "but you *do* know I'll turn into wind someday, right?"

"So? Everyone's going to turn into another version of themselves."

I wanted to ask what version of himself he had turned into—better or worse—but Nick called all the actors to the stage, and Robin left. In hindsight, that was probably the best possible ending to that conversation.

"Robin likes you," said Sylva, who had been quietly watching the whole scene.

"That's not a good enough reason for me to like *him*," I replied.

"He seems nice."

"He cut down a tree, Sylva."

Sylva thought carefully about this.

"I guess he wasn't always nice," she said, finally. "But he could be nice now. Oberon's nice now."

"*Nice?*" said Oberon, insulted (neither Sylva nor I had seen him approach). "Tea is nice. Going for a walk is nice. I shall have you know that I am not *nice*."

"Aren't you supposed to be backstage?" I asked.

"I don't have any lines in Act 1," he said. "What were you talking about?"

"About how Robin cut down a tree," said Sylva.

"Ah. Terrible business. I feel partially guilty, since he did it to get rid of *me*."

"I don't think you should feel bad," I said. "He *chose* to do that. He could have done something else if he didn't want to be your minion."

"Sometimes there are no other options. When I was stuck inside the tree, for example, there was nowhere to go."

"Maybe there was nowhere to go, but there *were* other options," I said. "You could have stayed in there planning your revenge. You didn't do that."

"Yes, well—don't tell Tania this, but I'm actually glad she locked me in there, or I would have continued being insufferable. At least I'm *nice* now—or so one of my sources tells me," he added, winking at Sylva.

"I've been meaning to ask you about the potion," I said. "What exactly does it do?"

"*Exactly* is not a word one associates with potions, especially gaseous ones," said Oberon. "They're not scientific. They merely magnify the sentiment of words."

"You lost me."

"One always needs to speak as one is preparing a potion," he explained. "This is so that the meaning behind the words takes effect when the gaseous potion is released."

"So what do you say while you're making it?" I asked. "Magic words?"

"No, none of that," he said. "I merely say that whoever breathes in the potion won't remember exactly what happened, but they'll be left with a sensation of wonder, a sensation that they've witnessed something they want to keep. They'll remember, like a dream, that they were fairies once, and that the forest is worth protecting."

"That's lovely," I said.

"I stole it from Shakespeare," he said, chuckling. "From the play's epilogue, you know—something or other about slumbering and visions."

"Those are Puck's lines," I said. "Do you know yours?"

"Mostly," he said. "I've been saying them to Caster, and he assures me they're good enough."

I had serious doubts about Caster's judgment, but decided not to say anything.

"There you are," said Tania, coming toward us. "How do I look?"

In a gorgeous gown made entirely of yellow flower petals, and a crown of tiny flowers? A-ma-zing.

"Like the queen of fairies," said Oberon, gallantly. "I hope the armor shirt won't damage the petals when you put it on."

"Armor shirt?" I asked, confused. "What armor shirt?"

Tania gave Sylva and me a smile full of mischief. "Let me show you something. Come with me."

"Don't take too long," said Oberon, "or the peasant will have a fit."

The *peasant*, of course, referred to Nick, who was watching the play several bench rows ahead of us.

"Stop calling him that," said Tania. "It's not nice."

"There's that word again," mumbled Oberon. "Pitiful word that's incredibly vague and means very little."

Tania ignored him, and we followed her behind a tree, where she made sure no one could see us before she waved her hand. We were suddenly transported to a hidden lane, a secret path several feet below the rest of the forest floor, dappled with tiny pools of light. It was almost completely covered by branches and shrubs, and therefore camouflaged to such an extent that no one could have imagined such a place existed.

"I love it!" said Sylva (she was saying that a lot since she had arrived in Florissant).

"What is this place?" I asked.

"It's a holloway, a sunken road," she said. "It was the path through which the fairy armies marched when we sent Welt and the other monsters back to the Underworld."

"It feels old," I said, breathing in the humid air. Tania was groping the wall, and I was about to ask what she was searching for when she let out a triumphant "Aha!."

"Found it," she said, placing her hand on a spot of root-covered wall that looked (to me) like every other spot of root-covered wall in the sunken lane. Immediately, the roots gave way to an old, wooden door that was plain except for a golden spiral line in the center.

"There's no door handle," I observed. "How do we get in?"

Tania traced the spiral line with her index finger. An unseen deadbolt within the door clicked open.

"Fingerprint recognition," I said, impressed. "Not bad for a place with no technology."

"Who needs technology when you have magic?" asked Tania. It was a rhetorical question, obviously.

Sylva and I gasped as we went inside after Tania. In front of us was a small room with two shirts of chain mail hovering in mid-air. But these were *fairy* chain mail shirts, reader: they were made of the finest enchanted gold, silver, and platinum threads, and ornamented with row after row of small gold leaves.

"The leaves are made of green gold, the only thing that can protect a fairy against iron," explained Tania. "They act like protective scales. You may guess who was skillful enough in alchemy to make this priceless artifact."

"Mom?" Sylva and I asked, in perfect unison.

Tania nodded. "She made them for me and Oberon."

I wondered if this was the treasure Welt had talked about.

"Will you guys wear them tomorrow?" I asked.

"*You* will wear one," said Tania. "You have the most dangerous task, since you have to push Welt to the Underworld."

"What about you and Oberon?"

"Oberon has insisted I wear the other," said Tania. "I have to address the audience before and after the play, so he thinks I'm more vulnerable."

"But Welt will try to kill both of you," I said.

"He'll try to kill you, too, when he realizes what you're up to," said Tania. "This is not open to debate, Wynd."

"I want to be with Wynd," pleaded Sylva. "Can't I do something to help?"

"You have to stay in the Academy, with all the other students," said Tania. "It's the safest place."

"But—"

"You *have* to stay there, Sylva," I said. "Promise me."

"Why?"

"If I'm worried about you, I won't be able to focus on Welt, and then something bad could happen to me."

Sylva didn't seem too happy about the promise.

"I promise to stay only if you promise to come back," she said. "No matter what happens, you have to come back."

Reader, is it ever okay to promise something you might not be able to keep? I wondered that, even as I used my most reassuring voice.

"I promise."

"Then I promise, too," she said.

We shook on it. I turned to Tania.

"You're sure the students will be safe in the Academy?" I asked. "What if Welt or DuBois decides to try something?"

"My fairy ladies will be there, together with the Guardians of Florissant."

I briefly wondered if Cobweb could turn into a giant spider if push came to shove, and decided not to ask. Not knowing was better.

"We have to get back to the rehearsal," said Tania. "Take one of the shirts, Wynd."

I touched the nearest shirt, and it dropped onto my arm, like a limp towel. It actually weighed less than that, which was incredible.

"Go ahead and put it on. They become whatever size you wear. They also become invisible. Once you put it on, no one can see them but you."

I let the shirt fall over my head. It was so light it felt like putting on a paper vest.

"Can you see it?" I asked Sylva.

"It's gone," said Sylva, wide-eyed. "Do you feel it?"

"Not really," I said. "It's got to be the most comfortable piece of armor ever made."

Tania put on the other shirt now. The minute it went over her head, it disappeared completely.

"That's amazing," I said. "It really works."

"Of course it works," said Tania, smiling. "It's magic. Now come on—we have to be on the other side of the door to handwave ourselves back."

As it turns out, there was no door handle to open from the inside. Tania simply pushed the door open, and there we were, back in the holloway.

A quick handwave—and we were back at rehearsal, behind the same tree.

"Where is she?" Nick was asking. "She just missed her entrance."

"I'm here," cried Tania. "Sorry. I had some costume issues."

She ran onstage, and I saw her wink at Oberon.

"Ill-met by moonlight, proud Tania," he said, with a charming smile.

"It's *Titania*," corrected Nick. "And why are you smiling? You're mad at her."

We all waited in suspense to see if the former fairy king would lose it in front of a bunch of parents, drama club kids, and the local sheriff. Thankfully, Oberon decided to ignore Nick's reprimand, and did the lines again—this time without a smile. He wasn't half bad, really, and he and Tania made a really attractive couple on stage. Together with Robin, they dominated the performance. The parents in the audience began to pay attention, and eventually every cell phone was forgotten.

When Robin came center stage to deliver the epilogue, Sylva whispered that this was the best play she had ever watched. I smiled. It was the *only* play she had ever watched, but she could have done worse than a production of *Midsummer Night's Dream* starring the former fairy queen and king themselves, as well as the ex-Puck.

"What did you think?" asked Robin, when everyone was leaving.

"It was great," I said. "You played your part really well."

I knew that he hadn't *played* anything, though. Tania, Oberon, Robin—the reason they had been so compelling was because they had been themselves. Robin, though no longer a fairy, had simply re-lived Puck.

"See you all tomorrow, then," said Sheriff Goodfellow. "Come on, son. We still have a while to walk before getting to the car, and I haven't been able to call your mom."

Robin said his good-byes, and they left on one of the lanes that Oberon had created, and that led directly to the dirt road where most people had parked their cars. I noticed the lane had light stakes on the edges. The lights were surprisingly bright: there was no way anyone could get lost or step off the path unless they were determined to.

"What if someone decides to go exploring, Oberon?" I asked.

"They won't," he explained. "I placed a spell on the lanes and paths. The moment the humans step on them, they'll feel a tremendous compulsion to get back to their metal boxes."

"I bet they all think the light stakes are solar," I said.

"They're actually lunar," said Oberon. "Lunar magic is the way to go when the moon is about to become full. Robin will know this—he used to be quite good with lunar magic."

"How come Puck has the last lines, Oberon?" Sylva asked him. "Aren't you the king?"

"Well-noted, and most unfair," said Oberon. "Confound that Shakespeare! I've half a mind to change some things."

"Over my dead body," said Nick, grumpily.

"That *can* be arranged," retorted Oberon, under his breath.

"You're not going to fight the night before opening," said Tania, decisively. "We have more important things to worry about. Let's all get a good night's sleep and focus on what we have to do."

"I won't be able to sleep," said Oberon, sounding almost childish with excitement.

"Then maybe you can run over those lines you always get wrong," said Nick. "You know, the ones from Act 2, scene 1: '*I know a bank—*'"

"I know the lines," insisted Oberon. He cleared his throat. "*I know a bank where the wild thyme grows—*"

"Blows," corrected Nick.

"*Where oxlips and the nodding violent shows—*"

"Grows," corrected Nick.

"*Quite over-canopied with luscious pine,*"

"Woodbine," corrected Nick.

"*With sweet musk-roses and with clementine—*"

"Eglantine!"

"See? It barely matters what one says, as long as there's a rhyme at the end," retorted Oberon.

"It *does* matter," cried Nick. "It's not like you can grab a bag of cuties while you're lost in the forest!"

"Cuties?" repeated Oberon, raising his eyebrows in surprise. "What in the forest's name are you talking about?"

"Forget it," snapped Nick. "I'm going home."

He turned around to leave, but froze as he saw Grimsby and his pack. They were glaring at him—and Grimsby, in particular, was growling and showing his teeth.

"I'll take care of this," said Tania. She walked to where Grimsby was. "For Florissant, Grimsby—stand down, please."

The green fire of her eyes met the yellow fire of his—and Grimsby stopped growling, though he kept his eyes fixed on Nick.

"Thank you, my friend," said Tania. "Can I count on you to stay out of sight and protect the Academy tomorrow?"

Grimsby gave her a soft bark and trotted away into the forest, the rest of the wolves following him.

"He still wants to kill me," said Nick, who had turned a shade paler. "I thought I'd be okay as long as I'm human."

"Never assume that, especially so close to the full moon," said Tania. "I'll take you to your car."

"I'll go, too," said Oberon. "Welt could be lurking there."

"I'm wearing armor, Oberon."

"And he's the King of the Underworld," said Oberon. "Armor or not, two is better than one."

"Okay, fine," said Tania, impatiently. "Sylva, Wynd—do you have acorns to get back home?"

Sylva and I showed her that we did.

"I'll see you back at the Academy, then," said Tania. She waved her hand, and the three of them disappeared.

Sylva and I went up on stage now. We walked around up there for a bit, enjoying the excitement that comes with knowing you're in a space of endless possibilities. The famous Shakespeare phrase "All the world's a stage" suddenly came to mind. Maybe the thing to do was not to accept the parts we didn't want to play, and to embrace the ones we did.

"Are you ready for tomorrow?"

It was Aynia. How timely. I glanced at Sylva, but she seemed upset, and kept her distance.

"Did you and the Old One like the play?" I asked, instead of answering the question.

"We thought there was rather too much talking and movement," said Aynia.

"I guess you'll still have to watch it one more time," I said.

"Hardly," she said. "My attention tomorrow will be on you, and on the King of the Underworld."

"I'll bring him to you," I said. "Just make sure you open that crack. I'll do my bit after that. And one more thing. Don't *ever* hold Sylva against her will again. If you do, she'll know you're not a worthy mentor, and she'll look for a different tree."

Then Sylva and I ate our acorns and were transported back to the Academy.

Chapter 17

A Night to Remember

THE DAY HAD finally arrived—the day that would determine *everything*.

I woke up from a night of tossing and turning to find that Sylva had left me a note. Yes, reader, you read that right: a handwritten note that said the following, in terrible handwriting:

SUN TO BREKFUST

I smiled. I guess Sylva had learned the alphabet. Now she just needed to learn spelling.

She was having a second bowl of oatmeal with maple syrup when I got to the kitchen, and I gladly joined her. I love maple syrup, reader—not the gooey, fake stuff you get at most restaurants, but the real thing. The one I was having, like everything else in Florissant, was the real thing.

Mustardseed, Peaseblossom, and Cobweb sat with us. Mariposa was busy in the infirmary, and Tania was in her office.

"What book are you reading?" asked Peaseblossom, noticing Gaoth's diary lying next to my plate. I had brought it with me, so I could take one more look through it.

"I got it from the library," I said. "It's a diary a wind fairy wrote."

I handed it to Peaseblossom, who started flipping through the crinkled pages. As she did so, the flowers in her dress seemed to tilt the same way as her face. I realized, with a thrill, that they were scanning the pages with her.

"This handwriting," she muttered. "Ladies—what do you think? Is it?"

Cobweb and Mustardseed peered over a few of the entries.

"Definitely," said Cobweb.

"Who did you say wrote this book?" Mustardseed asked me.

"Gaoth, a wind fairy who lived in Ireland," I said. "Why? Whose handwriting did you think it was?"

The three fairies exchanged uneasy glances.

"Never mind," said Peaseblossom.

I was about to ask again, but they scattered, claiming things to do, before I could.

"That was weird," I said. "I wonder why they didn't want to talk about it."

"Do you think Mom could have written it?" asked Sylva.

"I doubt it," I said. "An alchemy fairy wouldn't be able to give instructions on how to control wind magic. Only a wind fairy could do that, or a—"

Generalist.

"Or a what?" asked Sylva.

"Never mind," I said. "It's been super helpful, no matter who actually wrote it."

"Are you going to be reading it now?" she asked.

"Not if you want to do something else," I said. "What were you thinking?"

"A walk through the forest," said Sylva, cheerfully.

"I thought all the students had to stay in today," I said.

"We can go out in the morning," she said. "We have to be back for lunch, and we can't go out after that."

"Cool—we have tons of time, then."

So Sylva and I went out into the forest. It was a beautiful day, and we tried to find the sunken lane we had visited with Tania, but couldn't. We settled for picking berries and wading into a nearby stream. If you're wondering why I'm including all of this detail, it's because that entire morning was special to me—even more so because I knew there was a chance I might never see Sylva again.

"It's okay, you know," she said, as we made our way back. "It's okay if you want to go."

"Go?" I repeated, confused.

"Into the wind."

"Sylva! Don't say that."

"I don't want you to feel that you can't be *you* because of *me*."

"I *don't* feel that," I said. "I don't want to become wind because I want us to stay together. There's more to me than being wind, just like there's more to you than being a tree. Okay?"

"Okay!" she said. That was her standard happy answer, and I loved hearing it.

"Guess what?" she said, as we kept walking. "My tree has its first flower."

"No way!" I said. "That's awesome. You should have said something—we could have gone there."

"I didn't want to go there," she said.

"Is it because of Aynia and the Old One?"

She nodded. She was still upset at them.

"What's your tree called?" I asked.

"Aynia calls it the Young One."

"Do *you* have a name for it? What do *you* want to call it?"

"Mag."

"That's it? Mag?"

Sylva nodded. It was good enough for her—and, as far as I was concerned, far better than "the Young One."

"Then tell Aynia and the Old One that they should call her that," I said.

Sylva seemed encouraged and cheered by the idea—and then a cloud crossed her face.

"I don't want to live inside Mag, though," she said. "I want to live in the Academy."

"Right now Mag's not big enough for you to do that, anyway," I told her. "But the day she is, you still won't have to live inside her—no matter what Aynia tells you."

"Really?"

"Really. Tree fairies used to live in the forest before they withdrew into the trees. Aynia must have lived so long inside the Old One that she's more comfortable there now—but that doesn't have to be your case."

"Okay!" said Sylva. She looked so much happier that I realized these things must have been weighing heavily on her young mind.

When we were nearly back, Caster landed on a branch above us, cawing loudly. If you're wondering how we knew it was Caster, and not some other crow, chuck it up to the magic of Florissant. Once the magic kicks in, you can recognize animals the way you can recognize people.

"What's up, Caster?" I asked.

According to Caster, Nick was waiting for me at the dirt road. I had completely forgotten I was supposed to go to Welt's office to pick up the promised document.

"I better go," I told Sylva. "See you at lunch?"

She nodded and went through the front gate. I turned around and walked to the dirt road, where Nick stood outside the car, waiting.

"So hot today," he said. "It's already ninety-two degrees."

As he opened the door for us to get in, Tania emerged from the trees with Quince.

"Wynd, wait," she said, rushing toward us. "I've been thinking: maybe it's best if you don't go to Welt's office."

"Why not?" I asked.

"I have a gut feeling he may be up to something."

"He *is* up to something," I said. "He's planning to kill you and Oberon later."

"I worry you'll be in danger if you go," she said. "I don't know why I have this nagging feeling."

"I'm wearing the mail shirt, so I should be okay," I said. "Besides, if I don't go, he'll think something is wrong, and he may not show up later. Then the whole thing will have been for nothing."

"I'm coming with you, then," she said, getting into the back seat with Quince. "We'll wait in the usual spot. If you're not out of there in ten minutes, we'll call the police."

In spite of Tania's sudden nervousness, however, I felt confident. When we got to town, they dropped me off and I walked to Welt's office under the scorching heat of the midday sun. There were no trees on that entire block, and I decided it couldn't be a coincidence. Welt probably didn't want trees anywhere near him if he could help it, even if that meant the entire block wouldn't have shade in the summer.

When I got upstairs to his office, I expected the pale secretary to hand me the envelope, but Welt himself came out and called me inside.

"Here," he said, giving me the envelope. "Check that it's what you wanted."

I opened the envelope and took out the letter-sized document. My hands shook—I was so nervous even my fingers seemed to have turned cold all of a sudden—as I read this and that about relinquishing the claim to the forest. It had a signature. Everything seemed legit, so I nodded, and turned around to leave.

"Make sure you pick a spot where I get a good shot—especially at *him*."

"Oberon?"

Of course I knew it was Oberon, reader, but I was trying to get some more information out of Welt.

"He's had it coming for a long time," was all Welt said, so I had no choice but to leave after we agreed to meet at nine pm, in the place he had first put up the "Future Site—Welt Development" sign.

When I got to the car, Tania looked incredibly relieved.

"Weird," she said, when I told her he hadn't done anything strange. "I'm usually not wrong about stuff like this."

What I *wanted* to tell her, reader, was that Oberon should wear one of the fairy mail shirts. But I also knew that Tania would never let me *not* wear the shirt, so I decided to find a different way to get Oberon to wear it.

If you're thinking I was crazy, maybe you're right. Maybe the thought of a Florissant without Oberon clouded my thinking. The forest could do without a wind fairy, but it couldn't do without a fairy king—or queen, for that matter. Oberon and Tania were the heart and soul of the enchanted forest, and the thought of a fairy realm without one of them was unbearable.

"Why don't we have lunch in my office?" asked Tania, when we got back to Florissant. "We can't discuss our plan for tonight in the middle of all the students."

"But I told Sylva we'd have lunch together," I said.

"Sylva can come," said Tania. "She knows about everything, anyway, and she's a tree fairy. They tend to be discreet."

"I'll go find her," I said. "If she's not with Giniana, she's probably in the kitchen already."

I found Sylva in the kitchen. She was carefully listening to Mustardseed's advice on how to make the perfect stuffed eggplant—which happened to be what we had for lunch, together with rosemary potatoes.

"We're having lunch in Tania's office," I announced, to Sylva's delight. "Nick's also there."

"No Oberon?" asked Mustardseed.

"Not as far as I know."

"Get your dishes, then," said Mustardseed. "I'll put the queen's and Nick's on a tray."

When Mustardseed handwaved us to the door of Tania's office, Tania and Nick were talking about what a shame it was that he wouldn't see the performance.

"You're not coming?" I asked him. "It's not a full moon night yet, is it?"

"No," said Nick. "The full moon is tomorrow. I won't turn into a wolf until then."

"So why aren't you watching the play?" I asked, confused.

"I'm worried about those guys we met at the waffle house, remember?"

Could I forget them? Not easily.

"Dottie sent me a text saying she overheard them talking about the Academy. I'm worried they'll try something when everyone's at the play."

"The Guardians will be here, though," said Tania. "And trust me when I say my ladies can be frightening—downright terrifying, in the case of Cobweb."

"I'd feel better if I stayed," said Nick. "There's a spot off the dirt road where I think I can park the car. It's close to the school, and there's cell phone reception there. I'll just stay inside the car and watch. If I see something funny, I'll call the police."

"All right, but don't get out of the car," warned Tania. "Remember that Grimsby hates you, and that I won't be there to come between the two of you."

"Don't worry," said Nick. "I'll be careful."

"You've been a good friend," said Tania. "Thank you for doing this."

To her surprise (and ours), Nick took her hand and kissed it. I wondered just how many shades of green Oberon would have turned if he had been there.

"Anything for you," he said. "You know that."

"I know," she said, removing her hand with an embarrassed smile. "I'm sorry you got involved in our world."

"Don't be," he said. "I'm not sorry. I love the food here."

Tania laughed, relieved, and Mustardseed briefly took center stage as Nick went over all of his favorite dishes.

"I'm glad stuffed eggplant is one of them," said Mustardseed. "We had a surplus of eggplant in the walls. Jamarcus got distracted and spent too much time standing in that spot."

By the time Mustardseed handwaved herself back to the kitchen, we had nearly finished lunch. Our little group, by the way, included Quince: the shaggy wolfhound received generous scraps from the three of us, and no doubt would have eaten even more if Oberon had been there as well.

"How come Oberon's not here?" I asked.

"He's making sure the paths are clear," she said. "I'll see him soon, though. We're going over one of the scenes."

"Act 4, Scene 1?" asked Nick.

"How did you guess?" asked Tania.

"Reconciliation scene," said Nick. "You had a little trouble with it."

"That's because Shakespeare lets Oberon get away with everything," said Tania. "It's irritating."

"Can I come watch?" I asked. I *had* to find a way to talk to Oberon before the performance.

"Sure," said Tania. "But before we get there, I want to make sure you're clear on the plan for tonight."

"I meet Welt, and we hide in one of the Old One's branches until the perfect moment for him to shoot you—except that, by then, the Old One will have opened the crack to the Underworld, and I'll have pushed him in."

"Right," said Tania. "Remember: do *not* get into the crack yourself."

"Got it," I said.

"Meanwhile, we will take care of the audience," said Tania. "There's no way to know what'll happen or how they'll react if they see the crack or if Welt starts shooting, so that's where Caster and the gaseous potion come in."

"What about DuBois?"

"He hasn't been invited, but he'll probably be lurking there somewhere."

"So what do we do?" I asked.

"If he's there, the rest of us will deal with it," said Tania. "I don't want you to worry about anything but your wind magic. Focus, and you'll be fine."

"Why didn't you just teach me yourself?" I asked. "Why did you go through the trouble of writing a diary and pretending you were a wind fairy?"

"What do you mean?" she asked—but she looked nervous.

"If I look at a piece of your handwriting, it'll be the same as Gaoth's, won't it?" I asked.

Tania sighed with resignation.

"Fine," she said. "I figured you'd be more motivated if you had a role model who was a wind fairy. I wanted you think it's possible to be a wind fairy and control your abilities."

"Even if it's not possible?"

"It *is* possible, Wynd. But I'm sorry I deceived you," she said. "I thought it for the best."

"Anything else you lied about?" I asked.

"No. I swear by the forest."

I smiled. I had made the fairy queen nervous. Not bad for a mere wind fairy.

"Okay, then," I said. "If you swear by the forest, we're good."

Thank goodness Tania didn't ask if there was anything *I* was keeping from her. If those green eyes had focused on me and demanded the truth, I would have spilled all the beans about the fairy mail shirt I planned to give Oberon. Thankfully, Quince started whining and pacing, and the green eyes shifted to the window. Nick and I went to the window and looked out as well: the Guardians of Florissant were in the courtyard.

"Good thing I destroyed that liquid Welt gave you," Tania told me. "A whiff of it would have killed the wolves."

"I knew he was lying," I said. "I wonder what else he was lying about."

I was toying with the idea of asking her if the treasure Mom had left for us was also a lie, but she seemed too distracted by the activity in the courtyard for me to open that can of worms.

"I should tell the students to stop trying to pet them," she was saying. "The only one who likes it is Madog. I mean, look at Grimsby's face. It's a wonder no one's lost a finger yet."

"But I thought they were on our side," said Sylva.

"They are, Sylva," said Tania. "But they are also wild."

"And free," I added.

"Which is why I'll take Nick straight to his car," said Tania. "Ready, Nick?"

A slight nod, and they both disappeared. A moment later, Tania re-appeared.

"Now it's just the four of us," she said. "Sylva, you know you have to stay in the Academy, right?"

"Yeah," said Sylva, sadly.

Tania turned to Quince.

"Quince, you're not going to leave this room, are you?"

Quince wasn't. Not even to pee.

"Good thing the floor is grass," said Tania, chuckling. "Sylva, remind Mustardseed to bring Quince some dinner later, okay?"

Sylva nodded obediently, and then the gaze of her large eyes turned to me for reassurance.

"A promise is a promise," I said. "I'll see you later—for sure."

Reassured by my bluff, she gave me a quick hug and then ran out of the office.

"Now to that horrible reconciliation scene," said Tania. "Let's see if I can get through it."

She waved us to Oberon's cave. The former king of fairies was pacing, muttering something from a crumpled piece of paper. When he saw us, he clumsily inserted it in his cape.

"What were you doing?" Tania asked.

"Nothing," he said, evasively. "Are you ready to do the scene?"

"As ready as I'll ever be," she said. "Here goes. You've just released me from the spell. *My Oberon! What visions have I seen!*"

"Start with *How came these things to pass?*" he said.

"Okay. *How came these things to pass?*"

She really did look awkward—resentful, even—as she stood there. Oberon walked toward her, went down on one knee, and said the following:

> *Come, my queen, take hands with me,*
> *Mind what Ob'ron's pledge shall be:*
> *In your hands he puts his heart;*
> *Let forgiveness be your part.*
> *Life, and pride, and magic, all*
> *Yours to command, to rise or fall.*

Reader, his voice was quiet, gentle—like the whisper of wind on summer leaves.

"Oberon," said Tania, her eyes brighter than usual, "these lines are not from the play."

Oberon got up.

"I don't want to be Shakespeare's Oberon," he said, taking her arms and putting them around his waist. "I want to be *your* Oberon."

They were close to each other now. *Very* close.

"Did you write those lines yourself?" she muttered.

"Hmm."

"They're not half bad," she whispered.

They were *this* close to kissing each other when Robin ran in.

"People are beginning to arrive," he said—and then he noticed Oberon's glare. "Wait—did I interrupt something?"

"As a matter of fact, you did!" said Oberon. "You interrupted some pretty good bambic haymeter."

"Actually, that was neither iambic nor pentameter," said Tania, smiling. "But it was nice."

"*Nice?*" repeated Oberon, outraged.

"Let's talk after the play," said Tania. "I asked Robin to come early, so he could help me set up the reception, and then greet journalists and any early guests."

"You're wearing the mail shirt, yes?" Oberon asked, as she rushed out.

"Yes!"

"Be careful!" he called after her, but she had already left with Robin.

"Instead of mischief, now he just has bad timing," complained Oberon, sighing as he sat down on his hammock.

"Oberon," I began, thinking I probably also had bad timing, "what did you do for Welt to hate you so much?"

"You mean, besides hurling him into the Underworld?"

"Yeah—besides that."

"Maybe it was the fact that Tania rejected his offer."

"What offer?" I asked.

"During the war, he offered to make peace and let the fairies keep their remaining territories if Tania married him. She refused. Instead, the two of us used our combined magic to send him into the Underworld."

I understood Welt's hatred now. Oberon was Tania's other half. A monster could never be that.

"I think you should wear the other mail shirt," I said, pulling it from over my head so that it would become visible.

"Absolutely not," he said, as I tried handing it to him. "You are the one who will be in most danger—*you* wear it."

"I won't need it," I said. "Besides, the person he really wants to shoot is you."

But Oberon wouldn't hear of it, so I finally had to demonstrate how I could turn parts of my body into wind and escape any bullets.

"When did you learn how to *windify* so accurately?" he asked, impressed.

"I practiced a lot this past month," I said. "Will you take the shirt now? Please?"

"All right," he said. "But I'd like you to take extra care, regardless. You know what he is capable of."

My mother's murder. The thought never strayed far from my mind—and tonight Welt would pay for it.

"You look nervous," said Oberon. "Help me with my lines. It'll help pass the time."

So I did. And it did help. Finally, it was nearly time for the performance.

"Break a leg," I said, as we walked out of the cave. "That's what you're supposed to say when someone's in a play."

"What a strange custom."

"It's meant to bring luck."

"I'll need it," he said. "I may forget a few lines, but I hope I at least look the part."

Oh, reader. If he could have only known just how regal, mysterious, and wild he looked. I knew that even if he forgot his lines, people would adore him. Crown or no crown, he *was* the fairy king.

"Be careful, Wynd," he said, his brown eyes full of concern. "Do *not* break a leg."

I smiled, and we parted ways.

Showtime.

Chapter 18

UNEXPECTED

(Just a heads-up, reader: a lot happens in this chapter).

IT'S A STRANGE feeling, watching people watch a play. There's a lonely detachment about it.

About half an hour after the play started—the place was packed, by the way—I left my mossy seat and made my way through the trees. The sun had already set, but the sky hadn't darkened completely yet, and was still that dark indigo I loved. The moon shone brightly—not quite a full moon, but almost—and a very soft breeze wound through the leaves, turning the forest floor into a mosaic of moonlight fragments. I'm not usually poetic, but I remember thinking that. Moonlight fragments.

I walked slower than usual. Not sure why. I think I was nervous.

When I finally got to the dirt road, Welt was standing there, waiting. His shape seemed larger than I remembered (or maybe it was the shadow cast by moonlight). Even if I hadn't known *what* he was, I'm sure I would have found him eerie.

When he realized I had arrived, he let a flash of red escape from the back of his eyes. 'Nough said.

"This way," I told him. He gave me a grotesque grimace in return and followed. For a second, I wondered why he was wearing a jacket, then decided it was probably to conceal a gun. As we walked, I could tell he was skittish, nervous. The sounds of the forest made him jumpy. He must have been afraid of an encounter with the Guardians of Florissant.

To sum it up: it was probably the most awkward and uncomfortable walk I'd ever been on.

As we approached the Old One's radius, I began to hear the sounds of the performance—voices, laughter, applause, and so on. I looked longingly at the stage, hoping to catch a glimpse of the action. What I caught a glimpse of, however, was Sylva.

She was sitting on one of the lower branches of the Old One, and for a moment I couldn't figure out if she was part of the performance or if she was just watching. She could have easily been part of the scene—except for the fact that she wasn't wearing fairy wings.

I didn't know what to do. I wanted her out of there, but I also didn't want Welt to see her. I glanced back at him, to see if he had noticed— and then realized he was gone.

Not a good moment for me, reader.

I scanned the area. Nothing. He must have suspected something when we got close to the Old One. Now he was out there in the forest, armed with iron bullets, and I had to find him—quickly— and lure him back to the right place so we could trap him in the Underworld.

I scoured the area near the stage now. He wasn't there. I broadened the search area even more. Still no sign of him. Could he have gone back home? Had I done something to tip him off? As my mind went around in circles, Act 4, Scene 1 began. Titania was released from the love potion, and she and Oberon walked downstage to reconcile. Oberon kneeled to kiss Tania's hand. Then everything went down.

Reader, here's everything that happened, in (I think) the right order:

—Tania rushed unexpectedly in front of Oberon
—Several shots rang through the forest
—Tania collapsed and Oberon caught her
—The audience freaked out

I can't imagine what the impact of all those bullets—especially ones made of iron—must have felt like to Tania, even with the mail shirt on. Thankfully, she stirred almost immediately.

"I'm fine," she said, wincing as Oberon helped her up. "I caught a glimpse of him—he was aiming for your head."

"Look!" cried Robin, before Oberon could utter a word in reply. "Welt's over there!"

Oberon grabbed the nearest spotlight and directed it where Robin was pointing. Welt was climbing down a tree several feet away—so fast that I wondered if he was still fully human. It was hard to tell.

Oberon hardened his jaw. His eyes narrowed into slits.

"Wait—Oberon!" said Tania, but he had already waved his hand and disappeared after Welt. I went a different way, avoiding the crowd, until I was running through the woods, not sure if I was going after Oberon or Welt. I had never felt so disoriented before, and it didn't help that I kept thinking our plan would never work now.

"Wynd!" cried Tania, catching up to me. "Where's Oberon?"

As if in reply, more gunshots rang through the forest. In the moonlight, Tania turned pale as a ghost.

"Oberon," she whispered.

"Don't worry," I said, as we ran toward the gunshots. "I gave him my mail shirt."

To our horror, however, Oberon was lying on the floor, blood everywhere on his chest, on his hands, on the ground. So much blood you just knew he was dying. Welt and DuBois were standing over him. The mill owner had a rifle, and Welt was holding a bloody iron knife he had just pulled out of Oberon's heart.

I just knew, reader, that no amount of healing water could save Oberon.

Tania must have known it, too, because she went mad with grief. No other way to describe it. With a sound that was part wail and part scream, she turned into an eagle-like creature, with white feathers that looked like white leaves depending on the angle. She was large as an elephant, fluid like a school of fish—and her talons were massive and razor-sharp.

The burning green eyes of the white creature fixed themselves on Welt, and she went at him with a screech that echoed through the forest. He discarded his human body—it collapsed on the floor like flayed skin—and turned back into the monster he had always been.

Green eyes versus red eyes. White versus grey. Talons versus claws. The sounds they made as they fought were terrifying. Deafening. I covered my ears.

At some point, I realized that Tania was pushing Welt in the direction of the Old One. I looked at her roots, and thought I detected some movement. Then I saw a strange reddish glow, and realized she had opened a crack to the Underworld.

I ran after Tania and Welt—or whatever they were just then—and got ready to push Welt into the Underworld. I wasn't sure how to do it, though: Welt was monster-sized now. No way he'd fit into the person-sized crack the Old One had opened.

Tania solved this problem for me. As soon as they were over the crack, she shredded him to bits with her talons. Seriously. Powerful as he was, the King of the Underworld was no match for her fury. It was the fury of loss, and he had no defense against it.

There were several pieces of him—still moving—scattered on the floor, and I *windified* my hands to blow these pieces into the crack. There was one piece, however, I hadn't seen—an arm with a hand—and the hand grabbed my leg and pulled me down into the Underworld with it.

My head hurt—I had hit it on my way down—and my knees and elbows were bruised. Half-conscious, I thought I saw parts of Welt coming back together, like magnets that attracted each other. He'd be a monster again in a few moments.

But my head hurt so much I couldn't even remember I was a wind fairy. All I knew was that I was in the Underworld, and that, somewhere above me, the crack was closing.

Then, to my dismay, Sylva was standing next to me. She had jumped through the narrowing crack.

"Sylva! No!" cried Aynia, the anguish in her voice echoing from above. A root pierced the space we were in and wrapped itself around Sylva, then recoiled as sharp thorns erupted all over her body. I thought I was delusional, and then I realized Sylva was *defending* herself against the Old One. She was using tree magic, and the root could not get to her without being pierced.

"I'm not leaving without Wynd!" cried Sylva. "If you can't take *her* back up, you can't take *me*, either."

As my eyes focused more clearly, I realized all the monstrous pieces of Welt were nearly rejoined. In a moment, those glowing red eyes and sharp teeth would be upon us.

Then another root pierced the space and wound itself around me. Sylva lowered her thorns, and we were both lifted out of the Underworld and deposited on the forest floor. The roots released their grip on us and wound their way underground again, and the crack closed just as the pieces of Welt's hideous shape were all back together.

We were safe. Sylva and I had been to the Underworld and back.

I thought we were in the clear—at least for a few seconds—until I realized DuBois was standing there, rifle in hand.

"I still have one shot left," he said, aiming at me.

He fired. But it was Sylva he hit. She had jumped in front of me, protecting me yet again—and when she fell, I thought everything was over. I can't even begin to tell you, reader, what that felt like.

Then Aynia walked out of the Old One.

"I have had enough," she said, her voice so menacing that DuBois dropped his rifle and took a few steps back. "Do you know what it is like to watch, century after century, as people like you destroy *everything*?"

DuBois turned around to run, but instead tripped on one of the Old One's roots. More specifically, it tripped *him*—and then held on to his ankle so he couldn't escape. Another root immobilized his arms, and another wound around his neck—until I heard the sound of something snapping. I can only guess it was his neck, because after that he stopped moving.

"He may have been human, but he was as bad as the monster," said Aynia. "Do not worry about Sylva—she will awaken soon."

Aynia bent down to pick something from the floor: it was the iron bullet from the rifle, which she promptly showed me. The tip was flat, as if it had hit an impenetrable wall.

"Sylva is wearing the fairy mail shirt," explained Aynia, seeing the confusion on my face. "Oberon gave it to her."

Sylva opened her eyes now. She sat up, looking dazed and confused. I *had* to hug her. Tightly.

"Thank goodness you're wearing the shirt," I said, overwhelmed by relief.

"Oberon gave it to me and made me put it on," she explained. "He saw me on the Old One's branch."

Good old Oberon . . . and then the image of him covered in blood flashed through my mind.

"Oberon!" I muttered, horrified.

"What is it?" asked Sylva, alarmed. "Did something happen to him?"

"He's dying, Sylva—we have to hurry."

"You will not get there in time," said Aynia. "I will take you."

And she waved her hand.

Chapter 19

WIND

I DON'T THINK I'll ever forget the moment Oberon died.

Tania sat by him, her hand serving as a pillow for his head, her face soaked in tears.

"Tania," he whispered. "Do you forgive me?"

"I do forgive you," she said, in the shakiest voice imaginable, "but you must stay alive."

"I will always be here, in the forest," he said. "You will always be my queen, my eternal love, my all."

He closed his eyes, and his head fell to the side. He was gone.

I put my arm around Sylva. The two of us were crying.

"Oberon," whispered Tania, bending down to his face, "you will always be my king, my eternal love, my all."

She kissed him. Her kiss contained the soul of the forest, and the magic of love.

And, as you know, love is the most powerful magic of all.

All of a sudden, a pulse of light ran through the entire forest—so bright that Sylva and I had to cover our eyes. It washed the entire forest in a golden glow, and then faded.

"Wynd, look," whispered Sylva.

Oberon's wounds were gone. The blood had disappeared. And Tania seemed as amazed as we were.

"Most unexpected," muttered Aynia. I got the feeling it had been a *very* long time since she had been surprised.

"Like the ending of a fairy tale," muttered Sylva.

"Well, we *are* fairies," I said.

Oberon stirred, then opened his eyes.

"Well, my queen," he said, his expression a mixture of delight and mischief. "It turns out I was right."

"About what?" she asked.

"I heal a lot faster when you kiss me."

Tania smiled, and was about to kiss him again when Caster crashed down near them. One of his wings was injured, and he flapped around miserably, cawing loudly.

"DuBois shot him," said Oberon, carefully picking up the wounded crow. "My poor friend—I am very sorry. I know how much it hurts."

"He cannot deliver the potion now," lamented Tania. "And all those people will want to destroy the forest after what they've witnessed."

"I have worse news," said Aynia, grimly. "Florissant Academy is on fire."

We followed her gaze, until we, too, could see the smoke smothering the sky.

"Isn't there something we can do?" asked Sylva, nervously.

"It'll burn down before we can conjure rain," whispered Tania, sitting down and burying her face in her hands.

"Hang on," I said. "Could wind blow it out? You know, like we blow out birthday candles?"

"It would need to be incredibly strong to blow out the fire," said Oberon. "Otherwise, it would just feed it."

"I can do strong," I said, and I was the one with the mischievous smile now. "I can do *incredibly strong*."

I turned to Sylva. I hoped she'd be okay with what I was about to do. To my relief, she was.

"Save the school," she said, encouragingly.

"I'll do more than that," I said. I took the vial of gaseous potion that was still bound to Caster's claw and removed the cork. I sucked all the gas inside my mouth and swallowed it. Then I did what I had been wanting to do for a long time: I turned into wind.

"Five minutes!" I heard Tania call after me. "Stay under five if you can!"

Five minutes isn't long, reader—but that's only in the human world. In the wind world, five minutes is an eternity.

In that eternity, I flew to the Academy—and then really let go. Completely. I blew—no, I blasted. It was liberating, channeling all my anger at the fire.

I had a lot of anger, I guess. Most of us do.

The fire blew out like birthday candles, just as I had imagined. As I hovered over the Academy, I noted that it was mostly intact, though maybe a little singed. In spite of all my blowing, not a single tree around the Academy had actually collapsed, though several branches lay broken on the floor—enough to cause quite a bit of difficulty if you had to walk through them. Still.

Now it was time to spread the gaseous potion. When you're wind, reader, whatever is *in* you also turns into wind: your clothes, your memories, the air in your lungs, the blood in your veins, and the food in your stomach. I knew all I had to do was fly into town, and everyone there—including the people who had driven back from Florissant in a panic—would breathe in the potion.

But the thing about five minutes being an eternity, reader, is that you don't realize how hard it is to keep track of time.

As I circled the town, I began to forget. Why was I there in the first place? Who was I?

Whoever I was, I was free.

And yet.

Something pulled me back to Florissant . . . it was the distant memory of a little girl with wild hair and dark eyes as deep as the roots of the forest. That image made me fly in no particular direction around the trees, until I happened to pass a massive tree with white flowers— and then a young tree that had a single white flower blossoming.

Sylva.

In that moment, I stopped being wind and went back to being Wynd. I remembered who I was. I had my memories back.

What I didn't have back were my fingers.

I tried and tried to finish the transformation, to become a whole person again, but the tips of my fingers wouldn't take shape. I fell on my knees, exhausted, knowing that if I couldn't pull it off, it would be the end of me. Whatever life and soul I had in me were leaking out of those fingers, like water from a cracked vase.

I remember thinking this was it—I'd never see Sylva again. As my vision faded, I remember thinking I couldn't believe things would end this way.

When I opened my eyes again, everything was dark. I heard the sound of Aynia's voice.

"Welcome back to this side of the door."

Reader, I was inside the Old One. Don't ask me how I knew. I just did. It was the quietest and darkest place I've ever been in. It was as if nothing from the outside could get in. Not even time.

"What am I doing here?" I asked.

"You were poisoned. That is why you could not complete your transformation."

"But there was no poison in the gaseous potion," I said. "Was there?"

"The poison was in your fingers."

My mind flashed back to the moment Welt handed me the envelope, when my fingers had turned cold. It hadn't been nerves, after all.

"Poison from the Underworld is the most toxic kind of poison there is," said Aynia. "The one he used on you was designed to be dormant for several hours. In any case, it's entirely gone from your system now."

"How?"

"Trees can absorb quite a bit."

I couldn't believe it. Aynia and the Old One had saved me. What a plot twist.

"Thank you," I said, feeling humble and grateful. "I thought you wanted me out of the way."

"We did. We have now changed our mind and removed the mark from your hand."

"Why?"

"Sylva cares about you more than she cares about being a tree, and you care about her more than being wind. There are some bonds so strong that neither nature nor magic ought to interfere."

I could barely believe that an ancient, proud tree had come around to a new way of thinking. Maybe Aynia and the Old One would never like me, but they had found me worthy. That was something.

"Your sister is greatly worried about you," said Aynia. "I have told her to meet you outside."

Before I could so much as formulate a reply, I was standing in front of the Old One's trunk, and Sylva was running toward me, with Tania and Oberon close behind.

"I thought you were gone," she said, hugging me with all her strength. "I called and called, but you didn't come back."

"I *did* come back," I said. "It was your magnolia flower that brought me back."

"Really?" she asked, beaming.

"Really," I said, affectionately pinning some of her wild hair behind her ears.

"Well done," said Tania, giving me an unexpected hug. "You saved Florissant. You saved the Academy."

"I hate to break up this touching moment, Wynd," said Oberon, "but what were you doing inside the Old One?"

"Getting rid of poison," I said. "It's a long story, but Aynia and the Old One saved me."

"*I've* never been invited to go inside the Old One," he said, incredulously.

"Neither have I, Oberon," said Tania. "Let it go."

"I suppose I must," he said. "But I'm rather disappointed—not to mention envious."

I figured that, somewhere inside the Old One, Aynia was probably chuckling—if she was still capable of being amused. I had a feeling she was.

"We should get back to the Academy," said Tania. She was about to wave her hand, when Sylva asked her to wait and tenderly placed her palm on the trunk of the Old One.

"Thank you," she said, touching her forehead against the tree. "I'll be a good tree—I promise."

Of course she would be. One day—and I was sure of this—she'd be the queen of trees.

Chapter 20

The Crowns

WHEN TANIA AND Oberon handwaved us back to the courtyard, Grimsby was waiting with Gwaelrod, Whitby, Antrim, Etain, and Madog. The black wolf hurried over to Tania and whimpered.

"Dear friend" said Tania, worriedly. "What's wrong?"

He turned around and trotted away for a few steps, then stopped and turned back.

"He wants us to follow him," said Oberon, still cradling the wounded Caster in his hands.

"I don't like this," said Tania. "Something's happened, and he won't tell me what it is. I hope everyone is all right."

We followed Grimsby up the stairs and to the infirmary. We found out that Nick had been shot in the shoulder. Cobweb stood in one corner, with her customary creepy grin, while Mariposa poured healing water over Nick's shoulder. When she saw Caster in Oberon's hand, she immediately went to get some more healing water, and spent the next several minutes healing the crow's wounded wing.

"What happened, Nick?" asked Tania.

"Starveling, Snout, Snug, and Flute happened," said Nick. "They set fire to the school. Threw a bunch of home-made fire bombs from the truck."

"And you tried to stop them?" asked Tania.

"No—Grimsby and the wolves tried to stop them. You should have seen the pack go at that truck. I think the guys were terrified—so terrified they were trying to run the wolves over. I had to get out of the car and try to stop them. Then I saw Flute pull out a gun."

"He *shot* you?" cried Tania.

"He meant to shoot Grimsby," said Nick. "I could tell."

Tania turned to Grimsby, and he regarded her with his yellow eyes for a moment. Then he turned his gaze to Nick.

"That's why he's not attacking you," said Tania. "You took a bullet for him."

"I don't expect him to forget what I did before," said Nick, alternating his gaze between Tania and the great black wolf. "I just couldn't stand by and do nothing."

"What happened to the rest of those men?" asked Oberon.

"I had already called the police when I first saw them pull up," said Nick. "The cops pursued Flute, Snout, and Snug, and arrested them."

"What about that other one?" asked Oberon.

"Starveling, yeah," said Nick. "Something . . . something kind of happened to him."

And he went quiet—though not before darting an uneasy glance at Cobweb.

"What happened to Starveling, Cobweb?" asked Tania.

Cobweb shifted uneasily. "In the confusion, he somehow managed to get inside the school."

"And?"

Cobweb hesitated.

"And I ate him," she said, finally.

"You *ate* him?" cried Tania, in the most exasperated tone I've ever heard from her.

"I was in spider form," protested Cobweb. "It seemed like a good idea."

Tania actually had to sit down for a moment.

"Did anyone see it?" she asked.

"Only Peaseblossom," replied Cobweb. "Mustardseed had to give her some calming tea. They're in the kitchen."

Tania thought for a second or two. "Well, did he at least taste good?"

"Not really."

Tania glanced at Oberon, and then the two started laughing. Mariposa, Nick, Sylva, and I laughed as well. I honestly don't know if Grimsby joined us, because it's hard to tell with wolves.

"Thank you for protecting the school, all of you," said Tania, when the laughter had died somewhat. "It has been quite a night:

we have managed to save the school *and* send Welt back to the Underworld."

"What happened to DuBois?" asked Nick.

"The Old One got him," I said.

"Nice," said Cobweb, with a nod of approval.

"And how was the play?" asked Nick.

"Unfortunately, Robin never got to do his epilogue," said Tania. "But overall it was a success."

"Where *is* Robin?" asked Oberon. "Do you know, Caster?"

The convalescing crow, who was back on Oberon's shoulder with his wing healed, cooed several times, and ended with a caw and a click.

"So Sheriff Goodfellow took him away when the whole confusion started," said Oberon. "I see."

"Is everyone else accounted for?" asked Tania. "All the students?"

"Everyone here," said Mariposa. "Do you still need me?"

"Take the rest of the night off," said Tania. "Grimsby, you are free to go as well."

Mariposa turned into a moth and flew out the window. Grimsby trotted downstairs and met the other pack members in the courtyard. They all followed him out the open gate and trotted into the moonlit forest.

"It's very late now, so I suggest we all get some rest," said Tania. "Nick, why don't you stay in the infirmary tonight?"

"Thanks—I will."

"What about me?" said Oberon, in an insinuating tone. "Are you inviting me to stay over as well?"

"You can handwave yourself back to the cave," said Tania, flatly.

"If *I'm* not staying, *he's* not staying," said Oberon, with a disapproving glance at Nick.

"Then you can both sleep here," said Tania.

"What, *here*?" said Oberon. "You want me to sleep in one of these diminutive beds?"

"They're pretty comfortable, actually," said Nick, lying back with his hands behind his head.

Oberon didn't seem completely sold on the idea.

"Caster, what do you say?" he asked. "Shall we spend the night here?"

But Caster wasn't completely sold on the idea, either, and preferred to fly out the window.

"Your minion has abandoned you," said Tania, barely suppressing a smile.

"He's my corvid *friend*," corrected Oberon, "and he's got a nest full of young ones now, so I forgive him."

"Good night, then," said Tania, and without further ado turned around to leave. Sylva and I dutifully followed.

"Good night, my love," Oberon called after her. She ignored him.

"Wipe that smirk off your face, Wynd," said Tania, once we were in the corridor. "In spite of what happened, Oberon and I aren't officially reconciled yet."

"Maybe not *officially*," I began, "but—"

"Good night, then," said Tania. "Get some rest—you'll need it."

"For what?" I asked.

"For the holiday that I will declare first thing tomorrow," said Tania, her eyes two green orbs of excitement. "We must celebrate the departure of the King of the Underworld and the survival of Florissant."

So Sylva and I went back to our room. The hallways were empty—everyone was sleeping already. I was pretty sure it was past midnight, so whatever celebrations Tania had in mind would be happening *today*.

Although Sylva fell asleep almost instantly, I was too wired to sleep. My brain felt scattered. Maybe it *was* scattered. Maybe I was still recovering from being wind. From being poisoned. From being in the Underworld.

I sat in bed, looking out the window. The soft summer breeze felt like a visit from an old friend. I was happy. It was a deep satisfaction and calm joy I had never felt before. Everything had fallen into place. We had solved every problem.

Except for the missing deed to Florissant. If only we could have found that. I fell asleep on that thought.

But the next day, something funny happened. We had already had a pancake breakfast and a picnic lunch at that same spot my mother loved (Oberon, Nick, and Robin were all there too—Oberon had sent Robin an invitation through Caster). We were all just chilling in the water, several feet away from the waterfall, when I suddenly remembered I had dreamed of Mom. She and I had been sitting in that same picnic spot, and she had pointed to the waterfall.

"Go behind the waterfall, Wynd," she had said. "You will find what you are looking for."

So I waded my way to the waterfall. It was super slippery, what with mossy-covered rocks at the bottom and all, and my attempt was so clumsy I attracted the attention of everyone else.

"What are you trying to do?" asked Sylva.

"I want to check on something," I said. "I dreamed that Mom told me to look behind the waterfall."

"I'll handwave us back there," said Tania. "Ready?"

And there we were, behind the roaring curtain of water, staring at a wall of wet, dark rock. I felt pretty stupid all of a sudden. Then I slipped and had to steady myself against the wall of rock—and that's when the *click* happened.

Part of the rock jutted out slightly, like a drawer.

"It's a rock safe, set to open only if the right people touch it," said Tania, amazed. "No one in the world would be able to find it, let alone open it."

And what was inside the safe? A large, gold tube decorated with silver and platinum leaves. I pulled it out—it was heavy—and Tania handwaved us back to a shady spot near the edge of the water.

"Sylva!" I cried. "Mom left something for us."

Sylva came splashing through the water, followed by Robin and Nick. Oberon handwaved himself next to Tania, and they all waited, dripping, to see what I had found (if you're wondering why no one cast a drying spell, it's because it was one of those incredibly hot days, and being wet felt good).

"There's no place to open it," I said, puzzled. Tania tried it, and Oberon tried—and then Nick and Robin. No one could figure out how to open the tube.

"The case itself must be worth a fortune," said Nick. "Maybe that's what your mother left for you."

"I love it!" said Sylva. "These golden leaves are so pretty."

She traced them with her fingers—and that's when the second *click* happened. A golden lid popped open on previously unseen hinges.

"How clever," said Tania, as Sylva gasped with delight. "It's a gift for *both* of you, so each of you had to open something."

"It looks like there's a piece of paper in there," I said.

"Hang on—let's not risk it getting wet," said Tania, waving her hand and finally performing a dry spell on everyone. "Okay. Pull it out now."

Sylva and I pulled out the thick piece of paper and unrolled it.

"No way," I whispered.

"What is it?" asked Oberon. "What does it say?"

"Read it, Sylva," I said, encouragingly.

Sylva looked at the letters and concentrated.

"D-eed to Fuh . . . Fuh-lor-eessant," she read, so focused that our explosion of cheering and clapping startled her.

"You found the deed," said Tania. "Well done."

"So no one can cut down the forest now?" asked Sylva.

"No one," said Tania. "According to human law, the forest belongs to you and Wynd."

"But it doesn't just belong to us," said Sylva, confused. "It belongs to all the fairies, and all the animals, and all the trees and flowers and plants and mushrooms."

"And wind," I added.

"Exactly," said Sylva. "Doesn't Florissant belong to everyone equally?"

"Yes, tree child," said Tania, "but human law does not allow for that—which is why your mother left it to the two of you. She knew you would treasure this place."

"Can we show this to the lawyer?" I asked.

"I can see if he'll answer his phone," said Tania. "Now that Welt is gone, he might be willing to come back to town."

"Can we do it now?" I asked.

"*Now*?" repeated Tania.

"We can't risk it ever being lost again," I said. "We need everyone to know that the forest can't be auctioned off."

"I can call from the edge of the forest," said Tania. "Let's do that."

The lawyer, not surprisingly, was very happy to hear from Tania. When she told him that Welt seemed to have left the area for good, and that DuBois had been found dead in the forest, he agreed to meet us in his downtown office within the hour.

"We could leave now," said Nick. "I have to drop off Robin at the Sheriff's Office, and then stop by the waffle house to thank Dottie."

"That's already five of us in the car," said Tania. "How will Oberon fit?"

"Don't worry about me," said Oberon. "I'll see you all tomorrow, perhaps?"

"Tomorrow?" said Tania. She sounded disappointed.

"I have some things to take care of today," he said, cheerfully. "Good luck in town."

He waved his hand, and Tania stared at the (now) empty space in front of her.

"I thought he'd want to celebrate with us tonight," said Tania. "I asked Mustardseed to prepare a special feast with roasted apples, walnut loaf, potato pie, and leek pancakes—his favorites."

"He might turn up," offered Robin. "You know what he's like."

"Yes, I know," she said. "What about you? Will you celebrate with us?"

"I wish I could," lamented Robin. "It's my dad's birthday today, though, so we're going out. Mom's already made reservations and everything."

"I won't be able to stay, either," said Nick. "I mean, I'll bring y'all back to the dirt road, but it's a hundred percent full moon tonight, so you know what happens."

"All better excuses than Oberon's," said Tania, under her breath. She sulked the entire way to town, saying hardly anything and only replying to our conversation with "hmm" and "uh-huh." She only roused herself when we arrived at the Sheriff's Office and Robin was about to get out of the car.

"Did your father mention anything about Welt, or DuBois?" she asked him.

"DuBois apparently had a fall in the forest and broke his neck, and Welt skipped town after trying to shoot people in a school production. He's on a Wanted list."

"What about the others?" asked Nick.

"In jail," said Robin. "They're saying Starveling was Welt's accomplice, and that they're probably far from here now."

"Well, *that* part is certainly true," said Tania. "Good-bye, Robin. Pop by if you want to visit us before leaving."

"Leaving?" I asked. "Where?"

"College," he said. "My next adventure. I'm even thinking about auditioning for a play."

"Maybe you'll finally get to do that epilogue," I said.

"Maybe," he replied. "See you around, Wynd."

"See you around, Robin."

We drove off. I decided I was more relieved than sorry that Robin was leaving. We belonged in different worlds—worlds we had both been ecstatic to leave behind. His new world awaited, as did mine. If we ever met again, hopefully we'd have interesting adventures to share.

Nick pulled up to the waffle house's parking lot now, and we all went in. I kept expecting someone to come over to our counter seats and say something nasty to us, but Dottie came to serve us and was all smiles (I had already figured out that she liked Nick). She brought us sweet teas and went on and on about how awesome the performance was. She particularly enjoyed the ending, though we couldn't begin to guess what she was talking about. Two random people in there actually joined the conversation to rave about the ending as well. We all smiled and nodded along, trying not to appear too baffled.

We finished our ice teas and left to meet the lawyer. The rest of that meeting was pretty important, I guess, but not particularly exciting to write about: we registered the deed and took all the legal action we needed in terms of the human world.

On the way back, believe it or not, Nick's car broke down. He couldn't figure out what was wrong with it. After baking in the heat for over an hour, tinkering with it and not getting anywhere, he announced he'd walk back to town to get a tow truck. If you're wondering why he didn't just make a call, it's because his cell phone had died, and Tania hadn't remembered to bring hers.

"Will you be okay?" asked Tania. "It's nearly five o'clock, and tonight is a full moon."

"I still have a few hours until the sun sets," said Nick. "I'll try to catch a ride back to town. I should be back in Florissant for my sleeping spell by the time it gets dark."

"Okay. We'll walk back to the Academy," said Tania. "There's shade on the side of the road."

So we went one way, and Nick another.

"Should I have offered to turn into wind and find a mechanic?" I said, as we walked back.

"Absolutely not," said Tania. "Wind magic is dangerous. It's for emergencies only."

"I still feel kind of bad," I confessed. "I mean, now we all have to walk."

"There is nothing wrong with walking," said Tania, and she stopped abruptly to face me. "Listen to me, Wynd: do not risk yourself for convenience. Magic is not there to serve *us*, remember?"

"But you use the handwave all the time," I said.

"That's not the same thing at all," she replied. "A handwave does not put me in danger, the same way turning into wind does you."

"I thought the point of learning to control magic was so we could use it," I insisted.

"The more you think about magic in terms of controlling it, the more it controls you. Promise me you'll remember that."

"Okay. I promise."

So we walked all the way back to Florissant. By the time we arrived, we were so tired and sweaty that Tania handwaved us to the nearest waterfall—the smallest one in the forest—and the three of us just stood under the water until we felt refreshed.

"Let's just sit over there and catch our breath for a bit," said Tania. "It's still early."

We sat with our backs against a large tree, gazing up at the leaves and the sky—and the three of us dozed off. When we woke up, the sky was a pinkish red, and Oberon and Caster were peering down at us.

"Do you have any idea how worried I was when you never came back?" he told Tania, his hands on his waist with indignation. "And here you all were, taking a cozy nap."

"You sounded like you had other plans earlier," said Tania, rubbing her eyes. "I didn't think you'd even notice. What time is it?"

"Nearly sundown," said Oberon. "Even the peasant is back already."

"I already told you a hundred times not to call him—wait . . . how do you know Nick's back?"

"I've been at the Academy, waiting for you."

"Why?"

"Because, my queen," he said, leaning in, "I have a surprise for you there. Shall we?"

Oberon's surprise was this: he had attached long rows of string from one side of the courtyard to the other, and had also hung tiny bits of crystal from them, so that the entire courtyard looked as if it had been sprinkled with starlight.

"Silver web thread and moon crystals," muttered Tania, amazed. "Where did you find them?"

"I've been collecting them for a while," said Oberon. "I wanted to do something special for you."

"Dinner first," said Mustardseed, approaching in a stunning dress made of orange slices and peel, with green and red berries scattered throughout. "Formal wear, Your Majesties."

"I had better get changed, then," said Oberon. He waved his hand, and all of a sudden his pants and cape were all white (mushrooms, feathers, petals—everything stitched together with silver thread). Even his dark mane of hair had a few white flowers in it.

"That's what you wore when . . ." began Tania, and then her voice trailed off.

"When we had our first handbinding ceremony," said Oberon. "What do you say we do it again?"

Tania's eyes burned bright green as she smiled and waved her hand. She was now wearing a stunning long dress made entirely of white petals.

"That's not fair," I said, feeling shamefully underdressed. "Sylva and I are wearing the same thing we wore this morning."

"What would you like?" asked Tania.

"A dress made of leaves," said Sylva, immediately.

"Can I have something with pink petals?" I asked.

Tania smiled approvingly as her handwave changed us from shabby fairies to ones wearing gala-worthy outfits. We looked so good I was pretty sure we could have marketed these clothes to eco-friendly celebrities. Even Sylva's hair was somewhat under control with twig and pinecone hair pins.

"Where are Mariposa, Cobweb, and Peaseblossom?" asked Tania.

"Here," said Peaseblossom, coming forward in a dress of multicolored flowers.

"Here," said Mariposa, coming forward in a dress of moth and butterfly wings.

"Here," said Cobweb, coming forward in a dress of white and grey thread.

"You look beautiful, my ladies," said Tania, affectionately. "Where are the students?"

"All waiting inside the kitchen, together with Nick," said Mustardseed.

"You let Wolf Nick in the kitchen?" asked Tania, surprised.

"He never transformed," said Mustardseed. "The curse has been lifted."

"Grimsby forgave him," muttered Tania. "Hang on a second—I must talk to him."

She had sensed the wolf's presence even before we had seen him, standing under the doorway arch. In a way, it was fitting. He was as much Florissant as Tania and Oberon.

Tania walked over to him, kneeled down, and affectionately placed her hand on his chest.

"What a noble heart you have, my friend," she said. "Thank you."

Grimsby leaned against her for a moment—and then he bounced away, carefree. The rest of the pack bolted after him, and they ran joyfully through the trees, howling.

When they were out of sight, Quince shyly stuck her head out from behind the living room door.

"They're gone, Quince," said Tania, with an amused chuckle. "How do you fancy a feast? I bet that miserable man never gave you anything good."

Quince bolted to the kitchen with the kind of excitement that proved Tania was entirely right in her assumption.

Reader, you can tell I'm getting to the end here, can't you? Do I really need to say that the food and music were amazing, that everyone was laughing and happy, and that the evening ended in dancing? You probably guessed that already.

But here's something you probably didn't guess: somewhere in the middle of the dancing, Tania stopped the music and said someone was waiting to come in.

"The gate is open," I said, wondering why anyone would be standing outside.

"They're waiting for us to invite them in," said Tania.

Everyone was curious to see who it was. Everyone except for Sylva, who already knew. If you guessed Aynia, you guessed right. She, too, was dressed in evening wear, with a long-sleeved, straight gown made of magnolia blossoms and leaves. Her hair was contained in a perfect white braid bound with a single flower at the bottom. I'll say it again, reader: she was beautiful.

"Aynia!" said Tania, pleasantly. "I didn't think you'd come."

"You can't very well have another handbinding ceremony without the oldest one present," she said, dryly—but not unpleasantly.

"I may have mentioned something to her," Oberon whispered to Tania. "She did preside over our first one."

"Well, come in," said Tania, in high spirits. "Everyone is invited."

"Good, because I've brought friends," said Aynia. "They wanted to celebrate with you and show their gratitude for the risks you took to preserve the forest."

The "friends" Aynia was talking about were a variety of forest animals large and small.

"You are all welcome," said Tania, making a gesture that indicated everyone should come in. The courtyard filled with the animals of the forest. Tania and Oberon, standing facing each other, seemed truly to be the queen and king of all Florissant. All that was missing was their crowns.

Aynia placed Tania's hand over Oberon's, and then took a braided green and brown cord (don't ask me where she got it from—magnolia pockets?) and wound it over their hands.

"You said important words to each other yesterday," said the ancient fairy. "Would you like to add anything?"

"I have a collection of Shakespeare sonnets I'd like to recite," said Tania—and then started laughing at the look of dread on Oberon's face.

"You were joking?" he said. "Oh, what a relief."

"I'd much rather kiss you, if that's all right."

"Perfectly all right by me," he said, with his most dashing smile.

And so it was that Tania Greenwood, former queen of the fairies, kissed Oberon, former king of fairies. It must have been some kiss, because the chord tying their hands vanished, and a crown made of the purest green and yellow gold appeared on each of their heads. These crowns didn't look like the kinds of stiff crowns you see in a Shakespeare play, either. They looked uneven, asymmetrical, like a collection of forest twigs and leaves dipped in the shiniest, purest gold imaginable. They were captivating, mysterious, unique—like Tania and Oberon, and like Florissant.

"Welcome back, queen and king," said Aynia, smiling. "The trees find you worthy again."

Need I say more? Maybe just that on that special summer night, reader, the fairy queen and king danced until the sun came up—and so did I.

P.H.C. Marchesi is an English professor specializing in Shakespeare and Renaissance drama. She teaches at a liberal arts college an hour from Atlanta, GA. Her academic research into the role of trees and forests in Shakespeare's plays led to her discovery of how precious and rare old-growth forests are, and inspired her to write *Florissant*. Before embarking on the young adult fantasy genre, she wrote two science fiction novels for middle grade readers, *Shelby & Shauna Kitt and the Dimensional Holes* and *Shelby & Shauna Kitt and the Alterax Buttons*, both of which were self-published and won Children's Literary Classics gold awards.

Marchesi is originally from Rio de Janeiro, Brazil, and has also lived in Austria and England. In the United States, she has lived in New York, Delaware, Colorado, Arizona, and (now) Georgia.